Bells Are STILL RINGING

Sometimes the best gifts are the ones that make us wait

LORI LEGER

PRIME OF LOVE The Series

Book 4

CAJUNFLAIR
PUBLISHING

ISBN-13: 978-1-940305-44-8

. Main Character List - Connection by Series

La Fleur de Love
1) Some Day Somebody
    a. Carrie Jeansonne
    b. Sam Langley

2) Last First Kiss
    a. Giselle Granger (Co-worker of Carrie in Some Day Somebody
    b. Jackson Broussard (Co-worker of Carrie in SS)
    c. Scott "Red" McAllister (Carrie's cousin in SS and Jackson's friend)
    d. Dr. Tiffany LeBlanc (Jackson's doctor)
    e. Bill Broussard (Jackson's uncle

3) Brown Eyed Girl
    a. Dr. Tiffany LeBlanc (Jackson Broussard's surgeon in LFK)
    b. Red McAllister (Jackson's friend, Carrie's cousin LFK, SS)
    c. Tanner Collins (Tiffany's fiancé)
    d. Angelique Baptiste (Red's ex-girlfriend)
    e. Annie McAllister (Red's sister)
    f. Drake LeBlanc (Tiffany's brother)

4) Heaven in Your Eyes
    a. Annie McAllister (Red's sister in BEG)
    b. Drake LeBlanc (Tiffany's brother in BEG)
    c. Vivienne McAllister (Annie & Red's mom, BEG)

Halos & Horns Series
1) Green Eyed Temptation
    a. Angelique Baptiste (Red's ex-girlfriend in BEG)
    b. Liam Nash (Annie M's. body guard in HIYE)
    c. Det. Mike Harper (BEG)
    d. Sarah Richard (abused woman with twin infants)

2) Sarah Smile
    a. Sarah Richard (GET)

b. Tanner Collins (Tiffany's ex-fiance in BEG)
c. Mitchell Hebert (Sarah's brother)
d. Daniel LeBlanc (Tiffany and Drake's father)

3) Meagan's Marine
a. Meagan Hutton (Co-worker of Red McAllister, HIYE)
b. Mitchell Hebert (Sarah's brother, Sarah Smile)
c. Niki Reeves (Sarah's friend)
d. Matthew "Tex" Broussard (Mitchell's friend, US Marine)

4) One Year to Forever
a. Haley Broussard (Tex's sister in MM)
b. Lt. Cpl. Ben Bonin (Haley's boyfriend, US Marine sniper)
c. Niki Reeves (Meagan's friend in MM)
d. Tex Broussard (Mitchell's friend in MM)
e. Bo McAllister (Red's cousin)

5) Tinseled Up in Texas
a. Nicole 'Niki' Reeves (Appears in Meagan's Marine)
b. Matthew 'Tex' Broussard (Appears in Meagan's Marine)

Prime Of Love

1) Running Out Of Rain
a. Cynthia Robicheaux Ellender (Widow and old classmate of John Michael Ferguson)
b. John Michael Ferguson (Zach's dad from Full Circle Love)
c. Marilee Ferguson (John Michael's mom, married to J.D.)
d. J.D. Ferguson (John Michael's dad, Marilee's husband)
e. Bess Robicheaux (Cyn's mom)

2) Hanging On To Hope
a. Allie Sarver (Cynthia's sister ROOR)
b. Clay Andrews (John Michael's
c. Margie Andrews (Clay's ex-wife)
d. Jacques Bessette (Margie's fiancé)

3) Settling For More
a. Sandra Campion (Wife of Marshall, mother to Ella, Maddie and Brock)
b. Marshall Campion (Sandra's husband, father of her children)
c. Madison Campion (Mother to Isabelle, daughter of Sandra and Marshall)
d. Ella Chandler (Kevin's wife, Maddie's sister)
e. Kevin Chandler (Ella's husband, Maddie's old friend)
f. Brock Campion (Ella and Maddie's brother, fiancé to Vonna Rose)
g. Sharla Bowers (Brock's fiancée)

h. Brennan McAllister (Red's cousin, BEG, Bo McAllister's cousin in OYTF)

i. Vonna Rose McAllister (Brennan's wife)

4) Bells are Still Ringing (Ties Prime of Love series to La Fleur de Love series)

a. Bill Broussard (first appears in Last First Kiss, book 2 of La Fleur de Love, Jackson's uncle, friend to Carrie and Sam Langley)

b. Jackson Broussard (first appears in Last First Kiss, book 2 of La Fleur de Love, co-worker to Carrie and friend to Toby Granger)

c. Giselle Granger (first appears in Last First Kiss, book 2 of La Fleur de Love, as widow of Jackson's friend, Toby Granger)

d. Gwendolyn Perry (first appears in Last First Kiss as Bill's love interest)

DEDICATION

To those of you out there who can't seem to get a break when it comes to love … never give up. Dessert comes after the main meal, and is almost always worth the wait.

As always, to my hubs, Michael, who doesn't mind me bouncing ideas off of him now and then, who lets me read pages aloud to see if anything's off, who keeps the house from falling down around us when I'm in writing mode, and who loves me, despite my many flaws. We had to wait for our HEA too, and the older we get, the more we appreciate each other.

To my children, in-laws, and grandchildren . . . blood, step, adopted, almosts, in production, etc., I love you all and realize that life would be quite dull without you.

Chapter One

Billy: The Kid

December 24, 1960

Billy Broussard stood in the doorway of his room, his four-year-old mind trying to make sense of the comings and goings. His dad had already made several trips to his car, taking armloads of stuff with him. He made one more pass, spreading the smell that Billy hated—the one that always made him scrunch up his nose.

His older brother, Jamison, popped out of his own room long enough to pull Billy inside the bedroom across the hall. He eased the door shut behind them. "Don't leave this room, you hear, Billy? Pop's drunk and packing up his stuff. Mom says it's best to stay out of his way when he's like this."

Billy searched his brother's face for clues. "Is he gonna leave us again?"

Jay shrugged. "Sounds like it."

"You think he'll stay gone this time?"

"I don't know. I hope so," Jay admitted.

Billy nodded. "Me too. Mom's happier when Pop's not around."

Jay squinted in contemplation. "Seems like it, don't it?"

"Yep," Billy said.

Jay nodded a couple of times. "Can't blame her. I sure as hell am happier when he ain't around. A kid can't get a decent night's sleep around here with all his cussin', fussin', and door slammin'."

"Don't say *hell*, Jay. Mom will soap your mouth out."

"Mom won't know I said it unless you tell her." Jay narrowed his eyes. "You planning to tell her?"

"No, 'cuz I'm sure as hell happier when he's gone, too." Billy looked up at his brother, hoping he could answer a question that had been bugging him. "Jay, why does Pop stink when he argues with Mom? Is it like when you bother a snake or a stink bug?"

Jamison, a full five years older than Billy, frowned at him. "He doesn't stink because they argue, dummy. They argue *because* he stinks."

Billy shook his head. "I hate the way he smells."

"So does Mom. She says he comes home smelling like whiskey, cigarettes, and cheap perfume."

"What's cheap perfume, Jay?"

His brother released an impatient sigh. "You know that stuff mom wears that makes her smell good all the time?"

Billy nodded. "Uh huh."

"Well that's perfume. But Pop smells like some *other* lady's perfume."

Billy waved his hand in front of his face. "Well, whoever she is, she stinks. Mom smells *way* better."

"I think so, too," Jay agreed.

The two of them crawled into Jay's bed and lay there listening to the sound of their father's angry tirade as he left the house. Everything grew quiet and their mom finally opened the door.

"You boys alright in here?"

"Yup," they answered, in unison.

Jay sat up in bed. "You okay, Mom?"

Yvette Broussard sat on the edge of her oldest son's bed. "I'm fine, and you boys will never have to hear anything like that again. Your dad's gone for good, this time." She reached out to place a hand on each of her sons' heads. "Are you two alright with that?"

The brothers exchanged grins and Billy faced his mom. "I am."

"I am too," Jay piped up.

She nodded. "It's us against the world, boys. I don't want either of you to worry about a thing, because I'm going to take care of you both, okay? Now go to sleep so Santa can drop off your Christmas presents." She got up, walked calmly to the door and turned. "I'm going to cook us breakfast in the morning."

"But Pop can't stand the smell of food cooking in the mornings—" Jay stopped suddenly.

Yvette smiled. "We don't have to worry about that anymore. I'm going to cook breakfast for you boys from now on. No more cold cereal. What do you want for Christmas breakfast?"

"Bacon!" Billy said.

"And biscuits," Jay added.

Their mom beamed at them. "I love you, boys. Sleep tight."

Billy curled up next to Jay, thinking they'd all sleep better from now on. He sure did—and woke up to the smell of their mom cooking Christmas breakfast. He woke Jay and they joined her in the kitchen for bacon, biscuits, and eggs—cooked any way they wanted.

After breakfast, they opened the gifts Santa had put under the tree. They cleaned up the living room and hauled their gifts to the bedroom.

Billy stopped at his door and looked at his brother. "So far, everything's the same, Jay, only quieter."

Jay turned at his bedroom door and faced him. "That's because Yancy Broussard ain't around moaning and groaning about the high cost of Christmas and how he'd be better off without two kids and a wife holding him back." He shook his head and lowered his voice. "He made mom a nervous wreck with all his bitchin'. I like it better this way."

Billy pictured the smile on their mother's face this morning. "Me too."

From then on, Billy saw a huge difference in his mother. Yvette Broussard smiled more, even when, after teaching school all day, she had to take a part time job in the afternoons to pay for extras. He overheard her tell her best friend, Ms. Brenda one day that living without an alcoholic womanizer in the house was far easier than living *with* one.

As far as Billy could tell, he had to agree.

* * * * *

Christmas Morning, 1969

The tantalizing smell of bacon frying roused Billy Broussard from a sound sleep. Man, he loved bacon. He opened his eyes when the aroma of biscuits baking in the oven reached him. Biscuits, bacon, eggs—Mom's traditional Christmas morning breakfast. He smiled, and just for a few seconds, he forgot.

He rolled out of bed and went to the bathroom, doused his face with icy cold water from the sink faucet—still hearing his mom's words in his head.

"*Wash the sleep from your eyes, my boys—it doesn't cost a thing to start the morning with a clean face and clear eyes.*"

By the time he reached the kitchen, Jamison, nearly nineteen, had already dished out breakfast and placed it on the table. A visual sweep of the small room and over the half-wall into the same sized living area showed all the usual signs of the day. The same artificial tree they'd used for years, and the same ornaments and decorations placed around the room. He glanced at the Christmas placemats adorning the table. The ones his mom always used throughout the holidays—all images from some painter named Norman Rockwell, whoever the hell that was.

Jamison gave him a one-armed hug and slap on the back. "Merry Christmas, little brother!"

Bill returned the brief hug-slap. "Merry Christmas, Jay." The two of them sat, and began eating, careful not to disrupt the customs their mom had developed over the years.

They opened gifts afterwards, some from their mom due to her penchant for mail order catalog shopping throughout the year. They'd pulled several from her closet, already wrapped and hidden away, with inspirational messages added onto the gift tags. A few gifts they'd bought on their own and paid for with money they'd made by working odd jobs.

Billy stared at the half dozen gifts before him. "Just like mom to take care of us even after she's gone, huh?"

Jamison sat staring at his pile of loot. "Just like her. I guess she didn't want us to miss her too bad this first Christmas without her." He looked over at his little brother. "Not possible, right?"

"Right…"

Neither mentioned their father, still alive but non-existent as far as they were concerned.

Losing their mom had taken some major adjusting on both their parts. Billy remembered the day he entered the quiet house a few weeks before she passed away. He'd paused at his mom's bedroom door to listen in on a conversation between her and his big brother.

"I'm so sorry, Jay. I know how badly you wanted to go to college. But your brother will need you here at home."

"It's okay, Mom. I understand. You just concentrate on getting better. I'll take care of Billy."

But her cancer had beaten her. She'd left this world thankful for the time God had given her, but not without regrets. She'd held her youngest son's hand and smiled through her tears during their final conversation.

"I hate that I won't be able to see you grow into the fine man I know you'll be, Billy. I wanted to be here, to meet girlfriends, your wife . . . my grandchildren. I'm truly sorry for that."

"Don't Mom," he'd said, unable to finish the rest due to the lump in his throat.

She'd reached up and touched his face. *"I love you, son. Please be good for your brother."*

Bill had nodded. *"Love you too, Mom. I will be. I promise."*

She'd grown too tired to talk after that. A few hours later, she'd left this world for a better one. One with no pain, no nausea, no treatments, no more suffering.

But Yvette Henry Broussard had done what she could to prepare her boys, endowing them with her own strength and resilience, and teaching them self-sufficiency. Jamison had taken on the task of caring for his younger brother without a single complaint.

And thirteen-year-old Billy had always kept his promise to his mother.

* * * * *

May 1973

Bill threw the duffle bag into the passenger seat of his old Ford truck and faced Jamison. "I guess that's about it, Jay. I'll write every now and then to let you know where I am."

Jamison Broussard kicked one of the truck tires. "You'd better. And remember—call the Martins to let them know where you are when you move on to a new place. That way, if I'm out of town and can't get your letters I'll still be able to check in with her for updates." He shifted nervously from one foot to the other. "You sure about this, Billy?"

The younger brother hooked one thumb in a belt loop and adjusted his old straw hat. "Pretty sure."

Jamison scratched at his beard. "I promised mom I'd take care of you. Lettin' you loose on your own two days after high school graduation doesn't seem like a nurturing kinda thing to do."

Bill reached over and slapped one hand on his brother's shoulder. "Relax man. You've been looking out for me since you were nine, back when Pop left us. Considerin' how he spent the next ten years of his life—"

His brother's jaw tensed at the mention of their father. Jamison spoke, his voice hard and bitter. "You mean passed out drunk or in jail, and then croaking from a pickled liver?"

"Yep. Considerin' that—we were all a hell of a lot better off. I was only four when he left and I remember thinking I'd be okay because of you. Five years ago, at eighteen years old, you took over the job single-handedly when mom passed away."

Jamison stared at his boots. "Well hell, what was I gonna do? Put you up in an orphanage or some foster home?"

"You could have. But you didn't," Bill offered. "Here's *your* chance, man. Go do what Jamison wants to do for a change. Take that job overseas you talked about, or go work on your buddy's ranch in Montana."

Jamison shook his head. "Working cattle at fifteen below doesn't sound like fun to me, little brother. But that overseas job is a possibility—once I see proof you can take care of yourself."

"Proof? Well, hell…what's that gonna take?"

Jamison cocked his head. "I don't know. Maybe not getting a call to bail your ass out of some Mexican prison?"

Bill shook his head. "You're too cheap to pay for a phone, so I wouldn't call you anyway."

Jamison's mouth pulled down in a frown. "You're not helping, little brother."

Bill laughed at the worry lines on his brother's brow. "I'm just shittin' you man. There's too much of our own United States I haven't seen yet. I plan on driving through most of them, taking jobs where I can. You taught me everything you know, and a hell of a lot about hard work."

Jamison frowned, his face still contorted with doubt. "I taught you a little bit of a lot of different things. Hopefully, enough to keep you from starving to death." He pulled him close for his signature slap-on-the-back hug—finished it off by reaching up to ruffle his little brother's hair. "When the hell did you get taller than me, anyway?"

"End of junior year," Bill admitted. "I kept quiet about it so's not to damage your delicate ego." He chuckled at Jamison's brotherly shove.

"If you're goin', just go, smart-ass."

Thinking that may be as good a good-bye as he would ever get, Bill yanked open his truck door and slid behind the steering wheel. The engine turned over on first try, purring smoothly from the hundred or so hours of shade-tree-mechanic rebuilding and maintenance they'd given it over the years.

He rolled the window down and shut the door, resting his arm on it. "Later, man."

Jamison nodded. "Later."

Bill drove away, checked his rearview mirror once to see Jamison standing there with one arm raised and waving. He stuck his left arm out the window to wave back and kept driving.

Chapter Two

Billy and Lorraine: New Love

March 1975

"Can I get you anything else, good looking?"

Bill studied the waitress—from bleached blonde locks, to green eyes, lashes thick with mascara, down to glossy pink lips. The plunging neckline of her one-piece uniform revealed an enticing view of cleavage. Not even close to his type.

He pushed away the empty plate that had held two of the tastiest slices of pie he'd had in months. "No thanks, I'm good." Bill raised the white china mug and stared down at the bottom through three inches of unusually weak coffee, even for Washington state. He took one cautious sip, then another. How could a place with such tasty pie sell the worst coffee in the thirty states he'd inhabited over the past two years?

She leaned closer, her arms squeezing her breasts together to give him a better view of their plump fullness. "You sure? If you're short on cash we could work something out."

He pulled out his wallet, thick with cash, and threw a five on the counter, far more than enough to cover his meal. "I'm sure. Keep the change, though." He tipped his Stetson at her, slid off the stool and hit the exit, grinning at the waitress's farewell shot.

"Too bad, cowboy—we don't get many like you in here."

He walked several car lengths down the curb to his parked truck and got inside, taking the time to study the area map before starting his truck. Halfway to his destination, on a lonely stretch of roadway, he slowed at the sight of a blue car pulled over on the side of the shoulder-free road ahead of him, its hazard lights blinking. Bill stopped and got out of his truck, ready to help.

The driver's door opened and a leg appeared, wearing wide bell bottom jeans with tall chunky heels. A shapely woman followed, jeans covering a firm butt and wearing a fitted green sweater that displayed curves without revealing an inch of skin. She couldn't have been more than five feet tall without those stacked heels. But something about her screamed athlete, reminding him of Sallie Ann McHenry—the solidly packed cheerleader he'd dated off and on, then off again, during his senior year of high school.

As she turned, a gust of wind blew her light-brown, straight hair and covered her face for a moment. He approached as slender hands cleared the hair back from the prettiest face he'd ever seen. Intrigued by blue inquisitive eyes framed in long dark lashes, a perky nose, and plump pink lips, Bill cleared his throat. "Is there something I can help you out with, Miss?"

"Yes, please! My car just died on me out here." She cocked her head to one side, slight grimace promising a hint of dimples. "Are you in any way mechanically inclined?" She clasped her hands together. "Pleeeaase—" she said, following through on that promise by displaying a set of adorable dimples. "Say yes?"

He grinned. "Depends on the level of complication, I suppose. What kind of problems are you having?"

"It started spitting and sputtering. I'd hoped the darn thing would make it back home, but it finally just quit on me. It starts but coughs and stalls."

"Could be the fuel filter's clogged. Bad batch of gas?"

She sucked in her breath, showing straight, white teeth. "I tanked up at the Sure-Stop in town one morning earlier this week. I was running late for work and there was a longer line at the place I usually go to. Ugh!" She shook her head. "I can already hear my dad gloating 'I told you so'."

Bill chuckled as he pointed to her opened car door. "Mind if I give it a try?"

She waved her hand in one sweeping motion. "Go ahead."

He had to move the seat as far back as he could to slide in behind the wheel. One turn of the key had him thinking his suspicions were right on the money. He pulled himself out of the car. "Any chance you have a spare fuel filter with you?"

She leaned in the car to retrieve her keys. "My dad keeps a box of spare parts in the trunk. I'm not sure what's in there."

A quick search through the box produced an unopened filter along with a grunt of approval from Bill. He also grabbed an old hand towel and a couple of tools from the box. "Your dad obviously knows enough about cars to keep what's important in here. We'll see if I'm right in a couple of minutes."

Five minutes later Bill popped his head out from under the hood of her '72 Chevelle. "Give it a try." He grinned in satisfaction as the engine turned over on the first try and purred smoothly.

She jumped out of the car with a whoop of excitement. "You're a life-saver! Thank you so much." Approaching him slowly, she offered her hand. "What's your name anyway?"

He took her hand. "I'm Bill Broussard."

"It's nice to meet you. I'm Lorraine—Lorraine Stubbins."

His hand froze mid-shake. "I'm on my way up to Stubbins Logging Company right now. I'm applying for a job there in the morning and I like to scope out the area early. I missed out on a great position in Oregon last week because I got turned around on one of those mountain roads and got to the job interview late. That won't happen again."

Her smile reached clear to her eyes. "That's my dad's company. Are you meeting him at the house or his office?"

Bill pulled a folded slip of paper from his shirt pocket. "I'm supposed to be at this address at 8:00 a.m. tomorrow morning."

Lorraine glanced at the address and nodded. "That's his office." She scraped her bottom lip with her teeth and frowned. "This morning I heard him say something about there being far more applicants than job openings. Why don't you follow me to the house and I'll introduce you to him today?"

Bill recognized a great hand when the fates dealt him one—best not to turn his back on this particular stroke of luck. Besides, he wanted to know more about the pretty girl in front of him.

Ten minutes later, he followed Lorraine into her father's study. Once she made the introductions and stated how Bill had resolved her car trouble issue, Gary Stubbins pulled a stack of papers from his desk.

"I appreciate you helping my daughter out of a bind, but the logging industry can be dangerous work, Mr. Broussard. You'll have to prove to me why you can do a better job than the rest of the men who turned in applications."

"But daddy, couldn't you—"

Gary Stubbins cut off his daughter's comment with one look.

Bill stepped forward to diffuse the moment before it turned into a situation. "Now, hold on, Miss Lorraine. Your father's right. If he sends someone out there with no experience, he'd be putting not just me, but his entire team at risk. Logging is serious business."

He pointed to the papers in the other man's hands. "You should find my application in there, along with a list of recommendations from my former employers, complete with phone numbers for back up."

Gary shuffled through until he singled out a couple of pages stapled together. He studied it and looked up at Bill. "You've had several jobs in the last couple of years. That's not usually a good sign, son."

"Yes sir, but I give a hundred percent and always stay until the end of a job—never leave anyone in a lurch. Up until two years ago, I'd never been out of the state of Texas. Once I registered for the draft, I decided to see as many states as I could before Uncle Sam sent me to 'Nam. They never called my number, so I kept on traveling. The logging industry seems to agree with me."

Gary placed the application at the top of the pile and nodded. "I plan on calling every one of those numbers you listed as references, just so you know."

Bill nodded. "Never doubted it." He extended his hand. "I won't waste any more of your Sunday evening. Thank you for your time, sir."

Gary shook Bill's hand. "You come back in the morning and I'll give you my decision, young man. And thank you again for helping out my daughter."

Bill tipped his hat at the man he hoped would be his future boss. "Anytime."

Lorraine walked him to the front exit. "I think you'll get the job, Bill. And I have a feeling I'll be seeing much more of you around here." She gave him a wink. "I sure hope I will, anyway."

He touched the brim of his hat in a brief farewell. "Here's to you being right." He left through the front door, the image of Lorraine's beautiful smile giving him hope that she could be more than a simple acquaintance.

Chapter Three

Bill the young husband: Christmas Past

Bill and Lorraine fell hard and fast for each other after only one date. When he asked Lorraine to marry him two short months later, she said yes, providing he asked her parents. Within minutes, Bill stood before them, clean-shaven and dressed in his Sunday best. Lorraine stood next to him, their hands linked, both anxious and hoping for some form of parental blessings.

Gary approached him, his gaze stern and intense. "Look, Bill. I remember what it's like to be so wrapped up in a girl you can't see straight." He'd winked at his wife then. "God knows I still feel that way about Miriam." He poked his finger at Bill's broad chest. "But don't you go jumping the gun to make me a grandfather before I'm a father-in-law. You respect my daughter—you got me?"

"I do sir, I will—always." He squeezed Lorraine's hand, the familiar tug of emotion washing over him at her nearness. Like she was the half of him he'd searched for all his life.

Gary nodded. "You have my blessing." He looked at his wife.

"So long as you marry in the church." Miriam Stubbins peered down her nose at her daughter and her prospective son-in-law. "It'll take time to plan anything lavish."

Lorraine had laughed at her mom's supposition. "When have I ever preferred lavish over simple, Mom?"

"Never, but—well, a girl only gets married once, if she's lucky." She'd given them both a wistful sigh, as though recognizing that she'd already lost that battle.

Less than a week later, Bill and Lorraine stood before the Stubbins' family preacher in a local church to exchange vows before a handful of friends and family members.

Bill had existed in a constant state of elation since that day. He decided to make damn sure that neither his wife nor in-laws would spend a moment regretting their decisions.

* * * * *

December 23, 1975

Bill opened the door to the tiny bedroom, filled nearly wall-to-wall with their bed. He placed a steaming mug of cocoa with melted marshmallows on the night stand and paused to gaze at his wife. Six months into the pregnancy and she glowed with a beauty matched only by her kindness as well as her love for him.

He leaned over the bed, placed a gentle kiss on her plump lips. “Good morning, beautiful. It’s time to wake up.”

Lorraine’s long lashes fluttered several times before she cracked open one eye. “What time is it?”

He looked at his watch. “A little past four a.m.”

She groaned and pulled the covers over her head. “Ten more minutes.”

He pulled the covers down slowly. “Sorry, but your mom asked me to drop you off before I go up to the site this morning, remember? She said she’s too busy with baby shower preparations to drive up the mountain to get you.” He slapped her butt through the pile of quilts. “Come on, babe. It’s my last day of work before the holidays. Tomorrow we can both sleep late.”

A glance through the bedroom door revealed the other half of the two room cabin he and his wife had turned into a comfortable, cozy, honeymoon cottage. “I know you love our little place up here in the woods, but it’s too secluded to leave you alone in your condition.”

“I’m pregnant, not handicapped, sweetie. And all this seclusion gives me plenty of time and subject matter to paint.” A sweeping motion with her arm indicated a half dozen canvases covered with painted birds, squirrels, and even a fox she’d befriended over the last six months in their forest wonderland. “After this baby comes I won’t have nearly as much time to paint.”

The deep base of Bill’s chuckle filled the room. “Neither of us will have much leisure time on our hands but I suspect we’ll both be too busy doting on our baby girl to mind.”

She smiled. “You mean our baby boy.”

He patted her thigh under the blankets. "We'll see in a few months." He helped her to sit up and plumped pillows behind her for support before handing her the mug of cocoa. "Now drink up. We need to be on the road in thirty minutes."

One sip had her rolling her eyes in bliss. "Mmm … are you ever going to tell me what you put in this cocoa that makes it so much better than mine or my mom's?"

Bill grinned. "Nope. It's my secret ingredient. I figure as long as I'm the only one who knows, you'll keep me around." His comment wasn't such a stretch, considering he still couldn't believe his luck in marrying the girl of his dreams.

Her blue eyes softened as she looked up from her cocoon of quilts. "Like I'd ever get rid of you. You're the best thing in my life." She caressed her burgeoning belly with one hand. "So far, at least."

Bill placed his two hands on either side of hers and leaned forward to place a gentle kiss on her belly. He lay his face on Lorraine's belly full of baby. "I already love you, whoever you are—as much as I love your beautiful mama." He kissed his wife once more before standing. "I'll get your clothes ready for you while you finish your cocoa."

Bill rummaged through their closet, threw a few items of clothing on the foot of the bed. "How's this?"

Lorraine peered over the rim of the mug. "That's fine to wear over there. I left my outfit for the baby shower at mom's so she could hem the pants for me."

"Oh, yeah. What exactly happens at a baby shower, anyway?"

"Well, first we'll play silly games, like poking fun at how fat I am by guessing the circumference of my belly and how much weight I've gained."

He frowned, unhappy at anyone making fun of his wife in her condition. Especially when she worried over every new stretch mark that appeared on her taut belly. "Well, hell—that doesn't seem very nice."

"It's all in good fun," she explained. "Besides, they'll give us all sorts of adorable clothes and things for our baby."

"Hmph," he grunted, thinking he'd likely be comforting her later this evening. "I'm not sure if it's worth all that. You tell me if anyone gets out of hand and I'll have a talk with them later."

She cocked her head at him and smiled, obviously pleased with his devotion to her well-being. “Have I told you lately how crazy I am about you?”

Bill approached his wife again and leaned over for a kiss, sweet with the flavor of cocoa and marshmallows. “You have, but feel free to keep it up.”

She hooked one arm around his neck. “If we had more time, I’d show you.”

He smiled. “If we had more time, I’d slide under those covers and show you it’s mutual. But we don’t.” He slapped her thigh. “Drink that down and get going. Your mom’s waiting on us.”

Just under an hour later, Bill walked his wife to her parents’ door, leaving her with a kiss and a promise to pick her up as soon as he could make it back down from the site.

He didn’t know it then, but he wouldn’t be able to keep that promise.

Chapter Four

Bill: In Mourning

Please God, let her be all right.

Bill had repeated the same prayer dozens of times since his father-in-law had collected him from the job site. He pushed nervous fingers through his hair and shoved back the panic building in his chest. He faced the man behind the steering wheel. "Tell me again what happened, Mr. Gary."

Gary Stubbins down-shifted to turn onto the street leading to the hospital. "Miriam said she and Lorraine had just gone through the items she received from the baby shower. Lorraine started cramping and went to bathroom, then called out to her mother that she was bleeding." He swallowed hard. "Miriam got her to the hospital within fifteen minutes but by then she was hemorrhaging. As far as Miriam knows, nothing happened to cause it."

Bill shook his head. "I don't understand any of this. We both made sure she didn't lift anything heavy or overexert herself. I went with her for her last appointment and the OB insisted everything was fine." He pointed out a parking spot near the emergency room entrance, eager to get to his wife of just under seven months.

"Lorraine's always been healthy and Miriam and I know how well you treat our daughter, Bill. Sometimes these things happen through nobody's fault."

Bill answered with a grunt, shoved the door open and slammed it shut before the truck rolled to a complete stop. He sprinted to the hospital's emergency room entrance and pushed through the door, long having left his father-in-law in the dust. A quick scan of the room found him staring at his mother-in-law's back as she spoke to a tall man in scrubs. "Ms. Miriam!" he called out, running to her.

She turned, her face wet with tears, her eyes red and puffy. "Oh, Billy—" She fell into his arms, dissolving into tears.

Bill's gaze clashed with the doctor's as Miriam moved from his arms to those of her husband's when he joined them. Her heartbroken sobs echoed throughout the emergency room entrance. “Somebody tell me what the hell’s going on!”

“Mr. Broussard—I’m so sorry—”

“The baby?” Bill’s gut clenched at the sympathetic expression on the doctor’s face. “Oh God, no . . .” Lorraine would be devastated. “I want to see my wife. She’ll need me with her.” He faced his in-laws, both sobbing uncontrollably now. He looked down at the doctor’s hand on his arm, faced him again.

“Mr. Broussard, I’m so sorry. Your wife suffered from a hemorrhage and by the time we got to her she’d already gone into shock. Her heart stopped on the operating table and we couldn’t get her back.”

“I should have called an ambulance!” Miriam broke in, between her sobs.

“Don’t do that to yourself, Mrs. Stubbins,” the doctor added. “They wouldn’t have gotten to her any sooner than we did with you bringing her in. As I told you before, no one could have predicted this.”

“Wait a minute!” Bill cried out, tight-chested and damned near petrified with fear. “You’re not telling me my wife . . .” He gulped, swallowing bile. “She’s not—she can’t be . . .”

“I’m so sorry, Mr. Broussard. We lost both her and the baby.”

“No.” Bill shook his head. “No, that can’t be. I can’t accept that.” He grabbed the doctor’s scrub shirt in one hand and pointed with his other to the double doors marked with a MEDICAL PERSONNEL ONLY sign. “You get your ass back through those doors and do something to help her! Hook her up to one of those machines that’ll keep her breathing until she comes out of this. When she does she’ll want to see me. I guarantee it.”

The doctor gripped the hand clutching his shirt between his own two hands. “That’s not possible, sir. I’m so sorry.”

Four arms wrapped gently around Bill from behind. He turned and faced his in-laws—the two people who’d taken him into their family and treated him with nothing but kindness and respect, as he had them. Miriam rested her forehead on his upper arm. “Billy . . . she’s gone, honey. I know it hurts but we’ll get through this somehow—we’ll all get through this together.”

“Lorraine would want it that way, Bill,” Gary said, his voice thick with tears. “We know how much she loved you—how much the two of you cared for each other.”

Bill turned toward the doctor again. “I need to see her.”

“Of course—this way.” He placed a hand on Bill’s shoulder and led them all through the doors. The doctor held them up briefly and disappeared through a curtained off area. He spoke in quiet murmurs to bustling staff members on the other side. Several seconds later he opened the curtains and ushered them inside to the now empty area.

Up until that moment, Bill’s mind had held a tiny sliver of hope that this had all been some terrible mistake—that he’d walk into that room and see some stranger there instead of his beautiful young wife.

The first sight of Lorraine as she lay there—her face nearly the same shade of white as the sheet covering her—banished any promise of hope. He approached her side, stared down at the face he’d kissed thousands of times in the short but blissful nearly nine months he’d known her. Bill placed both hands on her pale cheeks, already several degrees colder than they should be. Undeterred, he leaned over and kissed her cool lips, then touched his forehead to hers. “I’m sorry, baby. I wasn’t with you when you and our child needed me most—and I’m so sorry.” Grief engulfed him—giant waves of it crashing over his heart like high tide at the beach. Laying his head on his beautiful wife’s chest, he broke down, clinging to her. Several minutes later he felt hands on his back and remembered he wasn’t alone—neither in the room, nor his grief.

He straightened, faced his in-laws, the parents who’d also loved his wife and child. Their faces mirrored grief as substantial as his. His voice thick with misery, he finally managed to speak. “It’s not supposed to be this way. This isn’t what we planned.”

Gary placed a large hand on Bill’s shoulder. “I know, son. None of us planned it this way, but it’s no one’s fault.”

“Of course not.” Miriam blinked back her tears. “There’s no way any of us could have known this would happen. You made our daughter so happy, Billy. We could see how much you both adored each other.”

He closed his eyes, lightheaded, overcome with a rush of memories. His first sight of Lorraine stepping out of that stalled Chevelle. Their first date one week later, when they both recognized an immediate connection. Their intimate wedding two short months after that. The honeymoon—consummating their love for the first time, and the multitude of nights and rainy afternoons of lovemaking that followed.

He remembered the worry lines on her brow when she told him about being six weeks pregnant only two months into their marriage. She'd expected he'd be upset. He pictured her face, washed in relief as he'd wrapped his arms around her waist and lifted her, spinning her around in his elation. The pregnancy had transformed his existence with her into a state of bliss he'd thought impossible.

And now this.

Heartbroken and miserable, he didn't dare give voice to the two thoughts running through his mind.

His dead wife was the lucky one.

And how the hell could he live without her in his life?

* * * *

His mind numb, he moved through the funeral like a zombie in one of those corny old scary movies Lorraine loved watching—not quite undead, but a far cry from alive.

His in-laws never left his side at the funeral home—probably because he'd never left the coffin, staring silently at the faces of his wife and the child cradled in her lifeless arms. He acknowledged everyone they introduced to him with a few polite words before turning again to the open coffin.

He stood there, stone-faced and silent, while Miriam and Gary Stubbins broke down when the box was sealed tight. The three of them walked behind the coffin carrying his wife and child to the church, then the cemetery. Long after everyone else had gone, he stood over the gravesite, staring at the wreaths and flowers arranged in the shapes of crosses and hearts.

His father-in-law joined him at dusk, placing a hand on his shoulder. "Come on, son. It's time to go home now. You're staying with us for a while."

Bill passed a hand over his face before turning to stare at the man. "Thanks, but I'm going to our cabin."

Gary looked doubtful. "Why don't you come with me and I'll send someone for your truck?"

Bill shook his head. "No. I'll drive to our place." He turned and walked away from Lorraine and his son's grave, with no clue that it would take him nearly forty years to return.

* * * *

He went home, sat staring at the Christmas tree he and his wife had cut down and decorated together.

He'd let her pick it out, kept quiet when she'd chosen one too big for their cabin. She'd kept quiet when he'd cut it in half in order to fit inside their home. Then again when he'd had to trim another half off the circumference so that it didn't overpower their tiny living area.

He'd made her mugs of hot chocolate while she popped kettle after kettle of popcorn for stringing. It had taken them until midnight to decorate it to her satisfaction. Exhausted, but thrilled with the efforts, they'd fallen into bed and used what little energy they had left on love-making.

His in-laws checked on him often, their faces plastered with concern. They'd leave—he'd sit staring at the tree. Christmas and New Year's came and went and Miriam suggested he take it down. He'd firmly, but politely put her off. By the end of January, she didn't ask, but arrived with her husband to help her dismantle Lorraine's tree.

Gary had pulled on a branch, releasing a handful of needles. "It's kindling, son. Don't make us come here one day to find you and this cabin have gone up in flames. We've lost enough for one year, don't you think?"

Bill had relented and helped them pack his and Lorraine's decorations, both store-bought and handmade, into a box. He handed them to Miriam, remaining stone-faced as she thanked him with a hug. They stayed long enough to help him get rid of the tree and clean the mess left behind.

Each day one of them would bring him a plate of food, creating one excuse or another to check up on him. He'd always thank them and place the food in the fridge, barely touched.

January rolled into February with more of the same. When the first of March rolled around, he opened the door to his mother-in-law, her face set with determination.

"You need to eat something, Billy. Lorraine wouldn't want you torturing yourself this way."

Miriam's words bounced around in his head, echoing as though spoken in a hollowed-out cave. "I tried, Ms. Miriam. I can barely get anything down. I just can't." He waved away the plastic covered plate of spaghetti with garlic bread. "Sometimes, it won't stay down. Not worth the effort."

Rather than perform any further useless methods of persuasion, his mother-in-law placed a gentle kiss on the top of his head. She turned and left him sitting alone and staring at the chair opposite his at the small table in his tiny kitchen—Lorraine's chair—as cold and empty as his heart.

He took care of his own basic needs—trips to the bathroom, showers, and brushing his teeth. One such foray into the bathroom had him staring at his haunted reflection.

The thin face with dark circled eyes staring back at him looked like some horror film character. His bloodshot blue eyes held no trace of emotion, his black hair dull and unkempt, and the scruff on his face had long turned into a scraggly, untrimmed beard.

He turned away from the gaunt specter. Lorraine *wouldn't* approve—he knew that in his heart as sure as he knew that it made no difference now.

Another two days passed before Gary Stubbins entered his small cabin followed closely by someone from Bill's life before Lorraine. "Son, your brother's here to bring you home with him."

"I am home," he said, to neither of the two men standing before him. He hadn't seen Jamison since that day he'd left their home nearly three years earlier. He'd only spoken to him a handful of times over the phone during the first year or two of his journeys. He'd written even less than that and he hadn't spoken to or heard from him at all since moving to Washington state. Likewise, he'd been too wrapped up in life with Lorraine to write to his older brother.

"Home to Texas, Billy. I could sure use your help right now and I'm not taking no for an answer. From the looks of it, you need to be there."

Too weak to put up a fight, he let his brother lead him outside. Jamison helped him into his truck, the newer model he'd bought from his father-in-law to replace his old Ford when it finally died. Jamison left him for a bit longer, returning soon with a few suitcases and several bags, along with Miriam and Gary. His in-laws both hugged him and bid tearful goodbyes before his brother took him away from the place that had brought him equal parts joy and heartbreak.

Jamison didn't make any attempts at conversation, but left him alone with his thoughts for a good portion of the trip back to Texas. Bill mostly slept, lulled by the monotonous rhythm of tires on pavement while songs played at a low volume from a combination of country and pop radio stations.

Every now and then they'd pull in at some diner for a break. Jamison would eat, and talk about his time working overseas in the oil industry—how the time he'd spent there had him longing for the Texas life again. After Bill had pushed his food around on a plate long enough, his big brother would have the waitress fill a thermos with strong coffee and they'd be off again. Occasionally, Bill would wake to find them parked at a rest area or pulled over on some side road, catching just enough shut-eye to keep Jamison going several more hours.

After nearly two days on the road, Bill felt a hand stirring him awake.

"Wake up, little brother. We're almost home."

Bill brushed a hand over his eyes and sat up straight, staring out the window at unfamiliar surroundings. "Where are we?"

"We're south of Houston in Brazoria County. My wife's dad owned a small ranch with a couple dozen head of cattle. I started working for him after I married his daughter. When he died a few months ago, it went to her and I took over the operations."

Bill studied his brother's profile. "You have a wife?"

Jamison nodded. "Yep." He shot a couple of cautious glances Bill's direction. "My company transferred me to Nacogdoches a couple of years ago. I met a beautiful girl named Elise Connor, an elementary education student at the university there. I fell hard for her. I don't know why but she did the same." He smiled, despite the exhaustion lining his face. "She dropped out of school and married me a year ago in January."

"That's great." His own comeback rang in his ear, sounding hollow. He tried again for something he could pass off as sincere. "Congratulations, Jay."

His brother paused and took a deep breath. "And…uh…we have a two-week-old baby boy now."

Bill stared straight ahead, swallowed hard. "You have a kid?" Somewhere in his brain, neurons fired, relaying a message that he should be happy for him. In his peripheral vision, he caught Jamison turning sharply to face him.

"Yeah, Billy. I hate that you had to find out this way. And I'm sorry if it upsets you."

The comment made Bill realize how taxing these past few days must have been for Jay, both physically and emotionally. He shook his head, reached over to grab his brother's shoulder. "Don't, man. I'm the one who should be sorry for taking you away from your wife and child for what—four days now?"

"Only two and a half. Your in-laws arranged for my flight over and insisted we drive your truck back home. Mr. Gary said he didn't know if you could handle the flight back in your condition."

"If I'd known about your situation I'd have driven myself." Even as he spoke he knew it was a load of bullshit.

"Anyway, I think he called it right. Makes me sad that neither of us knew what the other had been going through."

Bill stared out the window at a neat fence line and a dozen or so head of cattle. "Yeah, but you paid your dues, Jay. You took care of me after mom died, made sure I finished high school. I've done what I wanted to do since then—figured you'd earned the right to do the same."

"Still, we should have done a better job of staying in touch," Jamison insisted. "Mom would be ashamed of us."

Bill glanced over at him. "I figured you were still working overseas."

"I worked eighteen straight months in Abu Dhabi with hardly any time off." Jamison sent his brother a somewhat sober grin. "I made a ridiculous amount of money."

"Which you squirreled away, I'm sure." Watching their mom struggle with raising two boys alone had taught them both to budget and save. "I did try calling you once as soon as I settled in Washington but the Martins didn't answer and I never called back. When I left Texas, you didn't have a phone. I'm sorry, I should have written."

"We have a phone but our number is still listed under my father-in-law's name. And I had no way of knowing where you were to call or write to you," his brother added. "The last address either I or Mrs. Martin had from you was some place in Oklahoma."

Swamped with guilt, Bill realized he'd been so wrapped up in his own life he hadn't bothered to contact his brother in months.

He'd planned to try again once the baby came, winced when the thought sent a stabbing pain to his chest. "So, how'd you hear about—my situation?"

"Your father-in-law called a friend of his at the Harris County Sheriff's Department and gave him my name. That guy had a friend who had another friend. Trust me on this. When a Texas Ranger knocks on your door at four a.m., all kinds of images run through your mind."

Bill imagined himself on the other end of that early morning visit. "No doubt." He cleared his throat and made another effort to sit up. "Still, I'm sorry for causing you so much trouble, Jay."

Jamison whipped his head around to stare at him. "You're my brother, Billy—the only blood family I've got besides my son. I'd have gone through more trouble than that to bring you back home where you belong."

"I belong with my own wife and child." Bill nearly choked on the last syllable.

"Had they survived, absolutely. . ." Jamison turned the truck down a long, graveled driveway leading to a white house in the distance. "But they didn't, and after speaking to your in-laws, I think I learned enough about your wife to know she wouldn't want you wasting away from this loss, as awful as it is. You can hate me later but it's time you come back to the land of the living."

Bill stared at the slowly approaching house, a rambling wood frame farm house on tall piers with a wraparound porch. He thought about his mom and the home they'd spent a good portion of their lives. "What did you do with mom's place?"

Jamison slowed and swerved the truck to avoid a rut in its path. "It's still there. It's been rented it out since I started working overseas. I use a little of the money for upkeep but there's an account at the Bank of Pasadena with about two thousand in it. There used to be more but I gave the old place a facelift a few months ago between renters—new shingles and a coat of paint, inside and out."

Bill nodded, picturing the place as he'd seen it last. Before dying at forty-one of an inoperable brain tumor, Yvette Broussard willed their home, mortgage free, in equal shares to her two sons. At eighteen and thirteen, they'd been able to stay in their own place, thanks to their mom's careful planning, a life insurance policy, and Jamison's level of maturity and sense of responsibility.

Jamison pulled the truck into a horseshoe driveway and turned off the ignition. Bill gave the homestead a quick once-over. The house, barn, and sheds all seemed to be well-maintained with a neat yard and fence lines in good shape. He opened his door and stepped out. Somewhat weak and light-headed, he managed to get himself to a standing position.

Jamison appeared next to him. "You alright, man?"

Bill took one step, then another. "I'll live." *Unfortunately.* He followed his big brother up a set of wooden steps onto a wide porch spanning the entire front of the house and wrapping around both sides as far as he could see. Jay held the door open for him and he stepped through, pausing for a moment to take in the cozy interior. "This is a nice place."

"Thanks, man. We're comfortable here. Elise is kinda like mom—pretty good at making four walls feel like a home, you know?"

Bill nodded. *Like Lorraine.* He approached a group of framed pictures on one wall and studied them in silence.

Jamison joined him, pointing out several school shots of them, including graduation portraits. "Look at those knuckleheads, would you? A couple of country boys doin' the best we could with what we had."

"Except we lived in the city limits."

"Only because nobody gave us a choice. But face it, we're country boys at heart. Look where we both ended up. Me on a ranch and you up in the mountains."

Bill nodded in agreement, still studying the images of himself and Jay through the years. He paused on the last photo taken of his mom, healthy and smiling, before they discovered the tumor. Before the rounds of chemo and radiation changed her into the sunken-eyed woman she'd been the last months of her life—worried about leaving her sons alone and desperate to see them taken care of.

He stepped closer to study the smiling blue eyes she'd passed on to her boys. Had she been happy? Satisfied with the way her life had turned out? If she'd felt any hatred or bitterness toward their father, she'd never shown it. It sickened him, knowing his own father had betrayed her the way he had. *Poor mom.* He'd never have done that to Lorraine. A door opened and he turned toward the sound of footsteps in the hall.

"Jamison?" His big brother shot straight for the tiny woman who appeared in the doorway. "You're finally home!" She threw her arms around his neck, plastering his face with kisses.

"Hey babe—I missed the hell out of you . . ." He wrapped his arms around her, lifting her easily as he spun her around.

She squealed, begging him to stop. "Put me down now so I can meet my brother-in-law."

Jamison lowered her and with his hand on the small of her back, turned her to face Bill. "Elise, my brother, Billy. Billy, this is my beautiful wife, Elise."

Bill studied his sister-in-law. She'd plaited her black hair into a single long braid that hung over one shoulder. The dark hair contrasted sharply with her fair complexion, bringing to mind images of Snow White in the old animated movie.

She approached and held both arms open for him, her blue eyes sparkling with happiness, or tears, or maybe a mixture of both. "I'm so glad to finally meet you, Bill. I've waited forever to have my own brother and now I have one."

"Nice to meet you too, Elise."

She hugged him tightly then backed off to take in his appearance. "Excuse me for saying so, but boy, you look like you're about to pass right out. Sit. Now!" She pointed to a chair at the table. "I'm going to fix you something to eat."

"Uh, I'm not really hun—"

She put both fists on her hips and stared him down. "I did not stutter, my friend. You're on my turf now and you will eat what I put in front of you. I've got leftover meatloaf, mashed potatoes and green beans. I'll have it reheated for you in a jiff."

Jamison chuckled at the look Bill sent his direction. "It's best not to argue with her. She might look all soft and angelic but I haven't won an argument with her yet."

"Not one he hasn't lived to regret, anyway," Elise added, smiling sweetly up at her husband while pulling containers from the fridge.

"Right . . ." Jamison mumbled. "Is my son sleeping?"

"Yes, but he should wake for his bottle any minute. Go ahead and bring him in here to meet his Uncle Bill. I'll get a bottle ready for him."

Bill sat, watching his new sister-in-law flit from one corner of the kitchen to another, with more energy in her little finger than he possessed in his entire body at that moment. If she'd kept any of that 'baby weight' Lorraine had been dreading, she hid it well.

Before any thoughts of his own wife and child could tighten his chest further, Jamison re-entered the room, carrying a squirming, snuffling bundle swaddled in a blue and white blanket.

"I think this kid's grown an inch and gained at least a pound in the short time I've been gone." He sat in the chair next to Bill and began unwrapping his son. "How about it, Jackson Jamison Broussard—are you ready to meet your ol' Uncle Bill now?"

Bill leaned over to study his nephew. The infant's long arms flailed around, hands open, long, skinny, spider-monkey like fingers stretched and reaching now that they were free of the blanket. When Jamison's right index finger came into range, the baby wrapped his entire fist around it.

"Look at that grip, would you? Kid's gonna be an athlete, for sure, huh, Billy?"

Bill tapped the infant's opposite open hand and long fingers wrapped instantly around his finger. "Maybe he'll be a receiver like his uncle." The infant stopped flailing at the sound of his voice and opened his eyes. He stared at Bill, his tiny mouth opened and rounded in an 'O'. Bill stared back, mesmerized by the sight of his new nephew.

A distant click and flash to the left broke the spell, had him looking up at Elise. She stood there, camera in hand, tears streaming down her face.

"Are you okay, hon?" Jamison asked his wife.

She nodded before snapping another of Bill and Jamison facing her. "It's just so beautiful, seeing the three of you together." She put the camera down and excused herself to go to the bathroom.

Bill watched her disappear into the nearby bathroom, raised an eyebrow at his brother.

"She's okay." Jamison lifted his son to his shoulder. "Those post delivery hormonal swings are still affecting her, that's all."

Elise joined them seconds later and picked up where she'd left off in the kitchen. She piled up a plate and set it in front of Bill before lowering herself onto her husband's knee. "Now, I know you wouldn't dream of hurting my feelings by not eating these delicious leftovers." She took the baby from Jamison and snuggled closer to her husband.

Bill picked up his fork and took a bite. He couldn't pinpoint what made the difference—the cooking, the locale, or the company. But for the first time in months, he actually tasted that first bite of meatloaf. The second bite tasted even better so he kept eating until he pushed his empty plate away. "That was good. Thank you."

She smiled at him, cradling her baby. "Would you like more?"

He rubbed his belly, too full to risk another bite. "No, ma'am."

Elise's plump lips pulled down in a frown. "Ma'am! Do I look like a ma'am? I know I have a child now but I sure don't feel old enough to be a *ma'am*."

Jamison attempted to placate his wife before she had another melt down. "I think he's just being respectful, hon."

"That's true," Bill said.

"I appreciate that, but call me Elise, please." She rose from her husband's lap and adjusted her hold on the baby. "Would you like to hold your nephew now?"

Bill shifted uncomfortably. "I don't—ah—"

Jamison cleared his throat. "Maybe not just yet, okay, hon?"

Elise turned on her husband. "Why not?"

"Well, he—he may not know how to—"

"Don't be stupid, Jay. Neither of us knew what to do with a newborn two short weeks ago. He's got to learn sometimes." She turned to Bill. "Take him. There…support his head. Like that. See? Isn't that easy?"

Bill adjusted his nephew in his arms, still not comfortable with the bundle, and stared into the infant's little face.

Elise grabbed her camera again and moved in front of him. "Look up and say cheese, Uncle Bill."

He sent her a sober look, just long enough for her to get off another shot. He flinched at the pop of a flash. Bill blinked several times, trying to clear the black spots from his sight.

She chuckled from beside him. "Sorry, but I need to use the flash for these inside close ups. This is a pivotal moment in my son's life. He's a handsome little man though, isn't he?"

Bill blinked a couple more times. “I’ll tell you once the flash burn wears off.”

Jamison shifted from one foot to the other at his other elbow. “Kind of impossible for him not to be good looking, don’t you think, since he looks like his ol’ man?”

“I don’t know.” Elise leaned over Bill’s shoulder. “What do you think, brother-in-law?”

Bill grunted once he could see and faced his sister-in-law. “I see a lot of you.” Elise chuckled in triumph and Bill leaned close to whisper to the baby. “You dodged the bullet, kid.”

Jamison huffed his disapproval. “That’s great—you two conspiring against me already.”

“It’s not a conspiracy to state the truth, sweetie.” Elise stretched up on her tippy toes to kiss her husband on the cheek. “Oh, and don’t forget, we need to bring the truck in for those new tires at some point.”

“Glad you reminded me.” He tapped Bill’s shoulder. “What do you say, little brother? You feeling good enough to drive? I need you to follow me in your truck.”

Elise straightened and faced her husband. “Why don’t I follow you while Billy stays here with Jackson? I haven’t left the house in four days. I could use an outing and Bill can get acquainted with his new nephew.”

Panicked at the thought of being alone with the baby, Bill held up the child, hoping someone would take him off his hands. “M-maybe you should take him ba—”

“I think it’s too soon for that, hon.” The panic in Jamison’s voice matched his own.

Elise placed a hand on Bill’s arm. “You’ll be fine. I’m even going to let you feed him his bottle. He should be finished by the time we get back.”

Jamison reached out for his son. “I really think it’s too soon—”

Elise cut off her husband’s protest with one look. She leaned over Bill, cupping his face between her hands. “You listen to me. There is no kind of pain in this world that an innocent child can’t heal, Billy. Now you hold your nephew. You’re the only family he’s got besides his mama and daddy. He’s going to need you.”

She handed him a bottle, showed him how to feed the infant. "Now he's a little piggy so he never burps during feedings. If he finishes his bottle before we get back, just put him up to your shoulder and pat his back until he burps."

"How will I know when he does?"

She grinned at him. "Oh, you'll know. Trust me—like I'm trusting you with our son." She kneeled beside him, her tone soft, but serious. "I know what it's like to lose someone too, Billy. Family is important, and you're a part of ours now, so get used to it." She rose from her knees and turned to her husband. "Let's go. They'll be fine."

Bill locked gazes with his brother for a split second before Jay closed the door reluctantly behind them. He looked down at the baby in his arms, and remembered the last time he'd seen his own tiny son, wrapped in a blanket and arranged lovingly in his mama's arms in the coffin they shared back in Washington.

At the time, he'd thought he should have died along with them—couldn't see how he'd survive the loss. But somehow, he had—just barely. The forearms holding his nephew had lost a little mass and definition. His mind had grown foggy, along with his will to live. Why had God allowed that? No man should outlive his wife and child to spend his life alone.

Thoughts of what should have been threatened to overwhelm him again and he tensed. As though sensing his uncle's discomfort, the infant's big blue-black eyes widened. Within seconds the baby's face turned red and he began to choke on his formula.

"Oh, shit!" Bill pulled the bottle from Jackson's mouth and lifted him to his shoulder. "I'm sorry about that, buddy. Breathe, just breathe little guy!" After several gentle pats on the back, the infant took a deep breath and settled down. The danger behind them, Bill settled the baby in the crook of his arm and calmed himself before he proceeded with the feeding.

No matter how he felt, the needs of this child had to come first. "I get it now, Jackson. I do." The baby stopped sucking as though paying attention to him…took a deep breath and released it slowly. Had he imagined that, or had the kid just sighed in relief? Bill shook his head at the wonders of the universe, the wisdom of his sister-in-law, or the grace of a God that had somehow known that being needed rather than needing would be the key to saving his life.

Chapter Five

Bill: In Transition

One week passed, then another. Bill still woke up in a cold sweat each morning. Nightmarish dreams, wrapped around vivid memories of losing his wife and son still fresh in his mind. Each day he pushed them aside to go on with the chore of living without them. He realized soon enough his nephew's needs always trumped his own.

At some point during the day, something happened that brought Bill's loss back into focus. Maybe a song playing on his sister-in-law's kitchen radio, or some silly television ad that used to make Lorraine laugh. Small things, insignificant to others, cut his breath instantly. In seconds his calm vanished, replaced by a void in his chest—a hollow ache in the pit of his stomach.

Ever alert and empathetic to his feelings, Elise would invent some chore she had to do and place Jackson in Bill's arms. She'd give him a sweet smile and speak, her tone soft but with a touch of pleading. "Just until I finish this, okay Billy."

Somehow, his sister-in-law roped him into changing diapers 'muddy' enough to make a grown man gag, preparing bottles, feeding Jackson, administering pediatric vitamins, or bathing and dressing him. She even got him to go with her for Jackson's first outing to his six-week pediatric checkup.

Bill's close proximity to the infant resulted in him being sole witness to several milestones in his nephew's life. Like Jackson's first smile when his uncle lifted him from the crib after his afternoon nap. Bill kept quiet about it, though—instead, let Elise and Jamison think they'd been the firsts to witness that particular occurrence later the same evening.

He also kept quiet about finding Jackson's first tooth at six months—and again two months later when his nephew stood without support for the first time. At some point, he'd begun to fear that Jamison would feel jealousy over the bond he felt for his nephew. But his brother had simply turned to spending more quality time with his son, creating an even stronger father-son bond.

The living situation reached a tipping point when Bill entered the house after a long day of mending fences damaged by his brother's ornery bull. He approached the kitchen and leaned against the door jamb, quietly observing the scene. Eleven-month-old Jackson sat in his high chair, chewing on some kind of teething biscuit, his face and pudgy little hands caked with cookie.

Elise stood at the stove, stirring a pot of spaghetti sauce, singing along with her radio to a pop-song. She turned, holding the wooden spoon in her hand like a microphone as she sang to her son, her own voice in perfect harmony with Don Henley and the other Eagles. Jackson gave his mama a toothy grin and banged his teething biscuit on the tray as though trying to keep up with the beat. Elise laughed and leaned over to kiss her son's biscuit-caked cheeks.

Bill's heart ached at the sight, overcome by a feeling so strong it nearly knocked him to his knees. When the hollowness in the pit of his stomach didn't return, it hit him. Elise had slowly crept into his heart and filled the emptiness left there by the death of his family.

No. *Hell* no. This couldn't happen.

He didn't want anyone or anything replacing his wife and child in his heart. Not now. If ever it did, it sure as hell wouldn't be his kind, beautiful sister-in-law—the woman totally devoted to his own brother.

Overwhelmed by sadness, hope, and a tidal wave of conflicting emotional guilt from the clash of the two—he had to get out.

Bill cleared his throat and Elise pivoted towards him, her face transforming to a deep shade of pink at being caught. "Oh my gosh, I didn't see you there, Billy."

He gave her a boot-shuffling apology, stalled for enough time to compartmentalize his thoughts into a proper keep-your-distance approach. "Sorry, I didn't want to disturb your duet. You've got a beautiful voice—perfect pitch. I can't carry a tune in a bucket, but Jay can sing. Odds are Jackson will have a set of pipes on him, too."

Elise beamed at him. “Thanks—I hope so. I spent six years in junior high and high school chorus. Even used to sing with a band—we called ourselves *The Psychedelic Doves*. Catchy, right? Had our own tie-dyed matching dresses and everything.”

Bill walked over to the electric percolator, checked it to see if he could salvage a cup. “It is. Were they local?” He poured himself the last of the coffee and unplugged the appliance.

“Local to Nacogdoches, Texas—it earned me a little spending money during my freshman and sophomore year at Stephen F. Austin University.” She returned to stirring her sauce. “Probably why there was no junior and senior year of college.” Elise tapped the spoon on the rim of the pot and placed it in the spoon rest near the stove. She pulled out a chair at the table and sat in the spot nearest to her son. “Sit.”

Mindful of his newly discovered feelings, he pulled out the chair farthest from her and sat. “I thought you dropped out to marry my brother.”

She smiled, as though lost in the past. “Jamison attended nearly every one of my performances the last couple of months I was with the band. He’d always find a spot up front where I could see him but he never stuck around afterwards to introduce himself. One night, he finally did.” She lifted both hands and let them fall. “One look into those blue eyes and I had to see him again. The first time he serenaded me in that deep bass of his, I knew that part of my life had ended. I didn’t want to sing for any other man but Jamison.”

Shit. “I uh…” He swallowed the sudden lump in his throat, striving for the courage to say what needing saying—then do what needed doing. “I’ve been thinking I need to get my own place.”

“I know.” She stood and walked to his side of the table.

Panic hit him, hard and fast. “What do you mean, you know?” *Am I that transparent?*

“That was the whole point, right? For you to stay here until you didn’t need us anymore.” She leaned forward, placed a hand on his shoulder. “You’re good now.”

He nodded. “Sometimes I think I’m not quite to full capacity physically yet, but it’ll have to do.” He tensed at the lift of her brow, a sure sign that mind of hers was brewing up something fit to throw at him.

"Well, Billy-Boy—if that physique of yours isn't at full capacity yet, you be sure to let me know when it is. I can name a half-dozen girlfriends of mine who are itching to get their hot little hands on you."

He swigged his coffee and considered her offer. "Got their numbers?"

Her blue eyes sparkled with laughter. "Yes, but those girls are either married or out of your league."

Shocked by her frankness, Bill stood and faced-off with her. "I'm not good enough?"

Her brow wrinkled, as though his comment confused her. "I mean the opposite—they aren't." She cocked her head, her lips pursed. "Don't you realize yet how special you are, brother-in-law?" The look on his face obviously answered her question. "You and your brother are two of the finest men I know. You've already been through so much tragedy in your life—enough to break a lesser man. I refuse to let you settle for someone who isn't the absolute perfect fit for you."

Bill bit back any and all responses barreling through his conflicted mind. "I'm thinking you're a bit biased. It's time I find a place of my own, though."

Elise smiled big, her eyes sparkling with laughter. "You're in luck, Billy. As it happens, the renters on your mom's old place are moving out this weekend. Jamison doesn't seem to think they'll leave behind any damages needing repair. After a quick cleaning you should be able to move in immediately." She turned back to stirring her pot. "We have a few items you could use stored in the shed—a couple of chairs, a dining room set, beds, mattresses, washer, dryer—that family had their own furniture so Jay stored all the stuff that was in there when they signed a one-year lease."

"Sounds good." The sooner the better. No sense staying here. He'd witnessed enough of the bond between his brother and sister-in-law to recognize signs of a blissful marriage. Best to leave them to it.

He moved out less than a week later.

Chapter Six

New Year—New Heartbreak

Christmas Eve, 1980

Bill barely had time to shut his truck door before his nephew came barreling down the front steps towards him. Dressed in a long-sleeved blue chambray shirt, blue jeans, and boots, the kid looked like a miniature version of his daddy. Jackson threw his arms around his uncle's long legs, holding him captive. "Uncle Bill! What took you so long? It's almost time for Santa Claus to come."

Bill loosened the boy's grip and leaned over for a good look. "Hey, partner. Dang, boy—look at you—you can't be just four years old."

Jackson raised one hand, all five fingers splayed. "Mama says I'm almost five years old."

"Yessirree—in February," Bill agreed. "Still, you're growin' like a weed in a pasture full of chicken crap."

Jackson grinned, his blue eyes crinkling with laughter. "You better not let mama hear you say that or she'll tan your hide."

Bill smiled, kept the *I'd like to see her try* comment brewing in his mind to himself. "Oh yeah?" He grabbed the boy by his waist and threw him over his shoulder like a sack of horse feed. "Sounds to me like you're speaking from experience, bucko. Had your own hide tanned for cussing lately, Jack?"

The kid erupted in giggles. "I got my mouth soaped for calling something mom cooked *shit on a shingle* day 'fore yesterday."

Bill's laughter smothered lest he reap a dressing down from the kid's mom for encouraging bad behavior, he managed a comeback. "Well, I guess you did, boy. I'd have done the same thing if you'd said that about my cooking."

"Bull-oney!" Jackson cried out. "You can't cook."

Bill swung him down from his shoulder to his side, hooked his fingers through the back of the boy's belt and carried him horizontally to the front porch like a bucket of water. "Sure I can—steaks, and beans, and the best darn five alarm chili you'll ever taste in your life." He walked up the steps and set him gently on the porch.

Jackson scrambled to his feet and faced him. "What's that mean—five alarm?"

Bill chuckled. "It means it burns twice—going in and coming out."

The boy's face scrunched in confusion as the front door swung open. "I don't know what you're talking 'bout, Uncle Bill. You'll have to 'splain it to me."

"Don't you dare!" Elise opened the screen door, wearing a smug grin to go along with her tight jeans and curve-revealing sweater. "Good to see you, Billy—but don't encourage him. Believe me, that boy needs no help getting into trouble."

"That's what I hear. Jack informed me of a mouth-soaping incident. Is that a regular occurrence?"

"It's getting to be." She frowned at her son. "He didn't talk like that until he started Kindergarten this past August."

"Well, whatever she cooked that day sure didn't look app'tizin. Even dad said so." He leaned forward to speak in a loud whisper. "And it didn't taste good at *all*."

Elise rolled her eyes. "My beef stroganoff is delicious."

Jackson's deep blue eyes got huge. "Not to me, it ain't…or dad neither."

"Isn't, not ain't and it's or dad *either* . . . and there's more to life than steak and potatoes, son." Elise leaned over to swat her son on the bottom. "Go tell your daddy it's time to come in and get cleaned up." She watched him run down the steps and toward the barn. "That boy is Jamison through and through."

Bill stared after his nephew. "It's like he didn't have no mama."

"Didn't have *any* mama," Elise corrected. "I have a goal, Billy. It's to keep that child from becoming an uneducated heathen. Good future husband material, you know? To be respectful to women and his elders—have good manners, grammar, and hygiene. I expect to get some support from you and your brother. If you pay close attention you may even learn a thing or two."

He cleared his throat. "You mean I *might* learn a thing or two?"

She grinned. "Actually, in that context, either is acceptable, but thank you for playing along."

Masculine laughter filled the space. "I'm a simple man, Elise. No sense trying to change me into anything else."

Elise shook her head. "I'm just trying to keep from drowning in all the male testosterone floating around this place." She placed both hands on her lower belly. "I'll take another son, but I'm sure hoping this one's a girl."

Somewhat shocked at her comment, Bill paused to gauge his feelings. He pushed aside any lingering sadness over his own painful past to acknowledge her confession with as much of a smile as he could muster. Reaching out, he gave Elise a half-second, one-armed hug—the only contact he allowed himself to have with the woman who still dominated his dreams. "Congratulations, hon." He glanced at her flat belly. "Can't be too far along."

Her smile hinted at a combination of embarrassment, bashfulness, and euphoria. "A little over two months. Jamison and I agreed to put off telling Jack as long as we can. Our son will be relentless with his questions once he finds out. His teacher says he's the most curious nearly five-year-old she's ever known."

Bill took a deep breath, waiting for the wave of tightness in his chest to ebb. Five years of exposure to the most satisfied couple he knew still had repercussions. He held the door open and walked in behind Elise. "You know what they say—the only stupid question is the one that's never asked."

Elise crossed into the kitchen. "I don't think Jackson has ever encountered a question he couldn't or wouldn't ask." She approached the coffee pot. "Want a cup? It's fresh."

"Sure." He sat at the kitchen table. She placed a man-sized mug of strong coffee in front of him and took a seat on the opposite side. "How've you been, Billy?"

He took a sip of coffee—piping hot and black. "I'm good. I got promoted to lead operator on the platform." He put the cup on the table and shrugged. "I'm making damn good money, but I've gotta admit, I miss ranching with Jamison."

"Before he died, my dad said he'd never seen anyone more cut out for ranching than Jamison. He went from an oilman to a cattleman without taking a breath and it worked." She leaned back in her chair, arms crossed, her mouth pursed and serious. "So, besides work…how are you, brother-in-law?"

He took another sip, knowing what she wanted from him. "I'm not gonna discuss my love life with you, Elise. And please stop tryin' to set me up with Ms. So-in-So. You're good at lots of things, but match-making ain't—*isn't* one of 'em."

"Very good, William!" She clucked her tongue then. "I hate that every time I hear that 'third rate romance' song I can't help but think of you and your bevy of one-night-stands."

"It's all I need for now."

"But it's just sex—and you have so much more to offer than that."

"It's all I want for now," he insisted. Would she *ever* drop this damn subject? Thankfully, Jackson raced back into the room with his usual brand of energy.

"I'm hungry, mama!"

"Imagine that." She led him into the spare bathroom. "Let's wash your hands first, sweetie."

Bill breathed a sigh of relief at the reprieve from her badgering. Unfortunately, she re-entered the room with her son and picked up where she left off.

"The fact is, it's been five years, Billy. You're twenty-six years old. We want to see you settled with a wife."

He gave her a hard stare. "I lost a wife and child on the same day, Elise. I can't even think of replacing her right now."

"It can't happen if you won't let it."

He released a long sigh, considered for a split second blurting out the one thing sure to shock her into silence. How would Elise react if he admitted he used *her* as his benchmark for all women, rather than Lorraine, the wife he'd lost five years ago? That he upheld her, *his sister-in-law,* as the standard for all other women? After all, he'd known her a lot longer than he had Lorraine.

Jamison wouldn't be all that surprised. He'd actually told Bill once that all of his friends were half in love with Elise. "They can't help themselves." His matter-of-fact tone included more than a touch of pride. "I mean, hell, she's the perfect woman. She loves horses as much as her books, sings like a bird, can quote

General George Patton and Winston Churchill right along with Shakespeare. She's beautiful and a great wife and mom. I can't blame any man for wanting her."

Bill had replied with something along the line of "but God help 'em if they try for anything more, right?"

Jamison had grinned. "It keeps me from getting lazy where she's concerned, little brother. As long as I keep her happy where it counts, I've got nothing to worry about." He'd given him a shoulder bump then. "Trust me, I keep her plenty happy." Bill couldn't help but be a little green with envy.

The four of them ate supper together and followed the tradition they'd set up for the past three Christmases—with Bill spending the night with them in order to wake up as a family on Christmas morning.

Christmas Morning

Bill woke early Christmas morning, to the tantalizing aroma of homemade biscuits, bacon, and breakfast sausages. He entered the kitchen, bleary eyed and reaching for a mug and the nearly full pot of coffee. Eyeing his sister-in-law preparing the turkey for the oven, he cleared his throat. "Do you ever sleep?"

Grinning, she grabbed hold of the huge roaster. "Sure I do—open the oven door for me." She slid the pot in the oven and set the timer before facing him, her cheeks slightly flushed. "I woke up an hour ago, thought about Jackson's new filly and couldn't go back to sleep. Besides, you and Jamison are the ones who stayed up late to get her settled in last night. I thought you'd catch a few more z's this morning."

He lifted his nose to the air and gave a big sniff. "Not through all these delectable aromas. I woke up with a rumbling stomach."

She handed him a plate. "Go ahead and fill it then, Billy."

He'd popped the last of his biscuit into his mouth when Jackson came sliding into the room in socks and decked out in his superman PJ's. "It's Christmas, Mom—did Santa come?"

Elaine nodded toward the Christmas tree, set up in a corner of the living room next to the kitchen. "See for yourself."

Jackson spun around in the doorway, gasping at the sight of the tree with dozens of gifts under it. "Yep, Santa came while we were sleeping. Can we open them now?"

Elise smoothed down her son's thick, dark locks. "You know the rules. Not until your father is up."

"But, mo-omm!"

She laughed and placed a biscuit and two slices of bacon on a saucer. "You eat while I go wake your dad. I want that plate clean."

"Yes, ma'am." The boy popped a bite of bacon into his mouth and reached for a jar of homemade muscadine jelly Elise had canned in late summer.

"Let me get that for you, partner." Bill opened the jar and slathered a generous amount of jelly onto the boy's biscuit. "That's good stuff right there. I wonder if your mom would be willing to part with a few more jars of it. My supply is running a mite low."

"It wouldn't if you lived here." Jackson bit into his biscuit, dripping jelly down his chin.

Bill wiped the jelly from his nephew's chin. "Naw—your parents need their privacy. So do I, for that matter."

"For what?"

"For stuff—eat, Jack."

"But we're all family, aren't we?"

Bill released a sigh, deciding to let the kid's parents explain the nuances of immediate and extended families. "You'd better finish your breakfast if you want to check out those gifts under that tree anytime soon."

That seemed to jog the boy's memory and he dug into his meal with enthusiasm. Elise rejoined them seconds later and Bill allowed himself, just for a minute, to pretend they were *his* wife and child, rather than his brother's. He'd already admitted his selfish behavior and pulled himself out of that fantasy when Jamison joined them in the kitchen.

Sleepy-eyed, Jamison stifled a yawn and accepted the mug of black coffee from Elise, repaying her with a kiss and a hoarse "Thanks babe".

"Anytime, love of my life." She got up on her tip toes and kissed him squarely on the lips. "And thank you . . . for last night. I owe you one."

Although whispered, Bill caught the conversation and turned away from the intimate moment between husband and wife. The old ranch house wasn't quite big enough, it's walls not quite insulated enough, to stifle the sounds of late night/early morning love-making between the couple.

Elise reached for two more plates and Bill intercepted a wink from her husband. Jamison mouthed the words, "*plenty happy*", nodded, and gave him a toothy grin.

Bill reacted with an eye roll and shake of his head, garnering a chuckle from his older brother.

* * * * *

Jackson loved the new saddle his favorite and only uncle had given him, despite the confusion in his blue eyes. "I love having my own saddle, Uncle Bill. Only problem is, I don't have a horse to put it on."

Taking his cue from the boy's parents, Bill grinned at his nephew. "Are you sure about that? I thought sure I heard an unfamiliar whinnying coming from the barn this morning."

Jackson's gaze flew to his parents. "Do you think Santa brought me my own horse? Can I go see?"

Jamison nodded at his son. "I guess we should all check it out."

Elise called out to her son, already at the front door. "Put your coat on first, Jack. It's cold out there this morning."

Determined to have the pony saddled and ready for the kid at first sight, Bill caught up to him at the door and pulled him to a halt. "Ho-o-o-l-ld on there, partner. If Santa *did* bring you a horse, are you gonna let your first ride on it be in your PJ's? You're a rancher, for crying out loud. Dress accordingly."

Jackson turned tail and ran in the opposite direction, up to his bedroom. Bill, already fully dressed, grabbed the saddle and dashed outside with Jamison to saddle the two-year-old gelding the sellers had delivered the evening before. By the time a camera-bearing Elise came outside with the overzealous boy, they had the horse ready for Jack's first ride.

Jackson's mouth rounded in awe at the sight of the buff colored horse. In true cowboy fashion he checked the horse's gender first and straightened. "Is he mine?" He looked from one adult to another. "Is he all mine?"

Jamison nodded, holding out a piece of paper. "He must be, because I found this note attached to his halter."

Jackson grabbed the note and began reading the plain block lettering in a halting voice as he sounded out each word. “Dear Jackson. This horse is y-ou-ours now. Take go-oo-d c-ca-are of him or my e-e-el-v-elves will p-pi-pick him up and b-br-in-ing-bring him b-baa-back to the n-nor-th-north p-po-pole. And this says L-lo-love S-Sa-San-Santa. P.S. His n-name is R-Ri-co.” He looked up at the three adults. “Santa says he’s mine!”

“Yep, that’s what it says,” Jamison said. “But it’s hard work taking care of your own horse. You think you can handle it?”

“Yes sir. I sure can.”

Elise approached her son. “How about his name? Do you want to keep it or change it?”

Jackson’s mouth twisted, studying the yellow-brown bay colored horse with black mane and tail. “Rico.” He grinned when the horse turned its huge head his direction. “He likes that name.” He approached the horse slowly and let him smell his hand, like the three adults had taught him. “It’s okay, Rico. You and me are gonna be good friends.”

Bill approached Elise as she snapped several shots of Jamison helping Jackson onto his new horse. “Jesus, the kid reads now?”

“I taught him to sound out words using phonetics before he started Kindergarten,” Elise boasted.

Jamison joined them, watching as Jackson walked the horse in a circle in front of them. He leaned towards Bill and whispered. “His teacher says he’s far ahead of the other kids in his class.”

“Hmph…” Bill nudged his brother in the ribs. “Kid must take after his mom.”

Jamison crossed his arms and grinned. “We know he sure as hell didn’t get it from his uncle.”

Bill chuckled. “I guess not.”

Bill spent Christmas day and that night with them. He left for work the next morning, agreeing to return the evening of New Year’s Eve. He’d offered to babysit Jackson so Jamison could take Elise out for a rare night of dancing and cutting loose.

* * * * *

New Year’s Eve

Bill knocked briefly before opening the door at Elise’s call of “Come on in, Billy.”

"What's up, sis-in-law?"

"My feet, finally." She lifted her mug of coffee and pointed at her feet propped up on the chair beside her, ankles crossed. "Resting up before this evening. I've been chopping, seasoning, stuffing, and preparing as much as I can for tomorrow's menu."

He leaned in to give her a quick hug. "Hopefully, y'all won't be too hung over from your rare evening of toasting bubbly and dancing."

She smiled up at him. "I can't drink anyway because of the pregnancy, but I'll try not to overdo it. Thank you again for sacrificing your night out to watch Jackson for us."

Bill waved off her gratitude. "It's nothing. I like spending time with the kid. Besides, you two deserve to cut loose every now and then." He grabbed a mug of coffee and leaned against the counter to sip it. Even though he envied what his brother and sister-in-law shared, he couldn't think of two more deserving people.

Elise cleared her throat, pulling him from his thoughts before she spoke again. "Have you met anyone lately you'd even consider bringing here to meet us?"

He pictured the latest string of sex only, one-night-stands—sometimes twice—but never a third, for fear of complications. "Nope."

She sat back, falling against her chair. "You're hopeless."

He looked up as his brother approached from the side door. "Yep."

"And as dialog driven as ever," she added.

"I got plenty to say, when it's something worth talkin' about."

"Jamison," she called out to her husband. "Tell Billy he needs a wife."

Jamison entered the room and clapped his brother on the back. "Leave my brother alone, Elise. He'll settle down when he's good and ready."

"Yeah, mom…leave Uncle Bill alone," Jackson piped up.

Elise ruffled her son's dark hair. "Not a chance. But I want you to eat a good supper and then take your bath before your dad and I leave for the evening. You've got your uncle so wrapped he'll let you fall asleep full of junk food and filthy as a little piglet."

"Um…I'm right here, you know," Bill said.

Elise challenged Bill with a single, pointed look. "I can't do anything about the junk food after I leave but I can sure as heck make sure you've eaten some quality grub and had your bath."

Bill cocked his head to one side. "What you must think of me . . ."

She pushed away from the table and rose to her feet. "I think you're an overly doting Uncle who'd do anything to keep this kid from whining."

The four of them sat down to supper. Once they'd finished, Jamison suggested he and Bill clean the kitchen while Elise got herself ready for their date night.

She beamed at them. "Thanks guys, I appreciate that."

Bill rubbed his full belly. "It's the least I could do after that delicious meal."

She winked at him. "There might be hope for you, yet. Come on Jack—your choice tonight—shower or bath."

"Shower, because it's quicker."

"Fine with me, piglet. It means I won't have to scrub the muddy residue from the tub after you finish."

Jackson stopped and wrinkled his nose at his mom. "What's res-doo?"

Bill bit back his laughter as Elise sighed and escorted her son out of the room, mumbling.

"I'll tell you as soon as I get the smell of horse off you, son. You smell more like Rico than Rico does. How do you manage that?" She and Jackson left the room to the sound of her brother-in-law's and husband's laughter.

Jamison started loading the dishwasher. "I volunteered our kitchen cleaning services for a reason. I'm looking at a good two hours of her getting ready for the evening. We'd never get out of here if she had to do this too."

"No problem, man."

"By the way, thanks for sacrificing your New Year's Eve out on the town to babysit for us tonight, Billy. We appreciate it more than you know. We won't have too many chances after another seven months or so."

Bill paused from his duties of putting leftovers into smaller containers. "You hoping for another son, or a little girl?"

An ear to ear grin lit up Jamison's face. "I know Elise is hoping for a girl this time around, and I just want her happy."

The two men finished cleaning the kitchen amidst talk of NFL playoff games and their predictions. With the stove top and counter surfaces gleaming and all food put in the fridge, they decided to have one last round of coffee.

Bill poured his cup and sat at the table, wondering aloud about the recent pregnancy announcement. "I never heard either of you discussing more children. This new baby—planned or a happy accident?"

Jamison took the seat across from him and palmed his own mug of coffee. "It's something we've both wanted for a while. I guess we've put it off out of consideration for you."

Bill's coffee mug froze mid-air. "No shit? Why would you do that?"

"Bad enough you had to come home to see us with a new baby … a son, at that. We thought it would be insensitive to throw another one in your face so soon."

Bill's mug hit the table with a clunk. "That's some bullshit, right there. You shouldn't have to put your lives on hold for me. Besides—" He pointed towards the hallway. "Coming back here to that kid probably saved my life."

"Elise insisted that you needed to be involved in Jackson's upbringing—to be a part of it—and it worked. You're every bit as much of an influence on him as his mom and me are."

"That's what I hear—and it's his mom and *I*, not his mom and *me*."

Jamison stared at him over the rim of his mug. "Whatever, asshole."

Bill raised both hands. "Don't blame me. It's *your* woman who insists we all try to keep Jackson from imitating our heathenish ways and poor grammar skills."

Jamison gave him an eye roll. "That girl needs to go back to college and get her teaching degree."

"A second kid won't make that any easier on her."

"Think about what Mom accomplished with two kids and no husband around to help—*ever*. Elise has me here to help pull the load." He threw a look at Bill. "You could help too, if you've a mind to."

Bill gave his brother a brief nod. "Any way I can—just say the word. I owe you both far too much not to come running when you call."

"Good to hear. You helping us ring in the new year tonight is a big help. My girl wants to get some dancing in before she gets too big in the belly to jitterbug and Texas two-step."

The two brothers looked up at the sound of jingling wind chimes and something crashing onto the porch floorboards. They walked out onto the front porch and stared out at the inky black sky.

Jamison righted a plant stand and placed a large empty crock on it to weigh it down. "Feels like that Canadian frontal system is moving in already. It's supposed to bring a strong band of freezing rain along with it."

"Just in time for New Year's Eve and all the crazies out on the roads tonight." Bill braced himself as the first icy winds penetrated the flannel of his shirt. He shivered at the ominous feeling settling in his gut—a feeling that had nothing to do with the cold. He faced his brother. "You be careful driving tonight, you hear?"

Jamison reached for the screen door's handle. "You can count on it."

* * * * *

9:00 p.m.

Two hours later, Bill stood at his nephew's bedroom door, watching as Elise and Jamison tucked their son into bed.

The boy gave his mama a toothy grin. "You look beautiful, mama."

Jamison gave his wife an appreciative perusal. "She sure does, doesn't she, son?" He kissed Elise on the neck and winked at Bill. "Definitely worth the two-hour wait."

Elise brushed curled black locks over one shoulder, the gold sequined patches of her soft sweater catching the light from her son's lamp. "Thank you! It's nice to have my guys' approval." She sat on the edge of the bed and gave her son a big hug and kissed his face. "You be a good boy for your Uncle Bill. I love you all the way to the moon and back, Jack."

"I will…love you too, mama!"

Jamison leaned over the bed and hugged his son, giving his forehead a kiss. "Love you little man."

"Love you too, dad."

Jamison pressed one last kiss into his son's hair. "We'll see you next year." Jackson's expression transformed into one of horror that had Jamison scrambling for an explanation. "When your mom and I come in after midnight tonight, it'll be a brand-new year, son. That's all I meant by that."

"Oh, okay." Jackson's tone held a mixture of relief and confusion. His face brightened suddenly. "Just like Rudolph's Shiny New Year?"

Bill laughed at his nephew's grasp of the situation. He'd sat through the animated program with him earlier that evening while Jay and Elise were getting ready to go out. "Exactly like that." He walked over and whispered loudly. "Don't worry, Jacko—as soon as your parents are gone I'll spring you from that bed for some popcorn and hot cocoa."

"Okay," Jack whispered back, his volume equaling his uncle's.

"You are incorrigible." Elise approached her son's bedroom door with a low snort. "The least you could do is wait until I'm out of ear shot." She left the room, shaking her head.

Jamison laughed and turned to his brother. "Just remember, if he's sick tomorrow from eating s'mores at midnight, *you'll* be the one dealing with my wife. I'll be up early tending to my smoker."

"I hear you." Bill walked them to the door, his mouth watering from the thought of his brother's hickory and pecan smoked pork roast, accompanied by Elise's traditional New Year's Day favorites as sides. He waved the couple off. "Go on and get out of here, you two."

Jamison opened the front passenger door of Elise's car and helped her inside. Pulling up his collar against the icy wind, he returned to the driver's side and opened the door. He gave Bill one last look. "Take care of our boy."

Bill gave him a semi-salute. "You can count on it." He watched the car back slowly out of the drive and closed the door. It hit him suddenly that Jamison had spoken those exact words to him earlier that evening when Bill had urged him to drive carefully. His gut soured with the same ominous feeling he'd had then.

Chapter Seven

Bill and Jackson: More Bad Luck

Bill stood in the doorway, staring at the uniformed Brazoria County Sheriff's deputy who'd just asked him to believe the unbelievable. For a millisecond, he had the strongest urge to punch the man in the face. But Deputy Ryan Justice, an old friend and classmate of his, had a job to do. "Are you sure, Ryan?"

Ryan removed his hat, his eyes broadcasting sympathy along with a single nod. "I'm so sorry, Billy. I requested this because we're friends. There's no way to get around how bad this sucks for you and that little boy."

Bill looked over at Jackson, passed out on the couch, his belly full of popcorn and hot cocoa. He ushered the deputy out onto the porch and closed the door softly behind him. "I can't believe this shit. How the hell am I gonna tell that kid he's lost—that both his parents—" He cut off the painful words with a hand over his mouth, his heart already broken for his nephew, as well as for himself.

Weak kneed from an overwhelming rush of despair, Bill dropped into one of two ancient, but built-to-last porch rockers. He leaned forward, resting his head in his hands. "Tell me everything."

"Their timing couldn't have been worse. They were heading directly into the middle of that storm system at the worst curve between here and Houston. As far as we can tell, a car in the opposite lane crossed the center line and hit them head on. Witnesses driving behind the vehicle that hit your brother's car reported torrential rain at the time of the accident. No one's established whether it's alcohol related or not."

"Did they—" He swallowed. "Do you know if they suffered?"

"Seeing the destruction, we believe everyone involved died on impact." Ryan stopped to clear his throat. "I'm certain no one suffered, Billy."

Bill nodded slowly and took one deep breath to clear his head. He rose from the chair and gave the deputy's hand a single quick shake. "I appreciate you bringing me the news yourself, Ryan. What do I do now? Their son is asleep in there. I'd have to find someone to watch him before I could leave." He looked back at the door. "I'm sure as hell not gonna wake him or take him with me."

The deputy shook his head. "I wouldn't either if I were in your shoes. Just wait here for a call from the coroner, asking you to identify the bodies." He pulled out a pad from his pocket. "Is this the number to reach you?"

Bill stared at his brother and sister-in-law's phone number. "I s'pose so—for a while, anyway. Just have someone call me and I'll be there."

He entered the house and dropped into the chair beside the couch, his heart shattered. His older, wiser, big-hearted brother, who'd always put Bill first—gone. The beautiful, caring sister-in-law he'd never managed to replace in his own heart—also gone. He stared at his nephew, knowing that as horrendously empty as he felt at that moment, it'd be so much worse on the kid. There were few things on earth more devastating to a child Jackson's age than losing both his adored parents in one hit.

He sat there for another hour, too steeped in grief to move—too restless to fall asleep.

His brother's last words from earlier that evening came back to him. *"Take care of our boy."* He'd answered with an immediate *"You can count on it"*. Had he meant it? Or had it been one of those automatic but insincere reactions? The certainty of the situation slammed into him like a freight train. No way would he consider letting anyone else raise Jamison and Elise's son. He'd be there for the kid, as long as Jackson needed him.

At six a.m. he got up to answer a soft knock on the door. He pulled it open and sent Mrs. Brenda Martin, his mom's longtime friend, a somber smile. "Hey Ms. Brenda," he whispered, pointing to Jackson, still blissfully unaware of their unfolding tragedy and sprawled out on the couch. "I'd planned to call you in an hour or so."

"Joe's been up with his bad leg since two a.m. and heard the news on his police scanner. He woke me with the news. We're both torn up and I've been waiting to come over. I'm so sorry,

Billy." She pulled him close for a hug before joining him in the kitchen. She went straight to the coffee pot and helped herself to a cup of the strong brew, took one sip before turning to him. "I thought you might need me to watch him for you while you—" She paused to release a shaky breath. "Attend to some things today."

Bill raked his hands through his hair and took a deep breath. "I'm waiting for a call from the coroner to identify. . ." He swallowed, unable to finish.

She placed one hand on his arm. "I understand."

And she did. She'd spent enough time with him and Jamison when their mom, her best friend, died—the three of them sharing equally in their misery, as well as memories of times they'd shared, both good and bad. She'd also helped out Jamison and Elise by babysitting for Jackson occasionally over the past five years.

"You've always been here for us, Ms. Brenda."

She nodded. "Yvette and I were like soul sisters, Billy. Last week, when I discovered I'm going to be a grandma, I wanted so badly to pick up the phone and call her." She clucked her tongue and placed a hand over her heart. "I still miss her so much, and I know this is a devastating blow for you. You've already been through so much." She looked past the door into the living room and shook her head slowly before turning back to Bill. "That poor little boy—he's going to need you more than ever."

"I know that, ma'am, and I intend to be here for him, don't worry."

Her forehead wrinkled with doubt. "But your work?"

He knew she referred to the weeks at a time he spent on offshore oil platforms in his line of work. "I've already called the company I work for and explained the situation. I'll be staying here and running the ranch for Jackson until he either decides to take it over or tells me he's not interested. If that kid has even half of his mama's smarts and his dad's work ethics, he'll be able to do anything he wants to."

"Can you—I mean, is your financial situation—" She sighed, sent him a tired smile. "Is that possible?"

"If you're talking financially, Jamison and Elise were well insured. I'll be here for my nephew. We'll be fine." He wasn't talking out of his ass, either. Jay had discussed their wills with him, he knew they'd provided well for the raising of their son as well as his education. They'd left Bill in charge of seeing their legacy of love well cared for.

He whispered a silent prayer to the head honcho up there—asking for the strength and wisdom he'd need to raise his nephew into as good a person as either of his parents.

Chapter Eight

A New Friend, with Benefits

February, 1981

Bill sat back in his chair at the kitchen table. He inspected the cake slathered in chocolate icing, the four-layered creation leaning dangerously to one side. The slightest bump would probably send it tumbling over in seconds. "What do you think, partner?" Jackson studied his birthday cake, his face too serious. Bill couldn't much blame him. The kid hadn't had a reason to smile in two months.

"It don't look like mom's, that's for sure."

Bill winced at his nephew's poor grammar, knowing full well that Elise would chew his butt for letting him slide this way. He hadn't had the heart to do much correcting, considering the death of Jack's parents. But he'd noticed the boy slipping more and more as the weeks had passed.

Not on my damn watch.

"Say it *doesn't* … not it don't."

Jackson's head swiveled to stare up at him, a direct challenge in his recently turned five-year-old blue eyes. "*You* say *it don't* all the *damn* time."

Bill set his jaw and leaned over to get eye to eye with the kid. "Listen up, boy. I'm a lot older than you so I've been practicing bad habits a he-*e-eck* of a lot longer'n—longer *than* you. I'm going to try to speak correctly around you from now on, but I'm bound to slip up now and then. From here on out, we're operating on the 'do as I say, not as I do' system. You got that?"

Jackson nodded reluctantly. "Yeah."

Bill sent him the old I-mean-business lift of a single brow. "What'd you say?"

"Yes, sir." Jackson's grin turned sheepish.

Bill tousled the boy's hair. "I'm sure as he-*e-ck* not about to let you turn into a little heathen, just because your mom ain't around to correct you."

Jackson turned his blue-eyed gaze on him, the tiniest spark of laughter in his eyes. "*Isn't* around to correct me."

Bill winked at him. "Just making sure you were paying attention."

The boy snorted and looked back at the cake on the table. "It kind of looks like a cow kicked it sideways, Uncle Bill." He reached out to scrape a bit of icing from the cake plate and put it in his mouth. "But it tastes pretty damn good."

Bill slapped him lightly on the back of the head.

Jackson sat at attention. "I mean it tastes pretty *darn* good."

"That's better," Bill mumbled, turning his attention to the cake. "If it'll just hold up until this party is over with I'll be satisfied."

"Mom used to put some kind of sticks in hers to keep it from falling over."

"She did, didn't she?" Bill remembered making some crack to Elise when she'd handed him a slice with a wooden dowel inside it. She'd laughed and said that everything needed a little support now and then.

"Uh huh—she kept them in a drawer."

Bill rummaged through a couple of kitchen drawers until he found the items he needed. "Ah ha!" He held up a handful of wooden dowels.

Jackson's smile lit up his face. "That's the ones."

Bill studied the leaning tower of chocolate on chocolate, trying to decide where best to position the dowels.

"I think mom put those sticks in *before* the cake started leaning sideways."

Bill glanced at Jackson then back at the cake. "Yeah. Well, I'm afraid that steer's already been cut."

"What?"

"It's too late for that." Bill reached out with one of the dowels, his hand frozen in mid-air when someone knocked at the door.

Jackson jumped down from the chair. "Want me to get that?"

Bill palmed the dowel and stood. "You'd better let me get it." He looked at his watch on the way to the door. "It's a little too early for guests to be showing up for this shindig."

"What's a shindig?"

"Your party—a shindig is a party." He shook his head while reaching for the door knob. Sometimes he forgot he lived with a five-year-old. The door opened on a bodaciously curvy blonde holding a wrapped gift, her hand resting upon the head of a tow-headed little boy. He greeted her with a focused "Hel-loo there."

"Hi! I'm Maggie—Maggie Hannigan. My sister asked me to bring my nephew over to your little boy's party. This is—"

"Justin!" Jackson stepped forward to greet the kid. "He's in my class at school." He looked up at Bill. "Can he stay, even if it's too early?"

"Oh!" Maggie looked at her watch. "Are we? My sister, Jen, is home with Justin's newborn baby sister. She asked me to bring him shopping for a gift and get him over here—didn't mention the time of the party." She hitched her shoulders. "I'm sorry. I could kill some time and come back with him."

"Uh…we aren't quite ready. We just finished the cake and I haven't had a chance to pick up in here yet or set out the decorations."

She eyed the mess in the living room. "Or I could stick around and help you out." Her gaze surveyed him, head to toe. She bit her lower lip as she met his gaze again. "It kind of looks like you could use some…help, I mean." One corner of her lip curved upward, hinting at a not-so-subtle message.

Bill stepped aside, letting her and the boy inside. "Don't say I didn't warn you."

Maggie followed the boy into the living room with a feminine tinkle of laughter and a spicy scent that aimed a direct hit to Bill's olfactory center. On the way in she reached out and lightly brushed her nails across Bill's chest, one nail catching and popping open a single pearlized snap on his western cut shirt.

He snapped it closed, searching her face for signs in order to calculate the female's age.

She paused beside him and pulled out her driver's license from the back pocket of her tight jeans. "Don't panic, hon—I'm almost twenty-two." She gave him time to read her name and birth year on the license.

Satisfied with the unfailing ability of his judgement, he relaxed, allowed himself to enjoy the woman's company. Bill sent the boys off to play in Jackson's room while he straightened up the living room and she concentrated on the kitchen area and table.

He joined her afterwards, amazed at the spotless counters and cleared table. “This looks great, Maggie. I don’t know how to thank you.”

She sent him a full-lipped smile. “I’ll figure out a way.” She waved one arm at her work. “Is this it, or did I hear you say something about decorations?”

“Oh! Yeah! I found these decorations in a bag in the laundry room. Elise must have bought them a few months ago for Jack’s party.”

“This Elise—is she your son’s mom?”

He figured the confused narrowing of her eyes warranted an explanation. “Jackson is my nephew. His dad was my older brother, Jamison.”

Her eyes widened in gradual recognition. “I’m so sorry, Jen didn’t mention the party was for their boy. My brother-in-law, David, graduated with Jamison. As a matter of fact, he stood in as Jamison’s best man when he married Elise. It tore Dave up, hearing about that awful wreck on New Year’s Eve. It’s gotta be tough with the little boy.”

Bill nodded. “It’s been rough but I couldn’t let Jackson’s birthday pass without a celebration. They always made the day special for him.”

“Of course—I understand. It’s just that Jen called me last minute, asking if I could bring Justin. When I arrived this morning, Jen looked like she’d had a pretty rough night with the baby. She didn’t explain anything—just shoved the kid through the door and handed me money to pick up a gift and card on the way over here.” She leaned over, speaking out of one side of her mouth. “If Jackson doesn’t like the gift, I let my nephew pick it out. Truth is, I probably would have picked something totally inappropriate—like clothes, underwear, socks—a fifth of tequila.”

Bill laughed, for the first time in two months. It felt too damn good, made better by the sound of two little boys’ playful laughter drifting down the hall. He pulled a banner from the bag and they tacked it to the wall behind the table. He’d just complimented Maggie’s creativite results with crepe paper streamers when she pointed to the cake.

“Um—I think you’re about to lose the top layer of that thing.”

Bill picked up the dowels and turned his attention to the leaning tower of cake layers. "I was about to put these in when you knocked on the door." He gave her an uncertain smile. "You think it's too late?"

She grabbed a few dowel rods and studied the cake. Within a few minutes, she'd adjusted the top layer, secured it with three sticks, and touched up the icing to hide all signs of repairs. She stood back afterwards, observing her work. "What do you think?"

"Good as new." He grinned at her. "You're a life saver."

"Just needed a woman's touch, that's all." She swiveled around to clean up at the sink.

Bill's mouth watered at the sight of full, round hips and small waist. Her long silky-blonde hair hung straight down to the middle of her back, had him longing to tangle his fingers in it. "Do you live around here, Maggie?"

She turned off the faucet, taking her sweet time to dry her hands and hang the towel on a rack above the sink. She turned slowly, resting her butt on the sink and smiled out of one side of her mouth. "I do. I just finished my final semester at University of Houston. I'm waiting on results of the state exam I took a week ago. If I pass it, I'll be a certified registered nurse and working right here at Southwest Medical Center in Pasadena."

He nodded, considering the best way to ask her out. Maggie shocked him with her own direct take on the situation.

"I date some, but I'm not seeing anyone steady because I avoid anything serious. So, if you're available and willing, maybe we could 'not see anyone' together, cowboy."

Bill approached, placed both hands on the counter, pinning her in with his arms. He dipped his face close to her neck, breathed in a delicious mixture of her own essence and whatever perfume she wore. "Sounds good to me, Ms. Hannigan. You got any plans for this evening?"

She reached up with one index finger, tracing her nail from his chin, down his neck to the opening of his shirt. "Not a thing, Mr. Broussard—other than getting better acquainted with you."

He sucked in his breath at the implications, barely capable of a single approving grunt. He'd only started 'dating' again two years ago. The collective group of female acquaintances willing to settle for less than exclusive dating rights had grown, although slowly, since then. He'd never led any woman on; never let them think he needed or wanted anything more than the mutual benefits of good sex. His twice-broken heart couldn't handle anything more. Due to his work schedule, it'd been months since he'd enjoyed the physical closeness of a woman. His first priority being Jackson, Bill figured a night of mutually satisfying acquaintance sex with Maggie Hannigan sounded just about perfect.

Chapter Nine

Bill: Helping Out a Friend

February, 1983

Bill carried Jackson to the sitter's front door, toting the boy's overnight bag. He set him down in front of the door and rang the bell, taking note of his nephew's furrowed brow. "You okay with staying here tonight?"

"Uh huh, it's just that I hope Sweet Sue doesn't decide to foal while I'm not around to see it. She's my gift from Christmas, so she's my responsibility."

Bill ruffled his nephew's hair. "I keep telling you, it won't be for another eight or nine months. That's about the same amount of time you spent in the second grade."

"That's a long time to wait."

"It can't be helped, son. It takes that long for baby horses to develop in their mommy's bellies. That's how long it took for you to grow in there and just look how great you turned out." Bill couldn't help but remember one of his last conversations with Elise—how and why they'd waited to tell Jackson about her pregnancy and the endless questions he'd have. Maybe he should've kept the mare's condition to himself a bit longer.

"But what if she foals early?"

"She'll let us know in plenty enough time, boy, so quit your worrying about that. I figure by the time you're ready to go trick or treating for Halloween, we'll have another addition to our four-legged family."

Jackson's eyes rounded in wonder. "You think so?"

"I sure do. You better start thinking of appropriate names for that colt or filly—like Boo Boy or Ghost Gal."

Jackson chortled at his suggestions. "Those are awful names for a horse." He looked up as the door swung open. "Hi Ms. Brenda! Are the twins here?"

Brenda Martin leaned over to kiss the top of his head. "Hello, sweetie. They sure are, and they'll be thrilled to see you."

Bill grabbed Jackson's arm before he could run off and squatted before him, getting eye to eye with his nephew. "You be good for Ms. Brenda, okay son? Eat whatever she puts on your plate and mind your manners."

"Yes, sir, I will." Jackson started to run off, turned at the last second to throw his arms around his uncle's neck. "You're coming back to get me, right?"

The boy's words cut like a newly sharpened chainsaw blade through Bill's reserves, reminding him once more how much this kid had lost in his young life. He hugged his nephew tightly. "Always, Jackson. It's you and me against the world, son. You and me, for as long as you need me around."

Jackson released his uncle and stepped back. "Even when I don't need you around, I promise I'll always *want* you around, Uncle Bill."

Bill chuckled at the path his nephew's mind had taken. "Good to know, son."

Devastation and loss affected people one of two ways—either by crippling them emotionally or lifting them to a level of maturity well above their age level. Jackson had to be the oldest seven-year-old Bill had ever known in his life.

He'd taken to calling him son this last year. Didn't know why exactly, but Jackson hadn't seemed to mind, and it gave Bill a small measure of comfort. His plans weren't to replace his parents in the boy's mind…far from it. He found ways to bring up Jay and Elise at least a couple of times each day. He never wanted Jack to forget his wonderful parents.

He watched Jackson run off and rose to his full height. "Hard to believe I just threw the third birthday party for that kid since Elise and Jamison passed away." He turned to find his sitter wiping at the corner of her eye. "You okay, Ms. Brenda?"

She sniffed once and crossed her arms against her chest. "It still breaks my heart thinking about what that boy's gone through. You, as well." She reached out to pat his arm. "But you're doing an excellent job with him, Billy. Your mama would be so proud of you. And I know Jamison and Elise are smiling down from heaven when they see how close you two are. You're taking good care of their boy."

He sent her his best 'aw, shucks ma'am' smile. "I try."

She laughed and pushed him gently out her door. “If you could find a way to bottle that southern charm of yours, you’d be a billionaire, Billy Boy. Now, you go on and get out of here, and try not to have too much fun. Sometimes your kind of fun can come back and bite you on the behind.”

He touched a hand to his cowboy hat. “Yes, ma’am. I will. I mean, I won’t.” He pointed towards the direction Jackson had lit off to. “That kid has had his quota of birthday cake and ice cream today—I’m just warning you.”

Brenda waved him off. “I hear you. Be careful.”

Bill pivoted as she closed the door on sounds of his nephew’s laughter. Jackson loved going to the Martin’s when they had their grandchildren over. Ms. Brenda claimed the kid helped her tremendously when their twin grandsons were around. He’d be talking about tonight for days. Hard to believe the squirt had already turned seven. Harder to believe Jack had survived two years under *his* supervision.

He got in his truck, ready to shift out of ‘Uncle Bill/daddy’ mode for an evening of dinner and dancing with his date, that would hopefully lead into an all-nighter of tit-for-tat, mutually gratifying sex.

Ten minutes later, he knocked on a door in the same apartment complex he’d visited for nearly two years. Maggie pulled it open with her usual flourish.

“Hey there, Cowboy. Come on in while I put the finishing touches to my makeup.”

He grabbed her hand and pulled her to him before she could escape. “You finish up any more than you already are and I won’t be able to contain myself all evening.” He kissed her once then buried his face in her neck, breathing in the scent that tantalized him even in his dreams. “As usual, you look and smell good enough to take center stage on a dessert menu.”

“Mmm … I’ve missed you, Billy Boy.”

“Same here, Mags.” He gave her one last kiss and let her pull away to apply lipstick standing in front of her hall mirror. Instead of her naturally straight blonde locks, she’d switched to an equally flattering curled style.

She met his gaze in the mirror as she fluffed her curls. “What do you think of my new look?”

"I like it." He could hardly wait to tangle his hands in those curls. "Of course, you're always spot on gorgeous." He raised both hands and dropped them. "I can't think of a time when you didn't turn me on."

Her laughter filled the room as she dropped her lipstick in her purse. "That's because you're a typical horny SOB with only one thing on his mind."

Something about the tone of her voice had him second guessing their mutual agreement status. "You never seemed to mind before." He studied her carefully for signs. "Has something changed that I should know about?"

Her lips turned inward as she took her time closing her purse. "You are the most perceptive man I've ever known, Cowboy, I'll give you that."

He waited in silence for her to expound on her comment. Seconds dragged on until she finally sighed and met his gaze.

"I've met someone."

Her statement nearly cut his breath. "The hell you say."

"We have this new cardiologist at the hospital and—and I think I'm falling in love with him."

Well, shit—unexpected. He and Mags had relied on each other for two years—had been each other's go-to-partners for uncomplicated fun and sexual release—every bit as much friends as lovers.

"Really?" He took a deep breath and released it.

"Are you upset with me?" She bit her lip, waiting for his reply.

"Upset? No. I'm happy for you, Mags. Disappointed that we won't have *this* anymore." He waved his finger back and forth between the two of them. "I am assuming correctly, right?"

Maggie gave him her classic one-sided smile. "Assume away, but would it be too much to ask of you to go ahead with tonight?"

"For me, not at all, but—are you sure about this?"

She shrugged one shoulder. "You're the best I've ever had, Cowboy, and I love *you* in a way I could never love any other man. I just want to savor this one last night."

He grinned and held out his elbow for her. "Well, then come on, sweetheart. I'll wine and dine you so good tonight it'll bring a smile to your face when you think of me well into your nineties."

She slipped both arms around his waist and closed the gap between them. "Actually," she purred. "I thought we'd stay here and make the absolute most of our last night together." She stood on her tippy toes and kissed him.

His mind and body reacted to her tongue in his mouth, her nails scraping his back through the material of his shirt. He pulled her closer and kissed her back with the intensity of their first few meetings. She pulled away and took his hand, leading him with a smile, to her bedroom.

* * * * *

Weeks rolled into months for the two Broussard men, with Jackson's continued growth spurt struggling to catch up to his level of maturity. A good-looking mixture of both his parents, one look at the boy reminded him daily of his responsibility to their son. Jackson made that responsibility feel more like a privilege with the passing of time. The kid excelled in everything he put the slightest bit of effort into—from the classroom, to sports, to caring for his horses at home.

His mare, Sweet Sue, had foaled early on Halloween morning, a few minutes after midnight. Recognizing all the signs the evening before, Bill had stayed up with her while Jackson dozed in his sleeping bag in a nearby cot. He'd awakened the boy in time to witness the birth of the solid red filly with one white sock. All Hallows Eve—Eve for short—had come into this world with no complications. Over the next few weeks, the filly had formed an immediate attachment to Jackson, following him around the ranch like a puppy, until meal time. One whinny from Sweet Sue and Eve would leave Jackson in a second to suckle from her dam.

The boy helped his uncle muck out the stalls with no complaints, showing early signs of being a true horseman and rancher. But the kid showed potential as an athlete, as much as his parents had been. He excelled in both pee wee football and tee ball. Elise had excelled in basketball and long-distance running in track, while Jamison had shined on the baseball diamond.

Bill's preference had been football, having both the speed and necessary hand skills of a receiver. His chest swelled with pride that first Saturday in December when the coach awarded Jackson the MVP trophy after the last pee-wee football game of their season. They arrived back at the ranch excited and famished—

ready to dig in to the box of fried chicken picked up on the way home.

Bill unlocked the door and followed his nephew into the kitchen. He breathed in the fragrance of scotch pine, courtesy of the huge Christmas tree standing in the living room, waiting to be decorated. "Go wash up before we eat. As soon as we're done we can concentrate on getting that tree decorated. You don't have any homework in that back pack, do you?"

"Yes sir! I mean, no sir! I mean I don't have any homework!"

Bill had to strain to hear the last few muffled words since Jack had already reached his bathroom. For a kid that moved so slow in the mornings, that boy bounced around like a truck running on white lightnin' come Friday afternoons. The phone rang and he reached for the one hanging on the kitchen wall. "Heee-llooo," he drawled into the mouthpiece.

"Hey Cowboy."

"Mags! You're about the last person I thought would be callin' me today. What's up, buttercup?"

"I-I need a friend tonight. Are you available?"

"For you, Mags—always." He paused, none too pleased with the hint of sadness in her tone. He'd only spoken to her a handful of times since she'd relegated their relationship to a non-sexual, friend only status nearly ten months ago. Had that cardiologist broken her heart? "You okay?"

"N-n-ot really," she stammered. "I'll tell you all about it tonight if you can meet me somewhere."

Somewhere? They previously *met* at her apartment. "Like where?"

"W-would it be possible for us to meet at your house later this evening?"

"I'd have to make a phone call or two to get Jackson situated, but I'm sure I could manage that—" Bill cut off his desire for an interrogation, sensing a major meltdown in his friend's future. "Can I reach you at your old number when I get the sitter situation with Jackson straightened out?"

"No—I'll call you later, okay?"

"Alrighty then. Try back around seven-ish . . ." Before he could add a concerned "be careful" she slammed the phone down. "Well, shit." He hated the idea of her behind the wheel, crying her eyes out and too damn distracted to pay attention.

Jackson ran by him like a flash, headed straight for the bucket of fried chicken. "Hey kiddo—how would you like to spend some time with Ms. Brenda tonight?"

Jackson grabbed a drumstick and bit into it. "Does she have the twins?"

Bill grabbed a plate from the cabinet and placed it in front of him. "Is that the only way you'll stay?" He dished spoonsful of coleslaw and mashed potatoes into the plate.

The boy's face scrunched in seven-year-old concentration as he munched on his chicken and finally swallowed. "No, I like staying there. But I like it more better when the twins are there."

"Even better."

"That's what I said."

"No. You said more better. The proper way to say it is even better."

Jackson grinned. "You sound like my mom when you say stuff like that."

"That's the point, kiddo. And don't you forget it. Your mom and dad were special people."

"I know. I remember."

"Good to know. Stick around and I'll apprise you of the twin situation with Ms. Brenda."

"What?"

"I'll let you know…" A one-minute call had him addressing Jackson again. "She said she'd love to have you and it's not a done deal yet, but she'll call to see if she can get the twins." He pointed to the boy's plate. "Now eat, so we can get that tree decorated and some lights hung on this place."

Jackson's face split in an ear to ear grin. "Yippee!" he cried out, before grabbing a fork and digging into his mashed potatoes.

* * * * *

Bill stared at the woman clutching a handful of tissues and standing in his doorway. Her luscious curves had vanished, along with the carefree manner and sparkle in her eye she'd always possessed. He opened his arms to her and she came. He rubbed his hand on her back and shoulders, all traces of her former softness replaced by skin and bones.

"What the hell, Mags? You been locked up with no food for the last ten months or something?" Bill set her away gently from him to stare into eyes haunted with misery. He reached out and touched the circles under her eyes, removing a bit of makeup. "Good try but those are too dark to hide, especially from me. Get in here and talk to me. All I need is the name of the person whose ass needs kicking."

He dropped down beside her and pointed to the box of pizza on the coffee table in front of them. "I ordered your favorite. You need to eat something before you pass the hell out."

"I can't eat, Cowboy. My stomach is in knots." She opened her purse and pulled out a bottle of pills. "I'll take a glass of water though."

He watched her dump two pills in her hand before grabbing them and the bottle from her. "What the hell is this?" He scanned the prescription in her name. "Valium? The Maggie Hannigan I know doesn't need Valium." He studied the name of the prescribing physician. "Please tell me this Dr. E. Craig isn't the one responsible for your present condition. If he is, I'm sure it's a violation of some code of ethics."

She reached for them, her eyes panicked. "I need those, Billy. They help me cope."

He pulled them out of her reach and rose from the sofa, returning with a glass of water. He handed it to her, checked the prescription dosage, halved a single tablet, and gave it to her.

"That's not enough!" she protested.

"It's all you're getting." He pointed at the pill. "Take that and tell me what this is about. My patience is running thin and I'm about ready to go searching for a can of kick-ass to open up on a particular cardiologist."

She bit her lip and looked down at hands fidgeting on her purse. "Ev—Everett Craig is married."

Bill swore under his breath. Some guys were never satisfied. "And are children involved in this?"

"Two. The oldest daughter is a freshman in college already and he has one son at home, but the kid's almost thirteen years old."

"So…what? You think a thirteen old boy is beyond needing both his parents?" Bill scraped the fingers of his right hand through his hair. "Holy crap, Mags. You're having an affair with a married man with a kid at home?"

She faced him then, her eyes pleading for understanding. "It isn't like that. His marriage is in name only. His wife only married him for his money. She never loved him and doesn't even sleep in the same bed with him anymore."

Pieces of the puzzle started to fall into place for Bill. He'd bet the operating cost of the family ranch that this doctor's story wouldn't hold water. "She's probably afraid to catch something from the son of a bitch. Come on, Maggie—you're smarter than this."

"He loves me—he does! But *that woman* won't give him a divorce—not without taking him to the cleaners anyway. And Ev has worked too hard for what he has to lose it all to a woman who sits at home on her ass. He said she used to have a great job selling real estate but quit to stay home and raise their kid. I mean, this is not 1950—who the hell does that anymore? There are daycare centers all over the city."

"How long have they been married?"

"Almost twenty years."

Bill responded with a grunt. "And how old is Dr. *Love?* How long has he been practicing?"

"He's forty and . . ." She paused, as though making mental calculations. "Eight years, I think."

"Think about it, Mags. Twelve years, if not more, to get his education. If they've been married twenty years, she met him before he had money. Sounds like a classic case of wife working to put her husband's ass through college and medical school. And he repays her by sleeping with any pretty little nurse he can get his hands on."

"I'm not just any nurse."

He thumbed his own chest. "*I* know that already, but are you sure he does?"

Her eyes lit with fury. "He *loves* me."

He bent at the waist to get nose to nose with her. "Men who treat women this way don't love anyone but themselves."

She teared up and turned away from him. "You don't know him, Cowboy. He's not like that."

"I know this crap doesn't add up. Come on, Mags—stop lying to yourself. You weren't a naïve teenager when you started seeing this guy. You had to know what you were getting yourself into."

She leaned forward, her tears forming tiny dark wet spots as they dripped onto her jeans. "I just wanted this so badly."

"You *wanted* to break up a marriage and settle down with a man who'll more than likely turn around and do the same thing to you?"

"Of course not. And why should he be forced to stay in a marriage that exists in name only? We just need to be careful at the hospital so we don't jeopardize his career."

"*His* career?" Bill snorted, completely disgusted with the man he'd never set eyes on.

"We don't want anyone to get the wrong impression about our relationship, that's all."

"Oh—man!" Bill straightened, began pacing a back and forth trail in front of her, grumbling low curses under his breath. He stopped and faced his friend again, wishing he could force feed a good dose of common sense into her.

"How about the impression he's making on his own family? My brother always said that when a man disrespects his wife he's telling his daughter she should expect and accept the same treatment from men. He's telling his son it's okay to treat women the same way. He's telling his in-laws he doesn't give a rat's ass about their daughter. He's telling his co-workers he lacks what it takes to be a leader. And finally—" he pointed upward, continuing his tirade. "He's telling the man upstairs that he lacks basic Christian values."

"Your brother sounds like a saint."

"He sacrificed his first five years as a legal adult to take care of me. *That's* love, Maggie. Sacrificing for the good of your family, not catering to your own selfish desires." He stared down at the top of her blonde head. A taste of reality suddenly slapped him in the face. "Am I partly to blame for this?"

She dabbed at her eyes with the tissue and sniffed. "How could you be?"

He dropped beside her and took her hands. "Has the relationship we've shared the last two years made you feel . . ." He searched his mind for the right words. "Lacking—or less than—have I made you feel that you don't deserve any better?"

She answered with an eye roll. "Don't be stupid."

"I'm serious."

She released a sigh and faced him. "Look, Cowboy—we've always had a mutually satisfying relationship. As much as I enjoy your company, I've never been able to see us as—a couple."

Relief washed over him. "Well, that's good to know. I'd hate to think that I contributed to you thinking you should ever settle for less."

Maggie leaned forward, rested her head against his shoulder. "Don't do that to yourself, honey. You're my friend. The best friend I have in the world."

He hugged her tight. "Thanks, but that doesn't say much for your list of friends. Now set my mind at ease by telling me you're done with Dr. Love. Because, sugar, he's not gonna leave his wife. Even if he does, it won't be to marry you."

She pulled away. "Don't say that! I have to have something to hold on to."

Bill stopped short of telling her she'd have a better chance holding on to *him* than a man who cheats on his wife with her. But he didn't love Maggie the way he loved Lorraine, or Elise either, for that matter. He had no right to offer any more than he could give her.

He could and would, however, damned sure find out more about Dr. Everett Craig.

And he knew just the man for the job.

* * * * *

Wednesday morning, December 14th

It took a week and a half for Bill to get results from his private detective. He sat at his kitchen table, watching Maggie's face as she scanned the first page in a manila folder.

Her face blank, she turned on him. "What am I looking at?"

"It's proof that your boyfriend is a piece of crap who'll say anything it takes to get a pretty girl to sleep with him. You're far from the first, honey." Bill tapped the list of names on the paper she held. "These are the women he's had affairs with since medical school."

Her face paled as she scanned the list of nearly two dozen names. "How'd you come by this information?"

"I hired a private investigator I know. According to him, his easiest case ever. Your playboy doctor has never put forth much effort into covering up his infidelities. The last hospital asked for his resignation after the radiologist he knocked up miscarried their child and nearly died."

“He told me he left for a better position.”

“No doubt.” He pulled a tabbed photo out from the middle of the stack of papers and laid it in front of her. “And here’s the reason his wife quit her lucrative career in real estate to stay home. Their second child, a son born deaf, a trait passed down from your doctor’s side of the family. Rather than send him off to a school at an early age, she learned how to communicate with him and teaches him herself at home.”

She studied the photo of a pretty blonde woman signing to a boy, both of them wearing huge smiles. Maggie’s face remained expressionless. “What do you want me to say?”

“That you’ll end this and move on.”

She flipped through page after page of incriminating evidence, until she held up the last picture—a shot of the doctor and his family of four walking out of a church, hand in hand with his wife. The P.I. had circled the date on the bottom right corner of the page—taken the Sunday before.

Bill placed a hand on her arm. “Mags?”

She dropped the photo and rested her forehead in her hands. “Son of a bitch.”

“Yeah.”

She bolted out of the chair suddenly, nearly knocking it over in a rush to grab her purse and get to the door. “I’ve gotta go.”

“Where are you going?”

“To take care of some business.”

“Are you going to be alright?”

She turned at the door and gave him a hard stare. “I’ll be fine. Thanks for opening my eyes, Cowboy. I’ve been an idiot, but I guess it’s better to hear it now than later, right?”

He lifted one hand. “Be careful, hon.” Bill watched from the door until she drove out of sight, hoping she wouldn’t do anything stupid.

He called her that night to check up on her. Then again, the second night after revealing Dr. Craig’s past. She hadn’t answered either time. He pushed it from his mind to tend to Jackson, told himself she’d be fine. Maggie had the strength to put this behind her and move on.

Didn’t she?

* * * * *

December 17th

The clock on his nightstand read 3:27 a.m. when Bill reached for the ringing phone. His heart pounding in his chest, he braced himself and answered. “Bill Broussard here.”

“Mr. Broussard, I’m calling from the Southwest Medical Center in Pasadena. We have a patient, one of our own, actually—a former employee—who’s asked us to call you.”

Shit. “Maggie?”

“Her name is Margaret Hannigan.”

“Everyone calls her Maggie . . . is she . . .” He swallowed, dreading the answer.

“She’s okay. She overdosed on valium. We’ve pumped her stomach and she should be fine.”

“I’ll be there as soon as I can arrange for a sitter.”

It took thirty minutes for Ms. Brenda to get to his place, another thirty to get to the hospital. After inquiring about Maggie, a nurse ushered him into a tiny area near the back of the ER. She pulled open a curtain and stepped aside.

She lay there in the bed, nearly swallowed up by layer upon layer of paleness in the white walled, white-tiled room—from pristine white blankets, to bedsheets, to Maggie, her face absent of all color except for those dark circles under her eyes, even more prominent now. He stepped forward, took her pale hand in his and leaned closer.

“Mags?”

Her head turned on the pillow, as if in slow motion and she opened her eyes. Parched lips opened to croak out a single hoarse word. “Cowboy.”

“Hey Sugar.”

“You—” She paused, coughing. Bill grabbed a glass of water with a straw in it from the bedside table and held it up to her mouth. She took a long drink and dropped her blonde head back against the white pillowcase. “Throat hurts.”

“From the tube they used to pump your stomach, no doubt.” Bill pulled a chair closer to the bed and sat beside her, resting his chin on the rail. “What the hell were you thinking, sweetheart?”

Her face crumpled and he felt bad for getting on her case so quickly. He cupped her thin face between his hands and tried again. “Shhh…it’s alright, Mags. I’m gonna bring you home with me. I’m not lettin’ you out of my sight again until you remember how special you are. You are far too important to treat yourself this way.”

“I’m not your responsibility.”

“No, but you’re my friend, Mags. Simple as that.”

She sniffed and wiped her eyes with the hand that didn’t have an IV sticking out of it. “I can use one right now.”

He rested his chin on the bed rail again. “So, tell me what happened.”

“I confronted him about everything. He denied it, of course. You should have seen his face when I brought out that folder.” She closed her eyes and shook her head. “He accused *me* of hiring the investigator because I didn’t trust him. Said he could never be with anyone who had such a lack of faith in him. Do you believe that?”

Bill snickered under his breath, wishing for a chance to meet this guy face to face. “I can believe anything from a piece of crap like that.” He cocked his head suddenly. “He with you when you took the pills?”

She bit her lip. “No.”

“What happened to push you over that edge, Mags? What’d he say? What’d he do?”

“He—he got me fired.”

White hot fury rose from Bill’s chest, into his throat, then his face. “Are you serious?”

She swallowed loudly. “He told the hospital administrator that I seduced him—that I blackmailed him to keep seeing me.”

Bill bit back hard on the string of curses dying to spew forth. *Oh yeah. This guy had earned himself an ass-kicking of the first order.* “And what did the hospital administrator say when you showed him or her the folder?”

“I didn’t have it anymore. Ev took it from me.” She looked up at him, teary-eyed. “He destroyed all of the evidence. I’m sorry.”

The air rumbled with his deep laughter. “Well, there’s plenty more where that came from, honey. I only gave you one of a few duplicates.” He leaned over the bed. “What’s the name of your hospital administrator? I’ll bring it over myself.”

She wiped her eyes again and released a loud sigh. “And then what? Who’s going to suffer for his cruelty and bad judgement?

His wife and that boy will suffer." Her head fell back heavily against her pillow. "Seems to me his wife has suffered enough."

He gripped the bedrail in both hands and stared at his friend, wondering how someone could be so generous after what she'd been put through.

"Don't do that, Cowboy."

"Don't what?" he asked, baffled.

"Don't convince yourself I'm being noble. It's only guilt. I feel so awfully guilty for sleeping with the woman's husband. I knew this could happen and ignored my instincts. It won't happen again."

Bill stared down at her. "Are you talking about having an affair or trying to end your own life?"

She met his gaze then, her blue eyes wide and totally alert. "Both." She reached out to grab his hand. "I'm serious. You don't have to worry this will happen again. I'll be fine. Go home to Jackson. Love ya, Cowboy—and thanks."

He left then, thankful and certain his friend would be okay. But he wasn't quite as forgiving or gracious toward Dr. Craig as she seemed to be.

Later that morning, at his table and on his second pot of coffee, he made his decision.

* * * * *

"My word. Someone's definitely done their homework." The hospital administrator looked up at Bill from his desk. "I had no idea Dr. Craig had such a checkered past."

"So, you do see that his version of the story is a load of bull, right?" He pointed at the folder in the administrator's hands. "That man has never been seduced in his life."

The other man nodded and rested his elbows on his desk, fingers steepled. "What is it you want from me, Mr. Broussard?"

"I want you to reinstate Ms. Hannigan."

"Done, but are you sure she'd want to stay here? It's my experience that when things like this occur, the parties don't always feel as comfortable in their work environment as they did before."

"Are you saying situations like this are commonplace in hospitals?"

"The shifts for medical personnel are long, and can be both stressful and tedious, Mr. Broussard. As a result, hospitals are often breeding grounds for infidelity, and a hotbed for gossip and rumors."

"If she decides to stay, it's up to her. But if she wants to leave, I want to make sure this doesn't follow her. Is she good at her job?"

The man nodded. "She is one of the best."

"Then make sure she gets a glowing recommendation to take with her if she leaves here."

"Will do. And I *will* be talking to Dr. Craig about this, rest assured."

Bill stood and shook his hand. "I appreciate the gesture, but I doubt seriously your 'talking to' will land anywhere close to giving that man what he truly deserves." He left the office, satisfied with the outcome, so far.

His mouth salivating at the thought of giving Dr. Love what he deserved on a personal level, he pulled a slip of paper from his wallet and stared at the address. He knew this subdivision. Returning to his truck, he headed for the doctor's home.

It took nearly fifteen minutes to get to the Sherwood Forest subdivision, another ten to locate the address in the maze of creative names like Robin's Drive, Merry Men Street, and Friar Tuck Bend. Finally, he pulled into the driveway of a substantial home. Two people, a blonde woman and a pre-teenage boy, looked up from staking large red and white candy canes along the front walkway. He stepped out of his truck, manila folder in one hand, his Stetson in the other. He placed the hat on his head at the woman's approach.

She brushed a lock of hair back from her pretty face. "What can I do for you?"

"Hello ma'am. I'm Bill Broussard. I'm here to talk to you about your husband, Dr. Everett Craig."

Her eyes narrowed ever-so-slightly as she signed something to the boy. The boy glanced in Bill's direction but turned and went into the house. She faced Bill again. "This is about the woman who overdosed, isn't it?"

The traces of sympathy in her tone knocked him down from his righteously indignant perch a notch or two. "I'm a good friend of hers."

Her eyes softened in genuine concern. "Is she going to be alright?"

He nodded, wondering from what well of forgiveness and graciousness these women drank from on a daily basis. “She’ll be fine, physically. Mentally—” He shrugged. “She says she won’t try this again. At this point, all I can do is trust her at her word.”

“And do you?” she asked.

“Yes, ma’am. I believe I do.”

Tight-lipped, she nodded several times before she took a deep breath. “It must be nice—being able to trust someone that way. It’s been so long, I’ve forgotten how it feels.” She reached out for the folder. “May I?”

He handed it to her, watched her face transform from passivity to acceptance. “So, you knew about this?”

She looked up at him, not quite able to cover the hurt in her eyes. “It’s always going on, in one form or another.” She closed the folder and handed it back to him, clearly unaffected by the list of names.

“Excuse me for asking ma’am but, why do you take it?”

“At first, I had faith that he could and would change. Then, I had a baby at home, a little girl who adored her daddy. Our son was born with a congenital hearing disorder eight years later, and—it’s been—trying. Everyone told me to send him away to a school, but …” She stopped, swallowed. “I just couldn’t do it. So, I’ve trained myself to help him in any and every way I can to fully function in a world that he can’t hear.” She crossed her arms and glanced back at the house before returning her gaze to Bill. “Lately I’ve been thinking maybe it’s time to enroll him in that school.”

Bill shuffled his boots, hooking one thumb in the pocket of his jeans. “If you don’t mind me saying, I lost my second parent, my mom, at his age. I had my brother to raise me, but I still missed our mom a lot. I’m thinking if you sent him away now, he might feel like he’d be losing both his parents, too.”

“Oh, I wouldn’t be sending him away, Mr. Broussard. I’d be going with him—relocating without my husband to Austin so Brandon could attend day classes at a wonderful school for the deaf and come home every night. He’d be meeting other kids like himself, forming relationships he’d keep throughout high school. Hopefully, he’ll continue his education at the university there when he finishes high school—if that’s what he wants.”

Bill tucked the folder under one arm. “Sounds like you’ve put some thought and planning into this.”

She nodded. “For a few years now.”

“I think you should know that I went to the hospital administrator. Your husband had Maggie fired. Claimed she’d blackmailed him. Maggie says she didn’t—just blindsided her with it.”

“Sounds exactly like something he’d do.”

“I wanted to see that she’s reinstated.”

“Did they?”

“Yes. Whether she wants to stay there or not is up to her.”

“That’s good.” The woman shrugged. “Honestly, I’m past the point of caring what happens to Ev’s career. He’s made sure of that.”

Bill studied her features, her pert mouth tight with seriousness. “I think you’re a tough lady and you’ll do just fine with whatever you choose to do from here on out. Go out and find yourself a man who actually deserves your trust.”

She gave him a light snort of laughter. “Everett and I married when I was barely nineteen. I grew up with him. Twenty years of a marriage heaped with infidelity can change a person, Mr. Broussard.” She walked with him back to his truck. “I don’t know that I can ever trust a man again.”

He placed his hand on the door handle and did a half-turn to face her. “Don’t let one cheater ruin the rest of your life, ma’am. I’m telling you, there are plenty of men out there who actually appreciate what they’ve got at home.”

She smiled at him. “Are you one of them?”

He looked off in the distance. “We were only married seven months. I like to think I would have been had she not left this world when she did.” Her light intake of breath had him turning to face her.

“I’m sorry, you look too young to have faced that kind of loss already.”

“Death doesn’t distinguish the age of its victim—or in my wife and unborn child’s case, its victims.”

She groaned and shook her head. “I am truly sorry for your loss.”

“Thank you.” He adjusted his brown Stetson. “So, you see—I *do* recognize what a fool your husband is.”

She sucked in her breath. "That kind of makes my problems seem miniscule in comparison."

"No ma'am. Not from where I'm standing. Betrayal is its own form of death."

Her eyes closed for a moment as though she were testing the weight of his words. "You're correct. Betrayal is the death of trust, of peace of mind, of hope, of faith in my marriage. I can't keep doing this. I can't. It's taken too much from me and given me nothing to hang onto."

"Did you love him?"

"I did—once—but—"

He nodded, understanding completely. "He's finally hurt you more than you love him." Bill tipped his hat to her. "Good luck, Mrs. Craig."

"Natalie . . . my name is Natalie Benson," she said, her voice firm, her eyes hard with determination.

He smiled, glad to see her laying claim to her own name, and maybe along with it, that part of herself she'd lost. Lost in a marriage to a man who wanted to eat out of his own plate while sampling out of everyone else's at the table too.

* * * * *

Rather than seek out Dr. Love, Bill figured he'd let Natalie Craig—no...Natalie *Benson*...deal her husband the final blow. God knows she'd earned that right. When Maggie called to say her doctor had signed her release papers, he headed back to the hospital.

She looked up from her spot on the side of the bed when he walked in the room. "Hey."

"You ready to go, Mags? You're coming home with me."

"That's not necessary, Cowboy. A girlfriend of mine is expecting me."

"Let her know you're spending the holidays with me and the squirt. You still have a job, by the way."

Her eyes widened. "Last I heard I didn't."

"The hospital administrator reinstated you when he saw the evidence. What's more, he's putting the good doctor on notice."

She threw herself into his arms. "Thank you so much. I don't know what to say."

He hugged her then held her at arm's length. "Just say you're done with that asshole."

"I am. I swear I am, Cowboy."

Satisfied, he nodded and grabbed her purse. "Then let's get the hell out of here."

* * * *

Christmas Eve

Bill sat on the couch with Jackson, the two of them staring at the twinkling multi-colored lights of the tree. The gentle clinking of pots and pans drifted out of the kitchen, cabinet doors opening and shutting, and soft singing along with the radio. All of it sounds and traces of feminine domesticity in the house again—things not heard since Elise's presence in the old ranch house.

"Who wants hot cocoa with their popcorn?"

Maggie's call from the kitchen pulled him from his reverie. He exchanged a look with his grinning nephew.

"Told ya." Jackson held out his hand.

Bill fished around in his pocket and pulled out four quarters. "I don't have any singles. This'll have to do." He placed them in Jackson's hand.

Maggie appeared at the doorway as the kid jumped off the sofa and ran into the hallway. "Where's he going? I'm waiting for answers."

Bill grinned at her. "I had to pay up and he's hoarding his silver, the little miser."

She shook her head slowly. "Am I part of this bet?"

"He bet me you'd ask us if we wanted cocoa."

"I've asked that every night for the last two weeks. That's not much of a longshot."

"I know, but the kid is saving for a new glove."

She smiled and lowered her voice. "You mean like the one I wrapped for you that's hidden in the closet?"

"Just like that one. He said he didn't want to chance Santa not bringing him the one he wanted. That kid's always got a backup plan."

Jackson ran back into the room and jumped onto the sofa. He blinked at the two adults staring at him. "What'd I do?"

Maggie's light-hearted laughter rang out. "I'm still waiting on an answer from you two knuckleheads."

"I want cocoa!" Jackson cried out. "With extra marshmallows please."

"Sure, why not?" Bill agreed. "But—"

"I know, I know…" she called out, disappearing into the kitchen. "Without the marshmallows. There's something wrong with you, Cowboy."

"I prefer the taste of cocoa. If I wanted melted marshmallows, I'd—"

"Build a damn fire!" Jackson finished for him. He slapped a hand over his mouth and stared up at his uncle, and then Maggie when she reappeared in the doorway, open-mouthed. "Sorry. That slipped out."

Maggie pointed at Bill. "That's on you, Cowboy!"

Bill leaned close to his nephew, gave him his version of the old 'evil-eye'. "Son, you better hope Santa didn't hear you say that. I hear those elves of his have their ways of hearing what goes on up there at the north pole. They report everything directly to the fat man, himself."

Jackson grinned. "But Santa's not at the North Pole anymore. He's already on his way."

Bill cocked his head at the boy's matter of fact reply. "Maybe so, but I'm willing to bet they've got some magic dust or something that lets them keep in touch with him even when he's en route—on his way here."

The kid chewed his bottom lip as though contemplating the possibility. "I did apologize, Uncle Bill. It just slipped out and I'm really gonna try not to say it anymore, even though I hear *you* say it all the time." He raised one hand when Bill opened his mouth to speak. "I know. We're still doing that 'do as you say, not as you do' thing, right?"

Bill placed his large hand on top of Jackson's head, gave him a playful shove. "You are way too smart for your own good sometimes, son."

Jackson beamed at his uncle. "Mrs. Hanchey told me that very thing just yesterday."

"Oh really." Bill tensed, immediately on alert. "What'd you do—or say—to make your teacher tell you that?"

"She said she'd gained fifty pounds before she finally had her baby last month, and that it showed in her behind afterwards."

"Oh, sweet lord …" Bill covered his face and groaned.

"I told her my filly, Eve, weighed almost twice that much when she was born and afterwards, *her* dam's behind was the same size as before she got pregnant. Except Mrs. Hanchey thought I said her *damn* behind, you know, like the cuss word. But I told her no, that a dam is a mama horse, and she would know that if she'd been raised around them, like me." He let loose a suffering sigh. "And that's when—"

"She said you were way too smart for your own good," Bill finished for him. He looked to Maggie for assistance.

She snorted and shook her head. "I hope you're not looking to me for help. I'm just now learning, from a seven-year old kid no less, that a mama horse is called a dam."

Bill nodded. "Alright, then. I don't think there's a thing I can say to top what he already told his teacher."

Maggie turned away, leaving a second round of snorts and chuckles in her wake. "Y'all are something. I'm gonna miss being around you two crazy guys."

Jackson whipped his head around to face the kitchen door. "Where are you going, Maggie?" He looked up at Bill. "Where's she going?"

Bill lowered his voice to a whisper, deciding Maggie would tell them both when it suited her. "I don't know, son. But we knew she'd only be here for a little while. Maybe she thinks it's time to go back home."

"But I like having her here," Jackson hissed in a low whisper. His eyes widened suddenly. "She's not leaving before Santa gets here, is she?"

"I wouldn't think so since this is the first I hear of it."

Maggie reentered the room, carrying two bowls of popcorn, set them on the table and pointed at one bowl. "Here you go. This one has sugar, and the other has butter and salt. Cocoa's coming right up." She spun around on her heel. "I can hear you two bozos in here, you know. Let me finish what I'm doing and we'll talk."

Bill grabbed the sugared popcorn—his nephew, the salted and buttered bowl. They sat back and munched on the treat until she rejoined them carrying a tray with three mugs, a small container of marshmallows, and a third small bowl of popcorn. Maggie preferred her popcorn plain.

"You hang on to this, little man, or else your uncle will be digging popcorn out of the sofa for the next month." She placed the tray on Jackson's lap and sat beside him before grabbing one mug and her bowl of popcorn. She took a sip and released a satisfied sigh. "Mmm…so good."

The Broussard men followed her cue, rewarding her with similar grunts of approval.

Jackson placed his mug carefully on the tray and grabbed a handful of popcorn. "I like her cocoa as much as yours, Uncle Bill."

Maggie winked at the boy. "That's because your uncle kindly gave me his secret ingredient."

"Yeah, he's a pretty cool guy, isn't he?"

Maggie smiled at Bill. "He is that, little man. Cowboy is the best man I know."

"Then why do you want to leave him—and me?" He turned on his uncle. "Did you do something to chase her off?"

"Not that I know of, squirt. I like having Mags around."

Maggie followed up with a soft chuckle. "Your uncle didn't say or do anything to chase me off, Jackson. Cowboy and I realized a long time ago that we're much better off being friends than an actual couple. Some people are just like that." She did a half-turn on the couch, curling one leg under her and resting her left elbow on the couch back to look down at him. "I've loved spending time with you boys but I got a new job up in Dallas that starts on January ninth. I need to go back to my place and start packing up for the move."

"You're not gonna be here to watch the fireworks?"

Bill's heart broke seeing his nephew's big blue eyes tear up. "I bet if we promise to help her pack up her place we could convince her to stay with us until after New Year's Day. That way we could all go and watch the fireworks display together."

Maggie looked from him, to his nephew and then back at him, her smile growing even larger. "That sounds like a plan, boys."

* * * *

"Here, let me take him from you." Bill walked around to where Maggie attempted to exit the truck carrying an armful of sleeping Jackson. The transfer took place without waking the boy and Maggie opened the door to let them all inside. The two of them tucked him into bed and closed the door before entering the ranch home's cozy kitchen.

Maggie hung her coat on the hook by the door and faced him. "You want cocoa or something?"

He slipped out of his down vest and hung it on the hook beside hers. It felt comfortable—too damned comfortable. "I'm good."

She opened the fridge and pulled out a bottle of champagne. "I bought this today. Thought we could open it after the squirt went to bed. Kind of erase this crappy last year and toast in a new, better year—one with new beginnings."

"Hmph…" He watched her peel the foil off the top of the elegantly flared bottle. *For her, maybe.*

The stopper came off with a loud pop, but she kept the foam-over to a minimum. They entered the living room and stood before the fireplace. She poured them two glasses and handed him one. "To 1984. May it be a good one for both of us."

He lifted the glass and clinked hers. "To 1984." He took a sip and nodded. "Not too bad, for a sissy drink."

She laughed. "It doesn't hurt to expand your range now and then, Cowboy. There's more to alcoholic beverages than beer."

"Sure, there is. Lots of good stuff—like bourbon, vodka, and tequila." He grinned. "Don't look at me like you're just seeing this side of me. We've known each other for nearly three years. Let me get these logs going again to chase the chill from this room." He put the glass on the mantle and removed the screen from the fireplace.

"Yes, we have known each other awhile now," she purred, slipping one arm around his waist from behind. "In the biblical sense as well."

When he faced her, she took another sip from her glass and looked up at him, her long eyelashes fluttering. "How would you feel about spending one last night together—in that sense, I mean? One last going away celebration to mark our time together?"

He turned, grabbed the fireplace poker from the tools to get the glowing logs going again—all while contemplating her request. He stirred the embers before laying another log on the fire. The flames popped and sizzled, licking at the bark on the dry wood. Maggie had spent every night in the guest room throughout her stay. He'd never considered anything otherwise, out of respect for both his nephew and her situation.

Bill turned to her then. “How about we just sit in front of the fire and talk?”

“Oo-kaay, but . . .” She took a step back and stared at him, as though searching for clues. “Is something wrong?”

“Not yet.” He attempted honesty while still saving face. “But if we spent the night together like we used to, I’m thinking it could throw something out of balance in this carefully laid out relationship of ours.”

Her brow wrinkled, and she frowned at him. “How so?”

“I brought you here because I knew what you were going through. Jamison and Elise helped me through my bad time, and I wanted to be here for you.”

“I know that, Cowboy. I just thought maybe—”

He placed his hands on her shoulders, cutting her off. “I’m gonna have to pass, Sugar. We already had our last hoorah.” *Before you cut us off to have an affair with a married man.* “Let’s just leave it at that.”

She nodded slowly, her eyes alight with understanding. “I’m sorry, Cowboy. I didn’t realize that macho man ego of yours had taken such a big hit when I dumped you for a soft-handed doctor.”

Well damn.

He forced a smile and dropped onto the couch, pulling her down beside him. “Fact is, I’m afraid both the kid and I have grown too used to having you around. Don’t make me miss more than your company and your cooking.”

She leaned her head against his shoulder and sighed. “Alright. I understand now.”

Relieved by her answer, he stared into the fire and contemplated a life with no Mags in it. “We’re gonna stay in touch with each other, right?”

“Absolutely, Cowboy. Absolutely.”

He swung his arm over her shoulder and pulled her closer, forcing himself to be satisfied with the here and now.

Chapter Ten

An Eye-Opening Christmas

December 25, 1991

Bill pulled into the driveway to the last several notes of The Eagles version of *Please Come Home for Christmas,* brushing off the memories the song always conjured up in his mind. Memories of the first time he and Lorraine heard it together, to walking in on Jamison and Elise as they danced to the Charles Brown version in the kitchen. He walked around to the passenger side of his truck and opened the door, taking the tall, leggy redhead's hand as she stepped down. She peered around him at the old farm house.

"It's a little isolated out here, isn't it?" Hannah Harrison's green-eyed gaze narrowed on the structure, sweeping left to right in critical observation.

"Maybe so, but working ranches generally are. Even though it's small, considering the number of cattle we own, we still need land for grazing."

"We?" She focused her gaze on him, then.

"Well, my nephew and I. This place belonged to his maternal grandparents. His mom and dad, my brother, Jamison, took it over. Now it's his, legally, but I'll run it for him until he's old enough to either run it himself or decide what to do with it."

Her brow furrowed, as though struggling with her memory. "And Jamison and his wife . . ."

"Died when Jackson was just a little kid."

"Oh! Of course. I know that."

Did she? He'd mentioned them countless times. He brushed aside the prickle of warning. Stress from her latest round of job hunting—not to mention drained from her previous night of partying with a group of girl friends from high school in town for the holidays.

He escorted her into the house and helped her out of her coat, hung it on the hook by the kitchen door. Assaulted by the smell of roasting bird in the oven, he looked around at the otherwise empty room. "Jackson!" he called out.

"Yes sir…I'm here." His tall, lanky nephew came lumbering down the hallway, not quite out of that gawky adolescent stage. The kid had already passed the six-foot mark but from the looks of it, the high school freshman hadn't finished growing. He'd bet his left nut the kid would surpass his dad's height of six foot two inches—possibly even his own six foot three inches.

Jackson's blue eyes landed on Hannah, widening slightly as he brushed a hand through his hair, trying to smooth down the spiky flips and other remnants of his bedhead. "Hey."

"Hello there."

Bill introduced the two of them before turning on his nephew. "I forgot to ask if you had any homework over the holidays."

"I've got a book report to write that's due our first day back to school. I've only got a couple of chapters left to read and I can whip one of those out in a couple of hours." He raised one finger and reached into his back pocket for his wallet. "I almost forgot to give this to you. They need you to pick a time and date for the mid-year parent-teacher conference."

Bill reached for the paper and scanned it. He pointed to a date on the list and leaned toward Jackson. "You got anything going on then?"

Jackson shrugged. "Not that I know of. Baseball practice won't start up again until two days later."

Bill nodded and circled the date before signing the sheet and giving it back to him. "You got any friends coming over for lunch today?"

"Mike's dad is working offshore and his mom is sleeping late after an all-night emergency call. I talked to him a little while ago and he's kinda bummed because his older brother is at his girlfriend's house for the day. He's pretty much alone over there but I didn't want to invite him over until I asked you first."

Bill waved a hand. "Go over and pick him up. There's enough bird in that oven to feed a small army. Tell him to make sure he leaves a note for his mom though."

Jackson acknowledged with a silent nod before grabbing his truck keys and heading out the door.

Hoping Hannah wouldn't mind another hungry teenager at their table, Bill turned to give her an explanation. "His buddy, Mike Burnett, lives just down the road from us—his dad works seven-and-seven offshore and his mom's the best large animal vet in these pa-a-rt-s . . ." The look on her face held him frozen in his tracks. "What's wrong, honey? Did you swallow a gnat or something?"

"You're *raising* your nephew?"

"I am." He knew damned well he'd told her before. Had she really forgotten? Or just not paid him any attention? "Are you telling me you weren't aware of that?"

"Well, I mean I knew you talked about him *all* the time. It's always *Jackson* this, and *Jackson* that. I just thought y'all had this special bond or something."

He nodded. "We do. We did even before his folks died." He wouldn't remind her—again—about how caring for the kid had practically saved his life.

"Well, I think I should let you know, here and now, I don't want to raise a child of my *own*, much less anyone else's. I mean, I'm crazy about my little niece, but that's because I can spoil her rotten for one afternoon then drop her butt off to her parents and go back to living my life."

Deflated by her announcement, Bill attempted to salvage the situation. "You make it sound like that boy still craps his diapers and wakes up for two a.m. feedings. Jackson's pretty self-sufficient—has his own learner's permit to drive and everything. Hell, he'll be going off to college in less than four years."

"I don't care," she huffed. "I wouldn't be good step-mom material. Kids take up so much time. And teen-agers—ugh—my brother and I put my parents through hell when we were in high school. I absolutely *refuse* to go through any of that mess."

Should he waste time and effort by telling her that Jackson never gave him any trouble in school or otherwise? If he bothered, would she even listen? Would she even remember? He reassessed the woman before him and all her selfish traits. Recalled how, even after telling her he'd pick her up at 10:00 a.m. sharp because he had to finish preparing the Christmas meal, she made him wait until 11:00 so she could put on her make-up, fix her hair, and insisted on his opinion as she changed outfits…four times…before finally settling on the first one. How she couldn't seem to absorb a thing he told her about his life but had an uncanny ability to focus on the most minute details pertaining to her own self-interests.

Hannah had obviously never put the needs of anyone or anything before herself in her entire life. Had he really been so snowed over by her looks—her outward appearance? Deciding that all that pretty on the outside would never make up for the character she lacked on the inside, Bill sent her a definitive nod. "It's good we got this all out in the open now." He walked over to the door, grabbed their coats, and tossed Hannah's jacket over to her. "I'll take you home right away."

"But Bill—"

"No—you've made your point." He shrugged into his coat. "I'm doing the same." He reached for the door knob and walked onto the porch. He drove her home in silence, ignored her provocative come-ons after walking her to her door and left her there, open-mouthed, clearly unused to not having any man's world evolve around her.

By the time he returned home, Jackson and Mike were both busy in the kitchen. Jackson looked up from attempting to move the turkey from the roaster to a carving platter. "Mike doesn't like green bean casserole so I'm heating a couple of cans of corn. Where'd you go?" He looked around him. "And where's Hannah?"

"A situation came up and I brought her home. How's that bird look?" Bill hung up his coat and helped him transfer the bird onto the platter.

"Looks good, Mr. Bill—and smells even better," Mike said. The kid, with a head full of curly red hair and freckles, had been Jackson's best friend since third grade. "Thanks for inviting me over. Mom's crashed at home. It took all night to deliver a foal for some rich breeder whose regular vet left town for the weekend."

"I hope everything turned out alright."

"Better than alright. She impressed the breeder so much he asked if she'd be his go-to from here on out. Mom says his business alone will more than double her yearly income. She's been struggling to get clients since she finished school and started her own business a few years back. This is a big break for her."

"That's excellent news!" Bill slapped Mike on the back. "Tell her congratulations for me."

"I will, sir, but she'll probably give you a call later. The horse's owner told her you're the one who recommended her when he talked to you a few weeks back."

He gave the kid a nod. "She must be talking about Ol' man Thompson. I heard him at the feed store the other day complaining about his regular guy and I told him I had complete confidence in your mom's abilities. Hell, we'd have lost both my Palomino mare and her foal last year if I'd listened to ol' Doc Miller. I listened to my gut and called your mom over. She pulled them both through. You should be proud of her."

"I am, sir. I just hope dad will be too when he hears. I heard them arguing the other day about how he should be the one earning the big pay checks. Mom said that he'd worked hard to pay her way through vet school and he shouldn't let his ego outgrow his common sense."

Bill kept his mouth shut, deciding it would do no good to comment on another couple's marital squabbles. Mike's dad, Bobby, might be a prideful man, but he'd always been good to his wife, Sheila, and their two boys. Maybe the next time he saw that ol' boy he'd remind him how fortunate he is.

The three of them had just finished watching the Aloha Bowl—a nail biter between the Stanford Cardinals and the Georgia Yellow Jackets, when the ring of the telephone sliced through the air.

Jackson jumped up from the couch, heading for the phone. "Great game! I can't believe the Jackets pulled ahead with fourteen seconds left."

Bill rushed to the phone first in case Hannah called back. He sure as hell didn't need Jackson getting an earful by mistake. The kid's deep voice had people constantly confusing them. "Hello."

"Hey Bill, is my son still over there?"

Relief coursed through him. "He sure is, Doc Barnett. Hang on." He handed the phone to Mike. "It's your mom."

Mike hung up after a brief conversation with his mom. "She said to tell you thanks for having me over and that she's going to drop off some sweets when she picks me up."

"Did she have time to cook anything?"

"Nah…we went to my grandparent's place yesterday and have some leftover ham and some kind of nasty broccoli casserole in the fridge. She'd planned to bake a hen for supper but she's too wiped out to cook anything."

By the time Sheila Barnett knocked on the door, Bill had filled a plastic food storage bag with leftover turkey and another with rice dressing. He opened the door for her. “Come on in Doc, it’s getting colder out there.”

She entered, carrying a large plastic container full of sweets. “I came home from mom’s yesterday with all kinds of desserts and we can only eat so much. This is in thanks for feeding my kid today. But I owe you so much more for your recommendation of me to Mr. Thompson.”

He gave her a quick, one-armed hug. “I heard the good news. It’s well deserved and I’m happy for you. Here, I packed up some turkey and dressing for you to take home.” They traded containers and he peeked under the lid. “Holy crap, is that homemade pecan pie?”

“It is! My mom baked three of them and we only cut into one. My dad has a bad habit of cheat eating in the middle of the night.” She pointed to the rest of the items in the container. “And those are my pralines, divinity, and homemade fudge.”

Mike walked into the room at the end of the conversation. “Grandma Karen says she refuses to let Gramps go into a diabetic coma on her watch. I had to sneak all that stuff into our car yesterday during Gramp’s afternoon nap.”

Sheila laughed and shook her head. “The things we sacrifice for family, right?”

Bill grinned and nodded.

Sheila sobered, and approached him to whisper. “I’m sorry Bill. That sounded petty considering what you and Jackson have both been through.”

“It didn’t sound petty at all, Doc.” He looked at Jackson. His life had been so much fuller because of his nephew. “I haven’t sacrificed a thing where he’s concerned. He’s about the best thing that ever could have happened to me.”

“He’s lucky to have you.”

“We’re lucky to have each other.”

* * * * *

Later that evening, Bill and Jackson sat in the living room, watching back to back Christmas movies. They’d finished off the pecan pie during *The Christmas Story*. Halfway through *National Lampoon’s Christmas Vacation*, they’d put a good dent in the supply of pralines, divinity, and fudge.

Jackson rubbed his belly, his feet propped up on the coffee table. “I think I over did it.”

Bill propped his feet onto the same table and crossed them at the ankles. "That's what holidays are for—you'll survive. Were you satisfied with your Christmas gifts this year?"

Jackson's face lit up. "You're kiddin', right? A chance to watch Shaquille O'Neal play basketball for LSU against Kentucky in February? *And* another two tickets to watch Skip Bertman coach their baseball team in March. Off the chart Christmas gifts, Uncle Bill."

Bill sent him a satisfied smile. The kid would crap himself if his early birthday gift came through—three tickets to watch LSU battle Duke University at the Maravich Assembly Center. He'd already spoken to Sheila and Bobby about bringing Mike along. As much as Jackson loved taking road trips with just the two of them, he knew he'd have more fun with a friend along. "Yeah," he drawled. "Nothing like a road trip."

The kid grunted once and remained quiet for several minutes. Bill had begun to wonder if he'd nodded off to sleep when Jackson spoke up again.

"You brought her home because of me, didn't you?"

"What?"

"Your girlfriend, Hannah. I saw her face when we were talking about the parent teacher conference. She didn't look too happy about it." He turned his head to look at Bill. "I'm sor—"

"Don't!" Bill cut him off with a finger-point to his face. "That woman managed to keep it hidden until today, but she is the most self-centered person I've ever known. I still can't believe I let her fool me as long as I did. It just goes to prove that when a man lets his pecker do the thinking, he won't make the best choices. All my pecker could see was that she was pretty. But my mama used to say that pretty is as pretty does—and now I know what she meant."

"Well . . ." Jackson swallowed. "She was plenty pretty."

"On the outside, maybe. But on the inside, not so much. Just remember this, and learn from my mistake. Never judge a woman by her looks." He slapped a hand over his heart. "It's what's in here that counts."

Jackson sat there, pensive for several moments. "Uncle Bill—do you have any tips you could give me on . . ." He faltered, blushing down to his hairline.

Bill smothered a grin as memories came rolling in of having this same conversation with Jamison his freshman year of high school. "Are you asking me how to please a woman in bed?" Although, he supposed the odds of his first time being in a bed were slim.

"I-I-guess so," Jackson sputtered.

"Well . . ." Bill scratched his chin, tunneled his fingers through his hair, and finally clasped the back of his head in order to buy himself a little time. He really needed to be careful with this—he sure as hell didn't need to warp the kid's young mind. "I can give you some tips, but if you're anything like your dad or me, you won't need this information anytime soon."

"Really?" Lines of worry on the boy's brow eased off immediately.

Bill nearly laughed at the obvious signs of relief washing over his nephew's face. "I'm gonna give you two pieces of advice your dad gave me at your age. They've never failed me."

Jackson leaned forward, resting his elbows on his long legs, his eyes wide, his face a study of rapt attention. "My dad gave you advice?"

"Yep. First, never let anyone pressure you into doing something you aren't ready to do. Don't listen to your friends talking about all of their back-seat conquests. Most of the time that's all it is—just talk. Guys who can, do, and keep their mouths shut about it. Guys who can't, do nothing *but* talk about it."

"You think so?"

Bill chuckled. "I know so. Trust me on this, Jackson. The longer you wait, and the older you are when it happens the first time, the better it will be—for both you *and* your partner."

Jackson nodded, frowned when Bill didn't say anything else. "Is that it?"

"Just one more thing," he said. "Never *ever* expect any woman to do more for you than you're willing to do for her." He leaned in closer to him. "Never…I mean it." He pointed at him and nodded. "You follow those rules and you'll be respected by the ladies as well as your peers."

He stood then, a little uncomfortable at having this talk with the kid—or rather with the young man—if Jack had already contemplated having sex, he figured it might be time to quit thinking about him as a kid. "Did any of this sink in?"

Jackson nodded. “Yes sir, I think so. I mean, yeah—I hear what you’re saying.” He lifted one shoulder. “Well, I’m not quite sure about everything, but I’ll figure it out, I guess.”

Bill faced him again. “If you have any questions, ask me. Better me than somebody else.”

“Yes sir.”

“And do me a favor, will you? Don’t rush the process of growing up. You’ve had to deal with your share of shit in your life. Don’t be in such a hurry.”

Jackson stood also, wiped his hands on his jeans. “I understand, Uncle Bill. Don’t worry, I won’t.”

Bill watched him head down the hallway to his room. Would the kid listen to him about not being in a hurry to grow up? Do they ever?

He laughed at his own nerve. He hadn’t listened either. Why would he expect Jack to be any different?

Chapter Eleven

Jackson, the Jock

May, 1994

Bill stood, his own excited whoop lost in the roar of the crowd as Jackson pitched the last strike of his high school year. He, Sheila and Bobby Barnett, Mike's parents, along with the rest of the stadium full of fans, applauded as their kids' team gave the Panthers their final win of the season. Jackson had pitched first string for his varsity team since his sophomore year.

Jackson's pitching skills, along with a team effort, garnered their school three consecutive titles in district, region, and now state. Letters and calls from scouts in several states crammed both the mailbox and the answering machine at home, everybody wanting the kid for *their* college. Jack hadn't made his decision yet, but Bill suspected he wouldn't be attending any of the nearby universities, or even in The Lone Star State. Bill had silently pulled for Texas A & M at College Station, but it didn't look like that would pan out either. Ever since their Baton Rouge road trip freshman year, Jack had been obsessed with LSU.

They'd taken a walk-through of the campus, shopped at the student union, had come home with an armload of LSU Tiger T-shirts, sweats and other memorabilia. Bill hadn't seen Jackson that animated about anything since "Santa" had brought him Rico, his first horse. As selfless and undemanding as he'd been, Bill was happy to make it happen. He'd already found a small place east of Lake Coburn, Louisiana with enough pasture for their horses. The plot sat north of the I-10 corridor—about halfway between LSU and the independent oil company Bill co-owned with a friend of his based out of Houston. Not only would it cut the travel time between home and school for Jackson, and Bill when he drove to games, but he'd save a ton by not paying out-of-state tuition. He'd lease Jamison and Elise's ranch until Jackson decided to hang on to it or sell it.

Bill beat the rest of the crowd to the field, stood waiting patiently for the team to finish with pictures with this year's trophy. His nephew would most likely get the coach's MVP trophy for the third straight year. It would take its place in his closet with the other two—Jack didn't care for anyone singling him out for awards—a trait that made him a favorite of fellow classmates, teammates, teachers, and administrative personnel alike. He didn't have an enemy and never met a stranger.

He'd also never brought home a girlfriend to meet him. The thought bothered Bill. He'd had enough talks with the kid to know he was straight as a board. It concerned Bill that his own bachelor lifestyle had rubbed off on Jackson—and that's not the kind of life he wanted for his nephew.

Almost as though his thoughts had conjured up a ghost from his past, he heard the familiar ring of a feminine voice speaking.

"Bill Broussard! What are *you* doing here? I heard you were part owner of some big oil company now, and rolling in money."

He turned to stare at the tall redhead sidling up close to him. Hannah Harrison—*one of the biggest let downs of his adult life.* No need to be rude, however. "Hey Hannah. I'm doing alright—making a good living." *Better than good, actually, but there again, no need to rub it in her face.* "How's it going?"

"I'm good. You know how it is. Local team goes to state and every business in town closes up shop and goes to the game to show their support." Her eyes widened suddenly. "The Broussard kid pitching—is that *your* nephew? The one you were raising?"

Now she remembers. Bill nodded. "Yep, that's Jackson."

"He sure turned into a fine-looking young man." Hannah bumped his shoulder. "Good genes, am I right?"

"I can't take credit for any of it. That's on his mom and dad."

"So, he's a senior? He should be going off to college soon. That means you'll have plenty of time for yourself again." She looped her hands around his forearm. "Why don't you give me a call sometime? My number hasn't changed."

He stared down at Hannah, unaffected by her outright provocative behavior. There'd been a time when he'd had higher than average hopes to make a go of it with the gorgeous redhead. Memories of the day he brought her home to meet Jackson came at him like a bull targeting a rodeo clown. She'd informed him immediately there was no place in her life for a kid. He'd thanked her for her candor and driven her butt back to her own place.

He disengaged her hands from his arm. "To tell you the truth, Hannah, we'll be relocating to another state as soon as my boy graduates from high school."

"Oh really? Where to? I wouldn't mind a change of scenery." She pushed on, closing the gap between them.

"Hannah—" He extracted his arm from her grip and took two steps back. "I'm not interested in anyone who doesn't want kids, younger or older, to be a permanent fixture in their lives. I may want a couple of my own one day. You've made your stance on the subject perfectly clear. Hopefully, now I have too."

A group shout from behind him got his attention and he turned to see Jackson, tailed by his buddy, Mike, running straight to him. All thoughts of Hannah Harrison forgotten, he hugged him tightly, slapped him on the back several times. "Congratulations, son--you did good!"

"We all did, Uncle Bill!"

"Yes, you all did, but I'm so unbelievably proud of you, Jack. I know your mom and dad are both watching and smiling down at you right now."

"I hope you're right, Uncle Bill."

"I know I am, son." Bill grabbed Mike and gave him a half-hug and slap on the back. "You too, Mike. Your grand slam changed the momentum of the entire game. Congratulations!"

"Thanks, Uncle Bill! Have you seen my folks?"

Bill nodded at the kid he considered family. "We sat together but got separated when the crowd hit the field. They can't be too far." A couple of shouts had him pointing. "There they are!" The Barnetts made their way to them and Bill watched as Mike's parents hugged and congratulated both Mike and his nephew. Those two kids had spent enough time together over the years that they considered themselves more like brothers than friends.

Eventually, Jackson made his way back to him. Bill pointed to where the rest of the team had gathered up again. "You've got more celebrating to do with your team." Bill watched the kid embrace teammates and shake hands with coaches, as always, amazed at both his good fortune to be a part of this young man's life, and how quickly the years had passed.

The same thought crossed his mind three months later, as he stared at the taillights of Jackson's truck, headed for a designated athletic dorm on the LSU campus. Thirteen years as sole guardian of the kid—or rather, the young man—and now he had to let him go. Sure, he'd only be a little over two hours from him since their move across the state line into Louisiana. But that wouldn't stop him from worrying about him or missing his presence around their new home.

* * * *

December, 1994

As always, the weeks flew by and before he knew it the kid came home at the end of Christmas break. Bill stood at the door watching and waiting as Jackson hauled in a duffle bag and a suitcase.

He pointed at the duffle. "Is that dirty laundry?"

Jackson chuckled. "No, it's clean. I did it between my finals. I didn't want to spend an entire day catching up like I did on Thanksgiving break." He stopped in the doorway to hug his uncle. "Hey, I invited my roommate over for a couple of days. I hope you don't mind. Red's a good buddy of mine."

"Red—is that the McAllister kid that showed us around the athletic dorm that day we went to check it out?"

"That's the one. He's gonna spend tonight with his family and then come on over here to get some horse-riding in. He said their family's horse is too old to ride anymore and they can't afford to buy another one. He's one of eight children and so far, they've all gone to LSU."

"Eight tuitions—good grief! That's got to put a hurting on the old bank account."

"If his siblings are as sharp as Red, they all had full scholarships to help."

"No doubt; that kid seemed nice enough. Tell him he can come over and ride our horses any ol' time."

Jackson laughed. "I pretty much did that already. His mom also asked if I wanted to go spend a couple of days with them in Gardiner, about an hour east of here. She's the sweetest lady and the best cook, Uncle Bill. She's always bringing him cookies, brownies, and casseroles and stuff like that—and she always makes extra for me even though they have all those kids."

"They sound like good people. Sure, you can go. What about Mike? You plan on spending time with him over the holidays?"

"He finished up at UT a couple of days ago. He and his folks went to the Bahamas over Christmas vacation. They're supposed to be back in a week or so. We'll get together then."

"All right. I miss seeing that kid around. Whatever I have planned can wait until you get back from Red's place." It warmed Bill's heart to see his nephew making good friends at school. Every guy needed at least one good friend he could really count on. He'd worried a little when Mike had chosen University of Texas up in Austin, hoped they wouldn't lose contact with each other.

They picked up a tree from a local tree farm and spent the entire evening stringing lights and decorating it. Jackson hung the same wreath they'd used for years on the front door, one made by his mom. Bill placed *his* mom's Norman Rockwell placemats on the table, and the two bachelors called it good.

They spent the evening chowing down on take out fried chicken and shared a six pack of beer while watching a back-to-back *Lethal Weapon* movie marathon. Relaxed in front of the TV during the third movie, Bill gave his nephew a side-glance. "So—how's the old love-life?"

Jackson grunted. "Non-existent. Between classes, studying, work-outs and practice, I don't have time for anything else."

"But if you ever do . . ."

"Don't worry, I remember what you told me."

Bill nodded, hoping Jack's words weren't just that—words.

"Now it's your turn, Uncle Bill. How's the old love life?"

Bill scratched at his chin, thinking best how to answer. "Mutually satisfying."

"You know, now that I'm out of your hair—for the most part anyway—you might want to start looking for something a little more permanent. I know—" Jackson raised one hand when Bill started to speak up. "I know you've always said you didn't want any complications. But you're getting a little long in the tooth now. You might want to start considering quality over quantity."

Bill sat up slowly, and stared at his nephew. "Long in the tooth? I'm only thirty-nine."

Jackson sat forward to stare at him. "Most thirty-nine-year-old men have wives at home and have at least started on families of their own by now."

"We *are* family."

Jackson waved him off. "You know what I mean, Uncle Bill—kids of your own. I don't want you to look back when you're an old stallion and regret the sacrifices you made to raise me."

"I haven't sacrificed a thing, boy. And quit talking about me in horse breeding terminology like 'long in the tooth' and 'old stallion'. Sheesh—you sound as if you're ready to 'put me out to pasture'."

Jackson stretched out, putting both hands behind his head, his mouth twisted in a grin that could easily have passed for a smirk. "I'm just saying, you don't know how many more years you have left to throw some foals out there—"

Bill cut him off with string of low grumbling. "You can stop now." He stood quickly, and steered the conversation in a different direction. "When are you expecting the McAllister kid to come over?"

"He'll try to be here by three or four tomorrow afternoon. We wanted to saddle up a couple of horses and get a ride in. Are they all in good shape?"

Still a mite pissed over his nephew's digs about his age, Bill answered curtly. "Of course, they are." He entered the kitchen to start cleaning up the supper mess, but wondered if Jackson had hit a nerve. Maybe he should start looking for something a little more serious. But the move to southwest Louisiana had thrown him off his game. All of his previous female connections were over two hours west, across the Texas border. He'd have to start fresh from a whole new pool of women—women who didn't know a thing about him—and vice versa.

Jackson followed him into the kitchen, his grin sheepish. "You still pissed?"

Bill opened the dishwasher. "No." He threw a couple of plates in and faced his nephew. "Maybe you're right, but casual dating and serious dating are two different animals. I don't have that many connections around this area."

"You might want to get the internet set up over here. You can meet people online."

Bill turned on his nephew. “What the hell are you talking about?”

“If you had a computer I could set you up and show you how to meet people in chat rooms.”

“Chat rooms?”

“Yeah! You enter virtual chat rooms online and talk to people.”

“I don’t get it.”

Jackson nodded. “Well, you don’t actually talk to them. You type out messages back and forth to each other.”

“You’re shittin’ me, right?”

“Nope. I read the other day where some guy is about to start up an online dating service too. You’d fill out a questionnaire about yourself…about your hobbies, interests and such, and a computer uses its database to pull from and match you up with a woman with those same interests.”

Bill faced Jackson and raised both hands. “I don’t want to hear anymore of that bullshit. I don’t have or want a computer. I haven’t typed a thing since my sophomore year of high school, and I didn’t excel at it then. If I want to meet a woman, I’ll do it the old-fashioned way.”

Jackson shrugged. “Suit yourself, but if you change your mind, let me know.”

Bill turned back to filling the dishwasher. “I won’t.”

* * * *

By the end of day one of the McAllister kid’s visit, Bill could see why Jackson had hit it off with the young man. Raised sixth of eight children to a third-generation Louisiana rice farmer, Scott “Red” McAllister could have been the poster child for hard work, common sense, and loyalty to both family and friends. The auburn-haired sophomore had earned full double scholarships to LSU, in both academics and baseball, and had no trouble keeping either of them. According to Jackson, Red maintained his 4.0 GPA easily, while training as first baseman for the Tigers. As a freshman, he’d started several games, but barring any injuries, coach planned to start him the entire season his sophomore year.

It didn’t end with the two young men’s common love of baseball. Both stood well over six-feet-tall and were well-developed for their respective ages of eighteen and nineteen. Bill had grown accustomed to Jackson’s dark-haired, blue-eyed good looks attracting young girls. Contrary to most auburn-haired teens with green eyes, Red's eyes were as stunning a blue as Jackson's, only lighter in shade, and even more noticeable. According to Red, they'd come from his paternal side of the family, and every one of his siblings possessed what the residents in his hometown of Gardiner called "McAllister blue" eyes. Regardless of where their striking genetic traits came from, the two young men seemed to attract women wherever they appeared like catfish to stink bait. Each time they forayed out, either on a leisurely horseback ride, or in Jackson's pickup, shopping for items on the barbeque grocery list, they'd returned home wearing grins, their pockets stuffed with names and phone numbers of girls they'd met along the way.

Bill stared at the collection of slips of paper laid out on the table and shook his head. "You met all these girls while you were grocery shopping?"

Red gave him an enthusiastic snort. "The produce aisle rocks for meeting women, Mr. Bill. Honestly, all you have to do is stand there squeezing tomatoes or looking over a head of lettuce. I kid you not."

Jackson lifted a slip of paper. "But this one—this one asked me which steaks were best for throwing on the pit. Then I showed her the best charcoal and lighter fluid to buy, and she invited both of us over for a barbeque at her and her roommate's place tonight."

"You planning on going? Maybe she just doesn't know how to grill and wants to rope you both into doing the cooking."

"I don't mind flipping steaks or burgers to meet chicks." Red looked at Jackson. "Do you?"

"Nope," Jackson admitted.

Bill chuckled. "Maybe her roommate is a big ol' boy named Bubba."

Red's eyes grew wide. "If it is, we'll be home right away."

Bill shook his head and laughed before pointing at his nephew. "Just don't let all this go to your head and forget everything I've taught you about respecting women over the years. You hearing me, son?"

Jackson gave him an adamant nod. "I hear you, Uncle Bill. And I won't."

Bill's pointed stare at Red had him repeating Jackson's comeback. "Don't worry, Mr. Bill. I hear you, too. My mom and dad taught me the same things. I don't plan on doing anything that'll throw me off of my goals."

"What goals are those?"

"Help the Tigers win a couple of National titles, graduate Summa Cum Laude and become a respected, and eventually, wealthy business owner." Red shrugged. "I've never had money. One day I'm going to see what it's like to have it."

"A hard-working, single mom raised me and my brother, Red. Sometimes it's the struggle that teaches us better life lessons," Bill said, pointedly.

Red shrugged off Bill's comment. "My parents raised us all to work hard at everything we do, and I'm proud of that. I just don't see any shame in doing better. I'd like to be able to take care of my parents so they'll never have to struggle again." He settled his gaze on Bill. "And just like you, I don't want the complications of women dragging me down."

Bill opened his mouth to give him some kind of argument, but snapped it shut. What could he possibly say to this young man that wouldn't support his statement? Hadn't he always given Jackson the same excuses for avoiding relationships? He sure as hell didn't want his nephew to feel as though he'd sacrificed having a wife and kids of his own to raise him.

"We-e-l-l-l," he drawled. "It looks like you've got yourself a game plan. It'll be interesting to see if you can stick to it." Red answered with a smile that showed off a row of straight white teeth.

Bill wondered if those pearly whites were products of good genes and dental hygiene. Or maybe the kid's parents had to take out an additional lien on the family farm to keep the mouths of eight children in good form.

The phone rang and Bill grabbed the handset and scanned the caller ID before handing it over to Jackson. "It's Mike."

Jackson's brow furrowed. "He's supposed to be in the Bahamas." He pushed the answer button. "Hey buddy, did your trip get cancelled or something? Oh! Hey, Ms. Sheila, I thought you were Mike. You need to speak to Uncle Bill?" After a pause to listen he shrugged and passed the phone over to Bill. "I think something's wrong."

Bill's gut tightened as he put the phone to his ear, turning to face the kitchen window. "Sheila?" He got no response and checked the phone to make sure the connection hadn't been lost. "Sheila?" After some shuffling on the opposite end, someone finally spoke.

"Bill—"

Mike's dad, Bobby Barnett had barely managed to choke out the single word. Bill's gut did a somersault, expecting the worse. "What's wrong, Bobby?"

"Mike . . ." The single word came out in a gasp.

Bill turned slowly and faced his nephew, sensing he'd need the connection to hear Bobby's bad news. "Take a deep breath, Bobby. What happened?"

"He went swimming and—"

Bobby revealed the heartbreaking news in a succession of emotional starts and stops, knowing full-well what he was going through. He'd been there more than once.

Jackson had too—and now he'd go through it again.

Bill stared at his nephew, wondering just how many deaths, how many losses—of family—and now of his best friend—how much heartbreak could a kid his age take?

* * * * *

Bill sat in silence as the preacher spoke to the congregation about making sense of the senselessness of death, especially in a case like this. A family vacation turned tragic due to death by accidental drowning. He dropped his head back, stared up at the exposed beams of the church and sent up a silent inquiry. *God...what the hell were you thinking?*

After a phone call to Red McAllister's parents, Bill had sent Jackson over there for the three days it would take for Mike's body to make it back home to Texas. Vivienne, Red's mom, had assured him they'd do whatever it took to support his nephew and ease the loss of his oldest friend. When the time came to return for the funeral, Red accompanied Jackson and Bill, providing a bit of comic relief with stories of his large family.

According to Vivienne and Pete McAllister, Red's younger sisters had swarmed Jackson during his visit, providing him with the much-needed distraction that came from being around a boisterously large and loud family. Jackson would always feel the loss more at times for sure, but it had seemed to help. After a quiet Christmas at home, Bill had let him return to the McAllister's place for further distractions, working on their family farm until a few days before his return to LSU.

Their last night together, they sat watching a ball game on TV. After a quiet pause Jackson sat forward suddenly, resting his arms on his knees, his hands clasped tightly together.

Concern for his nephew nagged at Bill. “You okay?”

“I don’t know,” Jackson said. “I guess so. It’s just that sometimes I want to pick up the phone and call Mike so damned bad. Just to ask him how he did on his last math test. He hated math. I’ve helped him with his math homework for the last six years.”

Bill watched his nephew trying to work out the details in his mind. Could practically see him struggling to make sense of it. “I wish I could take it away from you, son. I wish I could say something to make it better for you. It will get easier eventually, but not for a while.”

Jackson’s jaw clenched tightly, his Adam’s apple bobbing as he struggled to swallow tears. Finally, he seemed to gain control over his emotions. He took a deep breath and blinked several times. “You know what I regret the most?”

Bill’s chest ached for his nephew. “What’s that?”

“That I’ll never get to introduce Mike to Red and the rest of his family. He would have loved it over there at the McAllister’s. It would have shocked the hell out of him, but in a good way.” He chuckled. “I keep imagining the look on his face the first time he’d have seen them all together.”

Bill couldn’t help but grin at the thought. He’d only met Red, but he could well imagine what Jackson meant. “He’d have fit in over there for sure.”

Jackson laughed. “I’ve never seen so much red hair and freckles in one place in all my life. Except their eyes are all blue and his are—were—green. I swear, Uncle Bill, Red’s kid sister, Bailey, acts just like him. I just kept thinking that I needed to introduce the two of them.” He wiped roughly at his eyes. “But I can’t.”

“No.” Bill reached over and grabbed him on the shoulder. “I’m sorry, son.”

Jackson nodded, blinked away the dampness from his lashes. “I know.”

The next morning, Bill stood at the foot of the front steps, watching and waving until the tail lights of his nephew's pickup faded in the distance. He turned back toward his empty home, comparing the two Jacksons—the one who'd returned home at the beginning of his break—and the one who'd just left him. Two versions of the same young man, not quite as much of a contrast as black and white. More like two shades of gray—one light and one dark.

And damn, he hated that for the kid.

* * * * *

The crowd roared in unison, everyone already on their feet when the ump signaled the second strike.

"Your boy is on his way to pitching his first college no-hitter!"

Several back slaps accompanied the comment called out from one of the fans seated behind Bill. He ignored the man, and checked the score board—again—for verification. Four to zero, with the home team ahead, bottom of the ninth. He exchanged a look with Pete McAllister, Red's father. The two of them shook their heads in silent agreement. They'd gotten to know each other well during these games, always sat together in seats reserved for the parents. The two men had formed a mutual bond over their LSU Tigers. Neither particularly superstitious under normal circumstances, they'd both taken the same stance—best not to tempt the baseball gods by taking anything for granted. No need inviting a round of unnecessary bad luck.

Bill shook his head. "It ain't over yet."

"Nope," Pete agreed.

Bill whispered a silent prayer to give his nephew strength for one more strike—just one more—if for no other reason than to put an end to this agony. For a man who prided himself on keeping his cool during stressful situations, he'd long reached and surpassed his limit.

Come on Jack—just one more out . . .

He took a deep breath, held it during Jackson's wind-up and release. He followed the ball's trajectory, watched as the bat barely caught a sliver of it—just enough to pop it into the air. The catcher threw off his face mask and raised his arm, catching it easily in his mitt. The stadium went wild, the fan behind Bill slapped his back several times as he whooped and yelled with unfettered glee.

But Bill's gaze had already returned to Jackson, on his knees at the pitcher's mound, his face twisted in pain as he grabbed his right shoulder with his left hand. Bill stepped into the aisle, took the steps two at a time until he reached a section in the fence low enough to drop down onto the field. He ran to the pitcher's mound, pushed his way through the crowd of teammates, coaches and trainers surrounding his nephew.

Jackson's gaze locked on him, his eyes huge and filled with pain. "Uncle Bill . . ."

Bill reached out to him, grabbed his hand and clenched it tightly. "It's okay, son. I'm here. Whatever this is—we'll get through it together, you hear me?"

Jackson nodded. "I hear you."

* * * * *

Bill closed the hospital door on Red, the very last of his nephew's visitors. Every one of his teammates and coaching staff had been there off and on, for the better part of the day. Red had been there for nearly two days straight and Bill finally had enough and sent him back to the dorm. Jackson lay in his hospital bed, the head section raised to the sitting position, his shoulder bandaged and in a dark blue sling.

"You need anything, son?"

"Nah, I'm good, Uncle Bill." He adjusted the head section with this good hand, lowering it several inches.

Bill sat in the chair nearest the bed, wondering how best to approach the subject of Jackson's baseball career—or its non-existence, according to the surgeon who'd repaired the blown-out rotator cuff the best he could.

"You feeling up to a talk, Jack?"

"Sure, but it's not necessary. I already know I'll never pitch again."

"Did your surgeon speak to you without me?" The thought irritated Bill to distraction. He'd asked the guy not to speak to the kid without him there to help cushion the blow.

"No, but I suspected the second it tore. There aren't enough pins, staples, or stitches that'll get my arm back to where I was before it happened." He shrugged. "I'm okay with it."

Bill stared at his nephew, amazed at the kid's resilience in all situations. "You are?"

Jackson nodded. "Baseball was fun, and I'm grateful I got to pitch a year in college, but I never figured on it for a career or anything. I'd just as soon get on with my life."

Get on with his life? Bill's gut tensed with dread. "Please tell me you're not thinking of dropping out of college." He relaxed when Jackson laughed at his comment.

"Of course not." Jackson's mouth stretched in a grin. "But that general studies curriculum seems pretty lame now. I'm thinking of a major in the field of engineering. Not sure which field yet but I'll figure it out." He placed his good hand on his right shoulder. "First I've got to concentrate on getting this thing healed."

Bill pointed to his nephew's shoulder. "That'll call for some physical therapy commitment."

Jackson turned his serious gaze on him and nodded. "I'm up for whatever it takes, Uncle Bill."

Bill didn't doubt that—not even for a second. His heart filled with pride at the young man before him. Even if he'd never have an actual son of his own, he'd always be grateful for the quality time he'd been able to spend with his nephew. Once more, his thoughts returned to Jamison and Elise, and how their combined DNA had produced such a fine human being.

But maybe—just maybe—he could claim a little of the credit for raising him the last fifteen or so years.

His nephew tackled his physical therapy with single-minded determination. Red spent a lot of time with him, ensuring he didn't slack up on his shoulder workouts. His presence kept him laughing more than anything else, and Jackson needed more laughter in his life.

Red's ever-present stories about his siblings were an on-going source of comic relief, in direct contrast to Jackson's overly-serious tendencies. Bill thanked the powers that be for sending his nephew the kind of friend he needed to fill the gaping space left from the loss of his longtime friend, Mike—especially when faced with one more course-altering milestone in his life.

Chapter Twelve

The Christmas Fiancée

December 1996

Bill's mouth watered with the combination of smells coming from his kitchen—roasted turkey stuffed with jalapenos and garlic, cornbread dressing, green bean casserole and the nearly done rolls about ready to come out of the oven—all Jackson's favorites.

His nephew had told him during Thanksgiving that he'd been seeing someone. Bill had been excited when Jackson asked if he could bring the young woman over for Christmas. Antsy and eager to meet his nephew's girl, he checked his watch again. He heard the crunch of tires on gravel and went to the window.

Jackson got out of his truck and walked around to open the passenger door, took the hand of a blonde woman. She stepped out and straightened, her thin body draped head to toe in black. Had he just picked her up from a funeral or something? He opened the door and stepped out onto the porch. "Merry Christmas, Son!"

Jackson faced him, wearing a huge smile. "Merry Christmas, Uncle Bill." He escorted the woman towards him. "Chloe Stansfield, this is my Uncle Bill."

Bill extended his hand. "I'm Bill Broussard, Miss Stansfield. Welcome to our home."

"Uncle Bill!" The blonde turned large, light blue eyes on him, and smiled, showing off a mouth full of teeth at least a couple of shades too white to look natural. She by-passed his hand and threw herself at him for a hug. "I've heard so much about you that I feel like I know you already."

Bill hugged her back gently, afraid to break the frail body that brought to mind a dried-out dragonfly carcass he'd pulled from his truck's grille a couple of months back. Hopefully her personality would make up for what she lacked in body mass.

Personally, he preferred women with a little more substance—soft curves rather than sharp angles. He supposed if this woman made his nephew happy, that's all that mattered.

Just before lunch, he opened the door to his own date for the day, a pretty, sweet-natured single mom he'd seen a couple of times named Amber Lee. Bill greeted her with a kiss to her cheek and led her into the kitchen for introductions. Jackson seemed to take her arrival amicably, but Chloe stared at the woman so hard he wondered if she and Amber were acquainted, and if they had previous issues.

Less than an hour after her arrival, Chloe entered the kitchen where he and Jackson had been cleaning up. "Uncle Bill, Amber is leaving. She said to tell you something came up with her kids, I believe."

Bill pulled aside the curtain to watch Amber's sedan back out of her parking spot and tear out of the driveway. "I hope nothing's wrong. Seems like she'd have said something to me." By the time he'd turned back to ask her for more info, Chloe had already retreated back into the living room. He shrugged it off, deciding to wait until later in the evening to check up on Amber's situation.

The remainder of the afternoon passed pleasantly enough, with most of it revolving around talk of Chloe's life, Chloe's interests, Chloe's classes in economics and accounting, Chloe's elective in interior design. Bill brushed off the first hints of annoyance, deciding it could be her way of opening up and sharing her life with him.

Later that afternoon she glanced at the clock on the wall and clasped her hands together, eyes shining with excitement. "Can we exchange gifts now?"

Bill checked the time. "It's only four o'clock. We usually wait until later, but I guess we could open gifts earlier this year." Before the words were even out of his mouth Chloe had pulled gifts from a medium sized bag she'd placed under the tree earlier.

"This is for you," she handed a square flat box to Bill and stood there, waiting for him to open it.

"Oh, we're taking turns." Bill laughed as he shook the box weighing absolutely nothing. He lifted the top and removed a gift card from a local home improvement store. "Thank you. Jackson must have told you I do lots of shopping at this place." He'd never stooped to buying gift cards, finding them far too impersonal—but, she wouldn't have known that about him.

He slipped the card inside his pocket and reached over for a beautifully wrapped box under the tree. Bill had grilled his nephew about what to get her for, insisting she should have something to open from him. Jackson had mentioned that Chloe didn't have a coat and wore a size zero. He'd enlisted the help of more than one saleswoman to find the perfect one for her, implementing a few suggestions from his nephew. He'd finally settled on a black leather jacket from a high-end shop in the mall. One of those places that insisted on calling itself a boutique rather than a store.

Chloe ripped the paper off with gusto and removed the cover. She pulled the coat out and gave it a critical once over before looking at the tag. "It's a size one, and I'm a zero."

Bill frowned, somewhat put off by her reaction. "The saleswoman said these run small so try it on."

She did, looking reluctant when it actually fit her. She zipped it up and passed her hands over the supple black leather. "I guess it'll work, but I'd like it to fit a little tighter."

"It looks great!" Jackson piped in and smiled at Bill. "I'm having a difficult time picturing you shopping for that thing. How many stores did it take before you found that one?"

"Four—no, five." Bill waited for some sign of appreciation from the young woman.

Chloe removed the jacket and threw it to the side before giving him a half smile. "Thanks."

Bill responded with a reluctant "You're welcome." He pulled out his wallet and pulled out a slip of paper. "I kept the gift receipt if you need to return it for something you like better." *Although the sales woman had assured him that considering the high quality of the garment and popular style, it probably wouldn't be necessary.*

Chloe reached over and snapped it from his hands. "That'll work."

Well shit.

Jackson cleared his throat. "Okay, who's next?"

Chloe looked up at him and smiled sweetly. "I've got something special for you, but mine first?"

Jackson grinned. "No, I think I'll save yours for last."

Her face drooped in disappointment. “Okay then, here’s yours.” She handed him a rectangular flat box.

Bill’s mouth tightened, wondering if Jackson had received an identical gift card. Thankfully, it contained a one-night stay in a bed and breakfast for tomorrow night. He’d expected to have his nephew here for two nights, but he’d be satisfied with one night.

Jackson hugged his girlfriend, thanking her profoundly for the gift before standing back. “I guess it’s my turn.” He handed Bill a large box. “Merry Christmas, Uncle Bill.”

Bill removed two pair of high-quality leather work gloves tucked inside a western hat. “These are very nice, son. Thank you so much.” He removed the hat and tried it on. “Perfect fit—how’s it look?”

Jackson stepped up to make a couple of adjustments. “It looks great on you. Now you can throw away that old stained work hat that you’ve worn for as long as I’ve known you.”

Bill laughed. “It’s a *work* hat, Jackson, and that old Resistol had been a gift from your mom and dad to me my first Christmas with them, so I think I’ll hang on to it. But I’ll wear this one in public when you’re around so I don’t shame you too much.” He reached for a box and handed it to him. “Here you go, son.”

Jackson showed equal amounts of admiration and appreciation for his new athletic shoes, even trying them on for size and walking around the living room.

Chloe cleared her throat loudly and stood there, hands on her hips. “Excuse me, but I think I’ve waited long enough for *mine*.”

The two men turned to stare at her, Bill trying his best to hide his annoyance at the young woman’s out and out rudeness. He didn’t know her well enough to judge whether her shortness came from Christmas excitement or plain old impatience.

Jackson laughed it off and reached under the tree for a box about four inches square and handed it to her. “Well okay, then. Merry Christmas, babe.”

Her eyes glistening with unbridled excitement, she ripped off the cover of the box bearing the sticker of a Baton Rouge jewelry store. She dumped the contents into her hand, a smaller box coated in royal blue velvet. Jackson snatched it from her hands before she opened it and got to one knee.

“I love you, Chloe. Will you do me the honor of becoming my wife?” He lifted the lid, revealing a diamond solitaire.

"Yes!" she cried out. Chloe grabbed the ring from the box, slipped it onto her own finger and launched herself at him.

Bill stood there, stunned as hell. Married? He planned to marry this girl? He wasn't twenty-one yet. But then he remembered the first weeks around Lorraine, how he knew in his gut she was the one for him. He walked away from his nephew and new fiancée, deciding to keep quiet and leave them to it.

They approached him in the kitchen a few minutes later as he poured himself a mug of coffee. He turned and gave her a hug. "Congratulations, hon. And best of luck," he added, giving Jackson a wink as he shook his hand. "I'm hoping there's no reason to rush this wedding." He lifted one brow and glared at the couple.

Chloe's face paled, as though the thought made her physically ill. "Definitely not! We've got at least a decade before we can even *think* about having a little snot-nosed brat."

Jackson put his arms around her from behind and chuckled. "I don't see a reason to wait *that* long before starting a family. I should be well-established with a firm long before that."

Chloe's mouth straightened in a hard line as she pulled away from him. "We'll figure all that out later, after the wedding in March."

"March?" Bill stared at Chloe. "This March?"

Jackson grabbed a coffee cup from the cabinet. "I doubled up on my course load to finish a year early but I still won't graduate until May. Maybe we could have a civil ceremony at a JP, or something along those lines."

"Oh, no, honey. I want a wedding!" she gushed. "With a *huge* reception."

"Then you'll have to wait a little longer for that," he insisted.

She pooched her lower lip out and approached him, running her hands down her hips seductively. "Okay, I'll wait. But if we aren't married by the end of June, this bod is going back on the market."

Jackson pulled her close for a hug. "June it is, then."

Bill waited for them to separate before pointing to the window. "It's looking like rain out there if y'all want to bring your luggage in from the truck. I changed the sheets in the guest room already and spruced it up a bit so everything's ready for you."

Chloe turned her wide-eyed gaze on Jackson. "Oh, this is awkward."

Jackson and Bill exchanged looks, obviously both equally confused. Jackson broke off the staring contest with his uncle to face Chloe. "What's awkward, babe?"

"Well-l-l . . ." She dragged out the last consonant. She looked at Jackson. "Sweetie, you know how much I detest surprises. I peeked at the ring a couple of weeks ago."

"You did?" he said, his face as impassive as his tone.

She gave him an unapologetic grin. "I assumed you'd be popping the question this afternoon, I'd say yes, and we'd leave here to celebrate. The woman called from the B & B yesterday to say they had a last-minute cancellation for tonight and asked if I wanted it for two nights instead of one—so I took it. With all the stress you've been under from the extra courses you picked up to graduate early, I thought you needed to relax."

"Oh." He checked his watch. "What time is check in?"

"Anytime we get there." She looped her arms around Jackson's neck and got up on her tippy toes to speak into his ear in a staged whisper—no whisper at all.

Bill turned away from the display, cleared his throat in embarrassment at overhearing her promise of what she'd do when they got to their destination.

Bill waved his hand at Jackson's look of apology. "Go on, you two. Y'all get out of here before the rain hits."

Jackson waited for Chloe's return to the living room to gather her things before facing his uncle. "I'm sorry about this, Uncle Bill. I had no idea we wouldn't be spending the two nights here with you."

Bill pushed aside the doubts, the warning flags waving, the nudge of gut instinct. Something slightly off about this woman. It wasn't his business and his nephew would figure it out for himself soon enough. "Don't worry about it, son. You go on now, and have some fun."

Five minutes later, he waved them off at the front door, then picked up the phone to check on Amber's situation at home. She didn't answer but figured she'd call when she had a chance.

He called twice more over the next few days, but she didn't pick up. Finally, he ran into her outside the post office. "Hey, what happened on Christmas Eve? Something come up with your ex and the kids?"

She stared at him, the look in her eyes cold and uncaring. "I don't think we should see each other anymore, Bill. I-I-don't think I'm your type."

"My type? What does *that* mean?"

She pushed passed him through the doors. "Don't call me again."

He stood staring after her, wondering what the hell had just happened.

He kept in touch with Jackson through phone calls over the next several months. The costs of the wedding and reception, originally intended to be "handled" by the mother of the bride, gradually shifted in small increments to the groom's uncle. By the day of Jackson's graduation ceremony, Bill had accepted financial responsibility of the entire production. Not that he minded. Jackson's wedding may be the only one he'd ever pay for. He could afford it, so why not?

* * * * *

May, 1997

The fact that the bride skipped her fiancé's graduation ceremony for a dress-fitting, perturbed the ever-living hell out of Bill. He stared at the empty seat beside him that afternoon at the Maravich Assembly Center, wondering again what his nephew was getting himself into. After the ceremony, he brought Jackson to a local sports bar in the city. He held back until the waitress had taken their food orders and brought them each a beer before tackling the subject.

"Jackson—you know I normally keep my nose out of affairs that aren't my business, right?"

Jackson sipped from his bottle of beer and set it on the coaster. "Yes sir, you do."

Bill nodded. "That being said—are you sure you want to marry this girl?"

His nephew blinked a couple of times and he grew pensive. "I love Chloe, and she hasn't had much of a family life, Uncle Bill. I want to show her what that's like."

"Last I heard, she didn't seem receptive to even having a family. Has her opinion changed?"

Jackson picked up his beer, began to peel the corners of the label on the bottle. "It will. I want that more than anything—and she knows it." He put the bottle down and met Bill's gaze. "She'll want to do that for me, even if it's something she's not crazy about. If I didn't believe that, I wouldn't be marrying her in a month."

"What does Red think about her?"

"They've hardly exchanged two words. I don't think he's in a position to judge her one way or another."

"He's your best friend. You've never spent time with the two of them together? No double dates or anything?"

"He's been busy with school and the team. I've been busy with all my classes. We haven't had the time to hang out together."

"Hmph . . ."

Jackson looked up at him. "What?"

Bill shrugged. "It's just that a guy's best man usually knows his bride well enough to have formed some kind of an opinion by now. It's less than a month before the wedding." Jackson's silence cued him into switching the subject to something more productive. "Have you heard anything from those engineering firms you've applied to?"

"I took the offer from the one in Baton Rouge."

"Oh. Well. That's good." Bill swallowed his disappointment that his nephew wouldn't be moving closer to home. He knew for a fact that a civil engineering firm in Lake Coburn wanted him—they wanted him badly.

He hugged his nephew tightly after their supper and drove on back to his own place.

* * * * *

In absence of a father, or either parent, for that matter, the bride walked down the aisle alone to meet her groom. Bill had volunteered to walk her, but she'd turned him down. At first, he'd wondered if it had to do with his choice of formal attire. He brushed a speck of dust from the tux sleeve, remembering how the saleswoman had smiled in approval for the fitting—just before she'd slipped her business card into his pocket.

Watching Chloe float down the aisle, totally alone, her head held high and glowing with self-assured radiance, he figured she simply hadn't wanted anything or anyone stealing the spotlight from her.

The sight of someone other than Red McAllister standing beside Jackson at the front of the church had been a shock, as had the complete absence of any, or all members of the McAllister family. Red and Jackson had been as close to brothers as they could be in recent years, and Bill couldn't imagine what could have happened to make his nephew strip Red of his best-man duties.

He sat there, staring at the young man he loved like a son, his stomach queasy, his chest tight with dread. Jackson stood straight and tall, his expression solemn. Bill would have given anything to know if the same thought ran through his nephew's mind as his—he was about to make the biggest mistake of his life.

His dread only increased when later, during the reception, he overheard someone claiming to have seen Jackson's new bride and his best man sneaking out of a storage room, both of them adjusting various items of clothing. Bill spotted Chloe a few minutes later sharing a private moment with the best man, a Tanner somebody, whom Jackson had described as a spoiled rich kid in pre-med. He ducked behind a corner to keep his presence unknown, watched her run her nails lightly down Tanner's cheek before turning away from him. She approached Jackson where he stood amongst several of his former teammates and plastered herself against him. She gave him a long, slow, wet kiss, producing a round of whistles and cat calls from the others in the group. She turned and left them, looking as regal as a queen who'd just ensured her position of total domination. Her gaze zeroed in on Bill and she smiled from one side of her mouth, her left brow lifted in—what—a challenge? A dare?

Bill turned away, sick to his stomach, wondering if Chloe had actually known he'd witnessed the scene earlier with Tanner, and just didn't care. Or worse, that she welcomed being witnessed. He pushed those thoughts aside, convinced that Jackson could never fall in love with someone that calculating.

He spied Tanner amidst a group of his own buddies, his speech punctuated by snickers and laughs. Could he be giving them a blow by blow account of his and Chloe's encounter? Tanner looked up at one point, his gaze clashing with Bill's. The man's mouth formed an undeniable smirk that had Bill's hands clenching in two fists.

He turned away as the group exploded in a robust round of laughter, made his way to the bar for a bottle of beer. Seconds later, he slipped out of the building's back door for a breath of fresh air. A leisurely walk to the side had him looking out onto one side of the front parking lot. He froze at the sight of Red, the ousted best man, searching the parking lot, apparently on some kind of mission. He watched as Red approached a fancy black sports car and paused behind it, looking at its rear license plate.

Bill had to squint to see the plate—a custom one that read FUTR-MD. He shook his head. Of course, that little shit, Tanner, would call attention to himself. People like that couldn't help themselves. Red kneeled in front of the plate and busied himself. He finished quickly and stood back to observe his handiwork. Bill's chest rumbled with laughter at Red's accomplishment, forced himself to keep quiet about what he'd seen.

Bill waited until Red left the area before he slipped back inside the building. When the spoiled med student took his leave, Bill followed him out, watching, waiting until the car left the parking spot, oblivious to Red's handiwork. He turned, went inside, laughing to himself. With any luck, that asshole would drive around the city a week or more, unaware that his custom plate had been altered to read DICK-MD.

He returned home that same evening, unsettled and sick at heart for his nephew. He grabbed a beer and, after not getting an answer from Red's phone, called the number he had on file for Pete and Vivienne McAllister in Gardiner. As luck would have it, Red answered the phone.

"Just the man I need to talk to." Bill smiled into the phone. "What the hell happened to get you booted out of Jackson's best man position?"

"Chloe happened, Uncle Bill. And I swear to God there's nothing to her accusations."

Bill chuckled at the sound of disgust in the young man's voice. "I've got my own reasons for believing you, Red. Just spit it out."

"She came to my apartment two nights ago looking for Jackson. They'd argued about something, apparently. When I told her he wasn't there, she threw herself at me. I mean, literally. She was all over me in two seconds flat. I pushed her away and she came at me again, scratched my face and neck in the process. Apparently, as soon as she found him, she tried to convince Jackson that I came on to *her*—tried to force myself on her. I don't think Jackson believed it, but she convinced him that she wouldn't marry him if I stood up as his best man." He released a long, miserable sigh. "I heard she's the one who chose that prick, Tanner Collins, to take my place."

"If it's any consolation, I doubt Jackson had any say in it at all."

"I can't figure it out." Red sounded disgusted. "Why can't he see through that woman?"

"Sometimes we don't want to see what's right in front of our faces. Sometimes the truth hurts too damn much. Jackson's such a good, decent guy, I doubt he can fathom the possibility of someone who's supposed to care about him being so deceitful." Bill's sigh matched the one Red had previously released. "Man, I hate this for him."

"With everything Jackson's been through . . ." Red began, then stopped himself, as though thinking better of it.

"I know, Red. I know. Makes you wonder if that kid's ever gonna catch a break."

Chapter Thirteen

Christmas and New Years - Y2K

The next eighteen months passed uneventfully, with Jackson establishing himself in the Baton Rouge engineering firm he'd chosen. Chloe switched her major twice more before dropping out of school completely, deciding she had more fun spending money than making it.

Bill kept his mouth shut about what he'd witnessed, as well as the conversation he'd overheard. He convinced himself that it could have been nothing more serious than a minor flirtation between two old friends. He kept in touch with Red, visiting occasionally with his parents, Vivienne and Pete, when passing through the area on business.

Jackson showed no interest in claiming his parents' property in Texas, and sold it for a hefty sum. Bill schooled him on investments to plan for his family's future. Chloe had reluctantly agreed to try for children, insisting it would ruin her figure.

Bill had whooped at the announcement, and promptly sold his tiny ranch for something bigger, in preparation for any future grand-nephews and nieces. The large ranch-style log cabin had been on the rustic side when he'd moved in. Within three months, he'd had it updated with all the modern conveniences and brand-new appliances. The place had a large pool when he bought it, and Bill enjoyed swimming in it every morning—so much so, that he built around it, enclosing and heating it for year-round use. The ranch had since become a regular setting for company barbeques and entertaining for new and established clients.

Christmas Eve of '99 found Bill greeting Jackson and Chloe at the side door of his home. He hugged Chloe's frail frame. "Girl, you're gonna blow away with the next gust of wind if you don't start eating something."

"That never gets old, Bill," she huffed, straight-faced and heading for the coffee pot. "Is the pool ready for me?"

"The pool is always ready." No doubt she'd spend the entire visit ensconced in the pool house and gossiping on her phone. He shrugged it off—it meant more quality time with Jackson. "Why did you come in two vehicles?"

Chloe cast a sour look at her husband. "Your nephew is a stick-in-the-mud who isn't interested in celebrating the biggest New Year's Eve celebration in a thousand years."

"Babe . . ." Jackson began, his tone low and placating. "I only meant that maybe we should take it easy on the celebrating, just in case you're pregnant already and don't know it yet."

She finished pouring her coffee and turned on him. "*You* can take it easy for both of us. *I'll* be celebrating with my friends." She walked towards the back door, stopping long enough to grab a shoulder bag she'd set on the floor. "Call me when it's time to open my gifts." She slammed the door behind her.

Bill clenched his jaw tightly, knowing she'd thrown in the last bit for him. He'd established the Christmas gift giving rules early in the couple's marriage when she'd mentioned during Thanksgiving dinner that she had no intention of accompanying Jackson for Christmas. "That's fine," he'd told her, wearing a smug grin. "I'll just get my money back for that big ol' gift certificate if you can't be bothered to show up."

"I'm sor—" Jackson began.

"Stop right there!" One look from Bill cut him off. "I can take a lot, but not you apologizing for your wife."

"She's not herself, Uncle Bill. Her medications are dangerous to fetuses, so she's off them in order to get pregnant."

"They've developed a treatment for rude, selfish behavior?"

"She's been diagnosed with bi-polar disorder."

"She's not—" Bill clamped his mouth shut, cutting off the rest of his comment. "What exactly does that mean?"

"She has mood shifts between manic and depressive—she's got classic symptoms. Highs, lows, out of control spending, talking fast, losing her train of thought, erratic behavior, guilt…there are a few others."

"Wee-ll-l," Bill drawled. "I guess accepting she has a problem is half the battle, right?"

"Ri-i-ght . . ." Jackson didn't sound quite convinced.

"You know I'm here if you ever need to talk about anything. Otherwise—" Bill raised both hands. "It's not my business."

Jackson released a long sigh. "I'm just hoping she gets pregnant within the year. Then she can get back on her medication. We'll have a child and life can go back to normal."

Bill kept quiet. No amount of medication would make Chloe any more pleasant to live with. Two hours with her left Bill with a full day's worth of tense exhaustion. He couldn't imagine how Jackson dealt with it. She could turn on the charm when she wanted to, for sure. He'd succumbed to it more than once, always wanting to believe that *this* sweet girl was the real Chloe. Those phases never lasted long, and soon she reverted back to her shrewish self.

He wondered if some childhood trauma had changed her. But then again, who'd faced more childhood trauma than Jackson? His nephew didn't possess a mean or selfish tendency. He decided to hope for the best concerning Chloe. If Jack could suffer through her, he could too.

January 1, 2000

Bill pulled open the door of the Quick-Mart, stepped aside to let a woman pass. Her mumbled 'thank you' had him stopping mid-stride. "Amber?"

She looked up, wide-eyed. "Oh, hello. I-I-ve got to go."

He placed a hand on her arm to keep her from running off. "Could you please tell me what I did to make you hate me?"

Amber brushed one hand over her hair and sighed. "I-I don't hate you. I am disappointed in you. I thought you were better than that. And frankly, I thought I was a better judge of character, so if I'm being perfectly honest, I'm also a little disappointed in myself."

He shook his head. "And I'm confused. One minute we were fine, and the next, Chloe came in telling us you had some kind of an emergency at home. What the hell happened?"

Her brow furrowed. "An emergency? Chloe told me you cornered her and threw yourself at her. She said you told her that I'm too—plump—for your tastes, but that I'd do in a pinch until you found something more suitable. How could you, Bill?"

"I couldn't! I would *never* do or say any of that because it's not how I feel. Why didn't you say anything at the time?"

"Because it's humiliating? My ex-husband used my weight as an excuse to sleep around on me for ten years. Why would I put myself through that again?"

Bill's heart ached for the pretty woman he'd so hoped to get to know better. "Amber, I'm so sorry. I knew that girl had some issues, but I'm beginning to think we've barely scratched the surface of her real problems. Can I please take you out to dinner sometime to make up for that day? I promise, I'm nothing like what you must be thinking I am."

"Is your nephew still seeing that girl?"

"He married her, unfortunately. And as committed as he is to her, I'm afraid she's there to stay. And—" He released a sigh. "—she'll continue to make everyone's lives miserable."

She stepped away from him, her chin lifted in resolve. "There's nothing more to say. Life is too short to spend another second of it in the presence of someone like that. If what you're telling me is true, she is cruel and manipulative and your nephew would be much better off without her."

He nodded, seeing her point. "I understand, of course. I wish things had turned out differently. And I'm sorry again, Amber."

She started to walk away then stopped and faced him again. "I'm thinking now that maybe if I'd said something to you about it you could have stopped the marriage."

"Maybe, but that wasn't your responsibility." He sent her off with a hug and a wish for a happy new year. He entered the store with a sick feeling, thinking that as twisted and as self-centered as Chloe seemed to be, nothing would have stopped her from getting whatever she wanted.

She obviously wanted Jackson.

Chapter Fourteen

Sexual Advances and Office Santas

Another Christmas passed, then a few more, with no pregnancies. Tired of the Baton Rouge traffic, Jackson took a job with an established engineering firm in Lake Coburn. Thrilled at having his nephew closer, Bill didn't much care why Chloe agreed to relocate. From what Red had told him, she'd pushed all the women associated with his old firm, both co-workers and wives of co-workers, to the limits of their endurance with her flirting and affairs. According to a friend of Red's, she'd worn her welcome thin within their entire social circle in the capital city.

Jackson seemed to take it all in stride, or outright ignored the gossip about his wife, always blaming her actions and daily emotional outbursts on her inability to conceive. Thankfully, he thrived at his new place of business, in part due to his co-workers, Carrie and Sam Langley. Sam, a former survey party chief for the state highway department, proved to be a wealth of knowledge when it came to roadways, bridges, and right-of-way boundaries in the five-parish district. Sam's wife, Carrie, drafted plans and basically became Jackson's right hand.

Bill had become good friends with the Langleys, and thanked God Jackson had such good people to turn to for advice and general support. He'd dropped in at his nephew's office on more than one occasion to hear Carrie, twelve years Jackson's senior, running interference with Chloe over the phone so her boss could have a quiet, stress-free lunch with his uncle.

They all kept a couple of facts from Chloe, for the sake of peace. The first, that Carrie came from Red McAllister's home town of Gardiner. She'd seen Red grow up and was, in fact, related on his mother's side.

The second, being that once Bill had disclosed the story behind the demise of Red and Jackson's friendship, Carrie had made it her goal to reunite the two of them every chance she got, usually at her and Sam's place in Kenton. Before long, the two college buddies were as close as they'd ever been.

It took a team effort to keep Chloe's advances towards men in check. Once, during the annual company Christmas party Chloe had insisted on hosting, it nearly came to an explosive head. Giselle Granger, a new member in Jackson's department, arrived at the party with her husband. Chloe took one look at Giselle's handsome husband, a brown-eyed version of Jackson, and headed straight for the man. Having been pre-warned about Chloe's 'condition', the man had been polite but firm in his rejection of her advances. As soon as Giselle had finished making her professional rounds to those in attendance, they'd left the party to avoid any further confrontations.

Annoyed and in full manic mode, Chloe zeroed in on the attending Santa. According to Carrie, nothing screams "shut this party down" quite like the lady of the house sitting on Santa's lap and grabbing his personal 'package'. Whether or not Chloe realized the same gentleman owned a full half of the company employing her husband, no one knew for sure.

The situation with Chloe reached a tipping point one afternoon in early February when he'd gone to catch up with Jackson after being out of country on a five-day business trip. Chloe answered the door, wearing next to nothing.

Bill faced the opposite direction, irritated that she'd answer the door in a get up like this. "Is Jackson here?" he asked, before her laughter had him cringing. More often than not, that sound accompanied some type of twisted behavior that amused nobody but Chloe.

"He's out running an errand for me but he'll be back soon. Turn around and give me your opinion on my new string bikini, Uncle Bill. A girl can't prepare for bikini season too early."

"I've seen enough of it. You're gonna turn to leather if you keep tanning like that. I heard some cancer doctor the other day saying how bad it is for your skin."

"This isn't from the tanning bed. Lake Coburn finally opened one of those salons that have a walk-in spray tan chamber. It's much better for your skin and it looks real."

"Oh yeah?" Curious, Bill snuck a peek to check it out, paid for his foolishness with the sight of a topless Chloe. He spun away from the sight, embarrassed and all kinds of pissed at her audacity.

"Dammit all—put your clothes on, girl! What the hell's wrong with you?"

She responded with that skin-crawling, wicked witch of the west cackle of hers. Jackson must have the patience of a saint, because condition or no condition, he'd have cut her loose years ago. Scratch that—he never would have married her in the first place.

"Oh, I'm bi-polar, manic-depressive with schizophrenic tendencies," she purred. "Didn't you get the memo?"

Bill shook his head. *Bullshit.* This crazy bitch might have his nephew fooled, along with a handful of money hungry doctors all wanting to make money from treating her for one particular 'condition' or another. But she'd never convince him that she was anything but manipulative with a heaping side serving of plain old nastiness. He sucked in his breath when she plastered herself against his backside, locking her hands around his waist to keep him from pulling away. "Get off, dammit!"

"Oh, come on, now." She released a high-pitched chuckle. "Show me some of that Bill Broussard magnetism that has all the women around here drooling over you. I've always heard older men were better lovers. Why don't you show me?"

He pulled her hands off of him and faced her to push her back into the house, lest some nosey neighbor get an eye full, and the wrong impression. He grabbed some flimsy cover up hanging from the back of a chair and threw it at her. "Cover yourself, dammit! You know, it wouldn't kill you to dial down that crazy a notch or two."

"Oh, but what's the fun in that?" She slipped the cover up over her nudeness but didn't bother to button it up.

He stared at her, shaking his head in amazement. "Aren't you even worried what I could tell Jackson about this?"

Chloe cocked her head at him, giving him that sweet, fake smile of hers. "Maybe you should be the one who's worried." She grabbed the sleeve of the cover-up with one hand and jerked, nearly ripping it off, before approaching him, reaching for his face. "He'll believe anything I tell him."

Thanks to Red's warning and the old saying "forewarned is forearmed", Bill stopped her before she could do any damage. He caught her right wrist in one hand, then her other as she clawed at him, no doubt wanting to leave marks on him as evidence of her defensive measures after he ‘attacked’ her.

He grinned at her frustrated growl, careful not to squeeze her wrists hard enough to leave bruises. “You’ll have to come up with some other method of getting your way. Jackson would never believe I’d force myself on someone like you. But you, on the other hand, have proven countless times that you’ll throw yourself at any man.”

She backed away from him, glaring—her eyes hard with ice cold hatred for him. “I can’t wait for you to die—for the day I don’t have to see your face anymore.”

Bill headed for the door, keeping her in his sight. He kept his mouth shut, struggling not to throw back the *“Ditto, you crazy bitch!”* seated there on the tip of his tongue. By the time he’d shut the door and left Chloe behind him, he’d already decided not to mention any part of the incident to Jackson. He wasn’t about to let anything “Crazy Chloe” did or said drive a wedge between them. His nephew had enough stress thanks to that lunatic—Bill sure as hell wouldn’t add to it by dumping anything more on him.

But that’s when he decided to put his own love life on hold. Jackson needed some kind of barrier against the vile woman he’d married. And if he had to, Bill would dedicate the rest of his life to providing one for him.

He owed it to Jamison and Elise to watch out for their son.

* * * * *

A couple of years after that incident, Bill began to notice a change in his nephew. Instead of getting upset by Chloe’s antics with other men, they rolled off of Jackson like water off of a duck’s back. By then they’d been married twelve years and Chloe had yet to conceive. They’d both been checked out and no one could find anything wrong with either of them, physically. Chloe had prescriptions for several types of mood-altering drugs, none of which she took in case there was the chance of a fetus being damaged.

Each month, they’d wait for the sign that she’d conceived. Each month brought on a new wave of disappointment. Each of those waves caused a tsunami-sized reaction from Chloe, usually culminating in blatant affairs with multiple men, and public displays in everything from four-star restaurants to the local grocery store. Jackson figured that as long as Chloe put forth the effort to conceive, he'd put up with the bad behavior that followed his wife around like flies to a pile of horse crap.

Bill cherished any time alone with Jackson, always asked him about his work. His nephew gave him regular updates on their company's latest project in road construction. More often than not, the subject veered off to whatever had been going on with Carrie and Sam Langley's boisterous family. Several times lately, he'd end up retelling some story relayed to him and Carrie by their co-worker, Giselle, involving her two kids.

"She keeps pictures of her little girls in her cubicle—she has the two cutest little girls you've ever seen, Uncle Bill. The three-year-old, Mac, she calls her, looks just like her dad. But the toddler, Lexie—she just turned one—that one looks just like her mama. She's beautiful . . ."

Bill studied him, wondering if he wasn't a little in love with this Giselle woman…or maybe he just lusted after the life she led with her husband and children.

"She's pissed off at me right now, though."

Jackson's statement got his attention. "When is Chloe not pissed at you?"

"Not Chloe—Giselle. She's not talking to me anymore."

"Aren't you her supervisor?"

"Yep, but she manages to find a way around that."

Bill chuckled. "What happened?"

"We had a plan-in-hand meeting with some contractors last week. I'd already had a bad morning before I got to work. One of those Chloe-induced-crap-moods that stay with me. My secretary, Joan, is out with her shoulder surgery so, during a meeting, I asked the temp to print out a list of chronological occurrences at an intersection. She gave it to Giselle to bring it into the meeting. When I got the list, I realized it wasn't in chronological order and accused Giselle of not being able to follow instructions. Of course, she didn't know what the hell I was talking about."

"So, you embarrassed her."

"In front of our peers." Jackson nodded. "And I've been paying for it ever since."

Bill grinned at the downtrodden expression on his nephew's face. "A woman scorned . . ."

"No kidding," Jackson admitted. "But she called me out before she walked out the office—told me to search my steel trap of a mind and remember who I'd asked to provide the list."

Bill burst into laughter. "Well, good for her," he said, as always, amazed at the resilience of people. Not to mention God's methods of keeping his nephew from losing his sense of humor, or all hope in the face of darkest situations.

Jackson groaned before shaking his head. "I hear Giselle and Carrie talking about *their* husbands—*their* kids, and I find myself wondering, why can't I have that? They're both so happy in their marriages."

Bill refrained from stating the obvious—that *they* hadn't married lunatics—opted for something more uplifting. "If you'll remember, Carrie had to wait for happiness too. She was married to a cheater for seventeen years before she got out of that marriage. Sam's wife left him. It took a while for them to find each other. Life pans out according to God's calendar, not ours." Bill could only pray that God had something special planned for his nephew—something that would keep him from losing all hope.

* * * * *

Bill spent the next three years wondering if Jackson would ever be happy. Tales of Chloe and other men circulated in a frantic whirlwind of rumors and insinuations.

Just as before, Jackson took the rumors in stride, in fact, seemed more upset with his co-worker, Giselle's, deteriorated opinion of him than his wife's. It had Bill scratching his head, and he wondered if Jackson had developed feelings for this woman. As always, his thoughts were his own personal observations, and he kept them all to himself.

But God's calendar flipped to one particular day—a day that would change his nephew's life forever.

Chapter Fifteen

Bad Endings

February 25, 2012

Bill opened his front door to the sound of his landline ringing, managed to reach it before the caller hung up. He smiled when his caller ID flashed Jackson's name and number.

"Hey son, what's up?"

"Uncle Bill . . ."

Bill's gut tightened as his nephew's voice cut off. "What happened?"

"I'm at the hospital—St. Luke's. We were involved in a pile up on the 210 Loop. It's bad, Uncle Bill. Chloe . . . she's gone."

"I'm on my way." Bill slammed the phone down and hit the door at a run. He didn't even think to ask him if he'd been hurt. Not likely that he'd avoid some injury in an accident bad enough to take the life of someone in the same vehicle. He'd taken the second detour to the hospital when he turned on a local radio station. At least six dead, dozens injured, some seriously. *The kid couldn't be hurt too badly if they'd let him make a call.* He snorted, amazed that after all this time, he could still think of Jackson as a kid.

He'd focused so completely on getting to him that he was halfway to the hospital before a cold, hard fact dawned on him.

Jackson's free.

Free to live his life. Free to find someone else. He gripped the steering wheel and spoke over the sound of the radio. "I hope you're listenin' Lord, because I've got somethin' to say. Seems to me you've put that boy through enough in his lifetime. How about you cut him some slack from here on out and send him a little happiness? He's a good kid—a good man. And you know he deserves it."

He finally got to the hospital and something else dawned on him. What if God *did* answer his prayers? How would Bill

Broussard spend his time if he didn't have to worry about the next crap hand being dealt to his nephew?

He headed for the hospital entrance thinking that maybe—just maybe—the good Lord could see fit to throw a little happiness his direction as well. Hell, he'd be sixty in a few years, and he sure wouldn't mind sharing whatever years he had left on this earth with a good woman by his side.

He headed for the information desk, turned when someone called out his name. Carrie hurried towards him, her eyes puffy and red, her face lined with worry. "I wondered if I'd see you or Sam here." He brushed a hand over his face. "This must have been a hell of an accident. It's all over the radio station and I had to take a detour to get here."

She nodded, gave him a hug when she reached him. "Fourteen cars and one jack-knifed eighteen-wheeler. It was awful from what I hear. Jackson called me about Chloe—" she bit back and sob before finishing with "—and Toby."

"Toby? The same Toby that Jackson met while building the deck at your place last year?"

She nodded. "The same. They grew to be extremely close friends the past several months."

Bill's heart sank for his nephew, knowing he'd lost yet another friend.

She pointed to the elevator with one hand and lifted her cell in the other. "Jackson called me a little while ago. He's been released already but I'm pretty sure I know where to find him. We need to go to the fifth floor."

They exited the elevator and approached a room to see Jackson standing beside a bed, staring at the sleeping woman inside it—a co-worker, maybe? Carrie approached his nephew, placed a hand on Jackson's shoulder.

"Jackson, I'm so sorry." She hugged him. "I thought you'd be here, so I brought someone up with me."

Bill clutched his Stetson tightly in one hand as Jackson turned, his face wreathed in a sadness he'd come to recognize on the young man.

"Uncle Bill."

"Are you okay, Jackson?"

"A few bruises and a sore knee . . . nothing." Jackson embraced him briefly, pulled away and shrugged. "It could have been a lot worse, obviously."

"I guess Chloe wasn't wearing her seat belt," Carrie said.

"She might be alive if she had."

Bill shook his head. "Senseless. Have you called her mother yet?"

Jackson's mouth twisted in distaste. "Oh, yeah. She said she was sorry for my loss but couldn't make it to the funeral."

Carrie gasped. "For her own daughter? Lord, it's no wonder Chloe was disturbed." She reached out to touch his arm. "Are you all right? I know how bad it was for you at home."

Jackson shook his head slowly. "I don't know how I feel yet. I mean, who are we kidding? We all knew Chloe was—difficult. I doubt either of us felt any love for each other in years, but to have her die like that." He lowered his head and squeezed his eyes shut. "God, I don't know if I'll ever be able to forget that. I wouldn't have known it was her if I hadn't recognized her clothing." His voice broke and he cleared his throat.

Bill started, in shock when Jackson spoke of being present when the doctor told Giselle about her husband. Bill stared at his nephew. *Wait...That's Giselle?*

Carrie's jaw dropped. "You were here?"

Bill listened as Jackson walked them into the corridor and said how awful it had been seeing the doctor sedate a hysterical Giselle.

Carrie dabbed at her eyes with a tissue. "Toby's poor girls. It makes you wonder what God could have been thinking, doesn't it?"

Toby's girls? Bill finally spoke up as all the puzzle pieces fell into place. "Wait a minute. Is that the wife of your friend, Toby?"

Jackson nodded slowly. "He died in the accident."

Bill's head fell forward. "I'm sorry, Son. I didn't realize. Isn't she the one you pissed off at work a few years back?"

"That's her." Jackson nodded. "She already didn't like me. After walking away from an accident that took Toby's life, she may never forgive me."

"She wouldn't hold that against you," Carrie told him.

He raised an eyebrow. "You didn't hear her." He shook his head and pushed away from the window. "She was right about one thing, though. She said I was jealous of their marriage. I was."

"Come on, Jack. Everyone was envious of those two. They were the perfect couple," Carrie said. "Now, you need to go home, take a couple of aspirin, and go to bed."

"I need to get to the Chevy dealership for a new truck. I can't drive Chloe's Vette around. I can't get comfortable in that thing. Are you ready, Uncle Bill?"

"Are you released yet?"

"It's taken care of. Will you be here all night, Carrie?"

"I'll be here until they release her." She reached up to touch a spot on his face. "I'm worried about you, Jack. You call me if you need to talk."

He leaned over to hug her. "If you need anything while you're here, let me know, and I'll get it to you."

"I've got your number. Get your new truck then go straight home. Bill, maybe you ought to stay with him tonight."

"I don't need a damn baby sitter," Jackson grumbled. He rose from the seat too quickly and winced.

Carrie clucked her tongue. "Now see? That's good for you, smart ass. Good luck, Bill."

Bill leaned closer to Carrie, as always, in awe of her ability to put his nephew in his place. "You can call *me* at home if you need anything, hon."

"So that's Giselle Granger." Bill followed him into the elevator and pushed the Lobby button. "Any children?"

"Two beautiful little girls, ages six and four."

"Bad ages to lose their daddy." If anyone knew how bad those two little girls would have it, Jackson did. He bit his lower lip, contemplating how life would change for his nephew now with no Chloe around to treat him like her own personal marionette.

Later, in his truck, Bill revisited the incident two years earlier—that unpleasant day when the woman had bared her all to him, in more ways than one. He'd made damn sure never to be alone with her again. He snorted at the memory, looked over to make sure Jackson hadn't heard, but he'd dropped his head back on the dusty seat of his truck. What could he be thinking right now?

Bill turned his attention back to the road, considering all the diagnoses those high-priced specialists had labeled Chloe with over the years. He'd put his money on the one doctor who claimed, *"She's simply one hell of an actress"*.

By the time Bill pulled into the dealership, Jackson had refreshed his memory, both on what he'd done to anger Giselle three years earlier, and how he'd become such good friends with Toby, a man whose wife despised him.

"Toby knew she hated me," Jackson explained. "Said he'd set a personal goal to 'patch things up' between us."

"You think he'd want you to look after his wife and daughters until they come to terms with things?"

Jackson let his head fall back on the seat again, paused before answering. "I know he would, but that doesn't mean she'll let me."

Bill pulled into the dealership Jackson had asked him to bring him to. "Do you want me to go with you?"

"No. Thanks for the ride, though."

Of course not. The kid had proven his resilience time and time again. "Call me if you need anything."

* * * * *

Bill left Jackson alone for the most part of the next day, figuring he had his hands full with Chloe's funeral arrangements. He took care of his livestock, wondering if he'd ever hear the laughter of children on this ranch. Logically, any offspring of Jack's would be his great nieces or nephews but Bill didn't care about that. He'd love having them call him Paw Paw. He worked in silence, waiting for a call from Jackson telling him when and where to show up. All day he waited and wondered.

After a long day of trying to keep his body occupied while his mind whirled with thoughts of his nephew, Carrie finally called—furious, fuming, and spouting obscenities that would make a Marine blush. It seemed Chloe had stated in a will she'd left with their lawyer that she wanted to be cremated and her ashes sent to her cold-hearted mother in California. None of that bothered Bill.

Details of a letter she'd left with same lawyer had his blood boiling. In said letter, Chloe had claimed to be 'condition' free…no bi-polar or any other disorder…just a well-played act to keep his nephew sympathetic to his wife's wants and need to manipulate everything around her. Turned out she'd never wanted children and had been on the pill for the duration of their marriage.

Hearing he'd been right about Chloe gave Bill no pleasure. It sickened him beyond words that his nephew had wasted fifteen years of his life with that twisted bitch. After reading the letter, Jackson had spent the previous night ridding his home of all things Chloe, and the entire morning shopping for an entire house full of furniture.

"There's more, Bill," Carrie said.

He braced himself. What could be worse than what she'd already told him?

Carrie sighed. "She'd taken two rounds of antibiotics previously that messed up her birth control pills. Chloe was pregnant."

"Oh . . . God." Bill headed for his truck.

"And she'd scheduled an abortion in Beaumont yesterday afternoon," she finished, with a disgusted huff.

"Son of a bitch!"

"I know. I'm worried about Jack, Bill. Please go check on him."

Bill started his truck, revving the engine. "I'm on my way, hon. I'll let you know."

* * * * *

He found Jack ensconced in his home, newly filled with furniture purchased and delivered the same day. He'd replaced all of Chloe's tacky choices with more masculine pieces that exuded classic style—lots of leather and wood—creating a comfortable haven for himself.

Bill glanced around the room, amazed at its total transformation. "Damn, you've been busy, haven't you, Son?"

Jackson nodded, keeping his eyes on the television screen.

"What brought this on?"

His nephew rolled his eyes and huffed. "Don't try to act like Carrie hasn't told you all about it. I know her better than that."

"All right, I won't. So, you erased all traces of Chloe."

"That was the plan." Jackson lifted his beer again.

"Well, I can't say as I blame you." *Crazy Chloe had always had god-awful taste in furniture.* "It looks a lot better than before. I don't know how you lived in this place."

"I didn't. I only existed here, but not anymore."

"It seems like you should be grieving a little," Bill said.

"I am grieving, just not over her. Never again over her."

Turned out Jackson grieved losing his friend, Toby, more than his own wife.

"—I keep thinking I'm going to call him and see what he thinks about this, but I can't. It's hard to accept." He grabbed the back of his head with one hand. "And if *I'm* hurting this bad, I keep thinking how hard it's going to be on Giselle and the girls."

"Are you going to the funeral home tomorrow morning?"

"If I don't, Carrie will send over the National freaking Guard."

Bill chuckled and agreed. "You mind if I go with you?"

Jackson's brow shot up. "You don't know them."

"I'd like to go as a show of respect. I know how you felt about Toby," Bill replied.

Jackson remained silent, but nodded his head in agreement.

* * * * *

Bill smoothed down the lapel of his dark brown western cut suit, made sure his boots weren't dusty before following his nephew inside the funeral home's foyer. Jackson looked sharp in a black suit, light gray shirt and dark gray tie.

Carrie approached and hugged Jackson. "I'm glad you're here." She faced him then, and he opened his arms to her. "Bill, you look absolutely scrumptious." She let him hug her. "Honestly, you two boys have every woman in this room drooling."

"Your ass," Jackson murmured. "You look nice, though."

"She sure does," Bill said. "Where's old Sam? Is he ready to give you up, yet?"

Sam Langley approached, maybe an inch shorter than Bill, but just as broad shouldered. He slipped his arm around Carrie's waist. "It's not up for discussion, Bill. Go find your own wife, this one's mine."

Carrie laughed and snuggled closer to her husband. "It's no use, Bill. Sam has me spoiled beyond belief for any other man."

Bill winked at her. "If he ever stops, let me know." He shook Sam's hand in a warm greeting. "Sam."

"It's good to see you two." Sam cleared his throat. "I wish it were under different circumstances."

He watched as Jackson approached Giselle, stood back to let them get the first difficult encounter behind them. He stepped forward to introduce himself when the woman placed her hand on his nephew's arm.

"I'm sorry about Chloe, Jackson. If you told me, I was too out of it to remember."

Jackson's jaw clenched. "Not as sorry as I am about Toby. He was one of the best men I knew, and a damn good friend to me. I know for a fact, how much he loved his girls. All three of his girls."

Bill grimaced when Giselle blinked several times, afraid she'd lose it. Instead, she wiped her eyes and smiled. That's when he recognized a strength in her—one that matched Jackson's.

"Thank you, I appreciate that." Her gaze landed on Bill. "I know you're his uncle, but you must have been his dad's twin, because y'all look so much alike. I'm Giselle Granger."

Bill shook her hand gently. "I'm Bill Broussard, ma'am. No, Jackson's dad, Jamison, was five years older. I'm sorry for your loss. Jackson always spoke highly of Toby. How are your girls?"

"I think we're in shock. It's difficult because there's no one but Carrie to help until I'm back to full speed. My girls are trying to be on their best behavior, but they're both so active."

Carrie grinned at the mention of Toby and Giselle's daughters. "If you haven't met them yet, you're both in for a treat. Ah, speaking of which . . ."

Bill turned when two little girls ran up to join them. The older had long, straight, dark hair and big brown eyes. The younger favored her mama, with golden brown curls and big curious green eyes, specked with gold.

Giselle turned the two girls around to face them. "Girls, I'd like you to meet some people. This is Mr. Jackson Broussard."

"I remember him, mama," the younger of the two girls beamed at Jackson. "He was in that picture on our frij-rator until daddy took it down because you drew on it. He's the tall man that works with you, except . . ." She scrunched up her face. "I thought his name was Satan."

"Lexie!" Giselle whispered harshly, covering the child's mouth.

Bill practically choked holding back a guffaw of laughter. *Yeah, that one's her mama made over.*

Jackson chuckled. “It’s okay, Giselle.” He squatted in front of the child. “Lexie, it’s true that your mom called me that sometimes, but I’m hoping that if I promise to be really nice to her, she won’t be mad at me anymore. Maybe if you just call me Jackson, your mom would too.” He glanced up at Giselle.

Lexie looked at her mom. “Mama?”

Giselle nodded, still embarrassed, no doubt. “I think that’s a great idea.”

Lexie nodded, obviously accepting the proposal without question. “You’re tall, Jackson. So is he!” She pointed at Bill. “They sure grow ‘em big where you come from.”

Bill chuckled as Jackson answered for both of them. “That’s my Uncle Bill, Lex, but he’s been like my dad for a long, long time.”

Her small face turned serious. “But why?”

“I lost both of my parents in a car accident when I was the same age you are now.” He placed a finger lightly on the tip of her nose. “I was lucky, because I had Uncle Bill.”

Lexie’s eyes widened. “You lost your daddy *and* your mama? You must have been really sad. I know how sad I am that I don’t have my daddy anymore. But I still have my mama.”

Giselle’s chin trembled as Carrie placed a hand on her shoulder in a show of support.

Jackson continued his talk. “You know, Lexie, your daddy was a great friend of mine and he always said how much he loved his girls.” He placed the tip of his finger over her heart. “But you’ll always have him—right here.”

“Yeah, that’s what mama says, too, but it’s just not the same.” Something caught the child’s attention and as quickly as she appeared, she ran off, her curls bouncing with each step.

Giselle wiped a tear from the corner of her eye. “Jackson, I’m really sorry about that.”

He rose slowly, in obvious pain from his knee. “Don’t worry about it.”

She placed her hands on the shoulders of her second daughter. “This is Mackenzie.”

Bill waited and watched, curious to see how his nephew would handle the second meeting.

“Hello, Mackenzie. It’s nice to meet you.” He held out his hand and she shook it.

"It's nice to meet you, too, Jackson. Everybody calls me Mac. I knew you weren't Satan. My dad told me you were a good dude."

Jackson beamed. "Well, thanks Mac, that means a lot to me."

Her brown-eyed gaze landed on Bill. "Are you his Uncle?"

Bill nodded, smiling at the beautiful little girl. "I sure am. I'm his Uncle Bill."

Her gaze moved to Jackson, then back to Bill. "You don't look old enough to be his uncle."

Bill grinned, immediately liking the kid. "Well, thanks, little lady. You just made my day. I promise you, I am."

She smiled shyly at him before running off to meet her sister.

"Photos don't do them justice, Giselle," Jackson said. "They're beautiful, and you should be proud."

"I am, most of the time. Oh, but Lexie!"

Jackson's reply held more than a hint of laughter. "That child is your clone, Giselle. She even has your mannerisms."

Giselle groaned. "I guess so." She glanced at Toby's casket then back at Jackson. "Are you ready?"

He nodded. "I guess I've put it off long enough."

Bill and Carrie stood back as the two of them approached the casket. He tensed when Jackson nearly lost it at first sight of his friend, had to clamp down on his jaw when his nephew reached for his handkerchief to wipe his eyes.

This would definitely be a rough couple of days on the kid. Heartbreaking memories washed over Bill, had him walking away in search of the kitchen area. He found it and poured himself a cup of coffee. Someone entered bringing an assortment of donuts and other pastries, followed closely by Giselle's two girls.

"Hello there," he said.

Lexie clasped her hands together. "I'm hungry and I smell donuts!"

Bill left his seat to open the two boxes. "I see plain and chocolate covered—and these are marked raspberry, lemon, and cream filled. What'll it be, ladies?"

By the time Jackson entered the room ten minutes later, he had them situated with jelly donuts and they were in the middle of telling him about their favorite singers. He joined them at the table with a cup of coffee.

Lexie gave him a raspberry coated grin. "Hello Jackson!"

Jackson laughed as he got up to dampen a napkin at the sink. "Hello Lexie." He wiped all traces of red from her face. "I can't let your mama see you like this, Lex. She'll think I'm not doing my job and fire me."

Mac stared at Jackson. "Mama gave you a job? Is she your boss now?"

Jackson grinned. "I told her I'd find you two and keep you out of trouble."

"Huh!" Mackenzie snorted. "Good luck trying to keep Lex out of trouble. Daddy says she's a trouble magnet." She frowned before continuing. "Daddy said a lot of things that made me laugh, and he made mom really happy. She said so all the time, and that she thanked God for him. Maybe God will send her someone else so she can be happy again."

Lexie turned her green-gold eyes to Bill. "What about you, Bill? You seem nice and you said you don't have a wife."

Bill started at the kid's suggestion. "Uh—I think I'm a little too old for her. Most men my age have children the same age as your mama. She may need someone a little younger."

Lexie turned her perusal to Jackson. "How about you? Do you have a wife? I didn't see you with one."

"No. Not anymore."

"Lex, shhh!" Mackenzie hissed. "Don't you remember what Carrie said? He lost his wife in the same accident as daddy."

Lexie's brow furrowed adorably. "If you lost her, why aren't you out looking for her? I lost my Barbie's horse once and didn't find it for two whole days." She shook her head. "But I never stopped looking."

Mac slapped her hand over her own forehead. "No! She's not lost. She's like daddy."

"Oh. She's sleepin', too." Lexie frowned. "Sorry, Jackson."

Jackson wiped his mouth. "That's okay, Lex."

"Were you and your wife as happy as mama and daddy were?"

Jackson shifted uneasily in his chair. "No, not really, Lex."

Mac locked up. "Why not?"

"Because she was a piece of work, wasn't she?" Lexie popped off. "I heard Daddy say that once. He said it just like that, too. "Jackson's wife is a piece of work." What does that mean?"

Bill joined his nephew in an attempt to smother his own laughter.

"It's, uh—" Jackson started. "It's kind of hard to explain."

Lexie's green eyes pinned him. "Was she mean?"

"Yes," Bill answered for his nephew.

"Uncle Bill, that's not necessary."

Mackenzie faced Bill. "Was she just mean to Jackson, or to everyone?"

"To everyone," Bill answered. "But she really liked to upset Jackson."

"Uncle Bill," Jackson admonished.

Lexie slapped both her hands on the table. "Well, I like you, Jackson. I'm glad she's not around to be mean to everybody and upset you anymore."

Mac threw her head back, rolled her eyes in exasperation. "Lexie! You shouldn't say things like that. Mom would be *upset* with you if she heard you."

Lexi seemed to weigh her sister's words. "No, she'd prolly be mor...mort...morti...What's that word she uses sometimes when I say things like that?"

The older child's brow furrowed in concentration. "I think it's mortified, or something like that."

Bill had to cover his mouth to hold back the guffaw of laughter as Jackson choked on his sip of coffee.

Giselle entered the kitchen, clearly in search of her girls. "Come on, girls. There are some co-workers of daddy's who would like to meet you both. You want to come with me now?"

The girls nodded and climbed down from their chairs.

"Lex, have you been in those jelly donuts?" Giselle examined her daughter's face and hands.

"I'm clean, Mama. Jackson washed my face just like daddy does."

Jackson and Giselle's gazes clashed.

Lexie's gaze moved from Giselle to Jackson and back to her mother. "Did I mortify you again, Mama?"

Giselle shook her head as Jackson and Bill worked hard to conceal their grins. "What am I going to do with you, Lex?" She herded the girls out the door, casting a glance back at Jackson. "I can only imagine what you four have been talking about in here."

* * * * *

Jackson opened the door before Bill could knock the next morning, keys already in hand. "I'm ready if you are." His nephew jutted his chin toward his truck parked in the garage. He closed and locked his door. I thought we could stop somewhere and pick up breakfast for everyone."

Bill nodded. "Good thinking."

Sam greeted them at Giselle's door later and let them inside. "Thanks for this, guys. Carrie's got a lot to do this morning, and about all I can manage for these ladies is cereal or toast."

They'd just set out the containers when Lexie peeked inside the room. Her face lit up when she spotted Jackson and Bill. She disappeared into the hallway and came in a minute later with Mackenzie.

Lexie ran straight to Jackson and climbed up on his knee. "I *me-rember* you. Your name's Jackson."

Jackson chuckled. "That's right and I *me-rember* you too, Lex. I hope you slept well."

She nodded. "I did. But I don't think momma did."

Mackenzie approached Bill shyly. "We heard her crying last night."

Bill pulled out the chair next to him and tapped the seat. "Climb on up here, little lady." Mackenzie climbed into it and smiled at Bill.

Jackson brushed Lexie's curls away from her eyes. "I'm sure she's sad and still in some pain. It'll take a while before she feels better."

Bill opened a couple of the containers. "Are you girls hungry? We have bacon, eggs, grits, and pancakes with lots of fixins."

Lexie cocked her head to look up at Jackson. "I like pancakes but what's a fixin?"

Bill laughed at the face she made. "In this case it's whipped cream with strawberries and sauce to go on them."

"That's what I want!" Lexie insisted, with Mackenzie chiming in her agreement.

The two girls were chin deep in "fixins" when Giselle appeared in the hall, her face pale and drawn. "Help…" she croaked.

Jackson shot to his feet to meet her, asking Sam to get her pain killers and some milk as he lowered her into a chair at the table.

Lexie's eyes were huge as she fixated on Giselle. "What's wrong with mama?"

Jackson gave her a reassuring pat on the head. "It's okay, sweetie. Your mom just slept through the night and doesn't have any pain medication left in her system. Here, Giselle, take them with milk and when you feel like you can eat something, let me know."

Giselle chased the two pills with a swallow of milk. She held on to the glass with shaking hands, and listed to one side.

Jackson took the glass from her and sat beside her to keep her upright. "Whoa, where do you think you're going?"

"I guess-I need-to set my alarm-to take a dose during the night." Her breath came in shallow pants.

"That may be a good idea for the next week or so. Try to drink the rest of this." Jackson pushed the glass of milk at her.

Bill watched the scene play out it quiet interest. Giselle pushed the milk away, but relented when Jackson warned her about the dangers of dry heaves.

She gave Bill and Sam weak smiles. "What's—going on?"

"I took Carrie's place this morning," Sam explained. "Jackson and Bill showed up with breakfast."

She checked out the spread, glanced at Jackson. "You brought us breakfast?"

"We stopped off at Shoney's and got an assortment from the breakfast buffet: scrambled eggs, sausage, bacon, grits, hash browns, mushrooms in butter sauce. What'll it be, madam?"

"A little of—everything. Don't want—dry heaves."

Jackson prepared a plate of food and sat it before her.

"You forgot to tell her about the pancakes with strawberry sauce and whipped cream. They're awesome, Mom," Mackenzie added.

Giselle frowned at Jackson. "You holding-out on me?"

"I didn't know if you could handle anything sweet."

She shuddered. "Right." Giselle looked at Lexie's face, covered in strawberry sauce and whipped cream. "Lex. Did you-get any inside-your mouth?"

Bill chuckled. "Don't worry, she's eaten plenty."

Jackson leaned forward to address her. "Do you want coffee or juice?"

"Coffee." She thanked him when he brought her a cup.

Jackson took his place beside Giselle. "Now eat."

She pointed her fork at him. "You're not—the boss—of me here," she gasped. "What time is it?" Her hand shook and scrambled egg fell off her fork before she could get it to her mouth.

"A little before seven." Jackson took the fork out of her hands. He cut off her glare with a pretty good imitation of dry-heaving.

Bill left them to it, turned his attention back to assisting the little girls.

"Why are you two up so early?" Giselle asked her daughters.

"I got up to pee."

"Lex. It's use the bathroom," her mom said.

Lexie sighed. "I got up to 'use the bathroom' and I heard them all talking. I was so happy to see Jackson, I stayed up and told Mac that Bill was here. Jackson's my favorite, but Bill is hers."

Giselle sent Bill and Jackson an amused glance.

Jackson shrugged. "We can't help it if we're irresistible to women."

She scowled. "Not all women."

"To the only two who count," Bill added.

"I could get used to being somebody's favorite." Jackson hugged Lexie.

"Me too." Bill tweaked Mackenzie's nose. He busted out laughing when Lexie went to give Jackson a kiss and burped in his face.

"Whoa! That's a first." Jackson joined in on the laughter.

Lexie giggled through an apology. "Sorry Jackson, that was on a asscident."

"Not a problem, Lex." He accepted a kiss from her anyway. When Lexie attempted to climb up on his knee, Jackson swung her easily onto his lap.

"She'll get strawberry sauce all over your nice suite," Giselle said. "She makes Toby late all the time—I mean—she *made* him late. He'd have to change his shirt . . . " She paused, finished up in a whisper. "Before he could leave the house in the mornings." She wiped at her eyes. "Excuse me, I have to get ready."

Sam reached for his cell phone. "Do you need me to call Carrie?"

"No, I'll be fine. Could someone clean Lexie up, please?"

"I got that," Jackson wet a paper towel and started to wipe the child down. "Between the three of us, we could probably get the girls ready for you and give you and Carrie a break. I can't do their hair, though."

"Mac can do her own hair, and I'll tend to Lexie's."

"Mom, can you braid my hair today?" Mac asked, running up to her mother. "Daddy liked it in one long braid, and I want to look nice for daddy."

"Sure baby, when I'm done." Giselle gently smoothed the child's bangs back away from her forehead before pulling her daughter close for a hug. "Daddy will like that." She placed a kiss on Mac's head and retreated down the hallway. "I'll lay their clothes out for you."

Bill exchanged a knowing look with Sam before hugging Mac when she returned to his side.

"I wish mama wasn't so sad," Lex said.

"I know, Lex. She'll be sad for a while, but it won't last forever," Jackson returned.

"Maybe God will send her someone else to make her happy."

"Maybe so." Jackson carried her to the sink.

"I don't think I'll like not having a daddy. You think he could send her someone who could be a good daddy for us?"

Jackson wet another paper towel and wiped Lexie's face again. "Maybe he will one day, Lex, but you can't rush something like that. You and Mac and your mom—you all loved your daddy a whole lot. It would be hard for someone to step in and take his place."

Bill froze when Lexie asked Jackson if he could take her dad's place, her reasoning being that Jackson already hugged and smelled like a daddy.

Jackson stared at the child, clearly puzzled by her comment. "I do?"

She nodded enthusiastically, sending her ringlets bouncing.

"I'm kind of curious, Lex. How do daddies hug and smell?" he asked the child.

Lexie's forehead scrunched up, as though she were struggling to find just the right answer. "My daddy always smelled good and so do you, but in a different way. And when daddy hugged me, I felt all warm and *comfable*. That's how *you* make me feel." She stared up at him, her eyes wide and questioning. "Did I 'splain it good enough, Jackson?"

Jackson blinked quickly then cleared his throat. "Yeah, Lex, you explained it fine." He kissed her lightly on the forehead. "I believe that's the nicest thing anyone has ever said to me."

Bill couldn't have agreed more.

* * * * *

They entered the funeral home as a group, with the men shaking the rain from their umbrellas. At the appropriate time, Giselle approached the casket, her two girls pressed close.

The sight of her leaning over her husband's open coffin nearly broke Bill. Memories overwhelmed him for several seconds—the history of his own painful goodbyes. First his mom, then Lorraine, and again with Jamison and Elise. He extracted his handkerchief when Giselle's whimpers transformed into full blown sobbing. Mac turned, her huge brown eyes brimming with tears as she focused on him. Bill opened his arms and she ran to him. He scooped her up, hugged her tight, his heart aching as she buried her face in his neck and sobbed. Lexie ran to Jackson and he lifted her easily into his own embrace as Carrie and her girls surrounded their mother.

The church service went quickly, and by the time they got to the cemetery, all that remained of the spring shower was a light drizzle. It too had disappeared by the end of the graveside service and the sun peeked out from clouds in a glorious display. Bill took Mackenzie and Lexie's hands and pointed to a rainbow on the horizon. "Look what your dad sent for his three girls."

Mackenzie pulled on her mother's hand as she pointed upward. "Mom, look at that!"

Lexie's squeal of delight pierced the air. "Did Daddy send it for us, Mama?"

"I bet he did, baby. I bet he asked God to send us that rainbow so that we wouldn't be so sad. He's still taking care of us, isn't he?"

Mac nodded and looked up at Bill. "That's just like daddy to do that for us."

Bill had never met Mac and Lexie's daddy, but he'd bet the deed to his ranch that it would be just like him to do that for his three girls.

They ended up at Giselle's place afterwards, eating delicious food prepared by women of the bereavement committee from the local Catholic church. Bill sat with Sam and Jackson, telling Mac and Lexie all about the animals on his ranch.

When Giselle joined them in the dining room, Lexi went to her. "Mama, did you know that Bill has a ranch, and he has horses, and cows, and even some little piggy goats that don't grow very big at all."

"I think he may have Pygmy goats," Giselle corrected.

"I guess so. Anyway, he also has a big pond on his ranch where we could go fishing. He wants to cook us all a barbeque when your ribs don't hurt you anymore. He said our whole family could go—Carrie's and Sam's, and our school friends, too. Can we go, Mama?"

Giselle smiled at Bill. "Maybe by the time school ends I'll be feeling better and we could plan a day like that."

"Can't we plan it now, Mama?" Lexie pleaded.

Giselle placed her good hand on her daughter's shoulder. "Lex, you're putting poor Bill on the spot."

Bill stepped forward, lowered himself into the chair beside her. "It was my idea. As a matter of fact, Mac told me she and Lex both have birthdays coming up in July. One's on a Friday and the other is the next Tuesday. How about planning a joint party for them on the Sunday? I'd love it if you'd say yes, Giselle. It would give this old man something to look forward to."

She gazed at him for a moment then smiled and nodded. "All right."

Satisfied, Bill followed Jackson and Sam onto the patio and discussed maintenance issues on Giselle's place for the next hour. He looked up as Carrie joined them outside. "How's she doing?"

"I just got all three of them tucked in for an afternoon nap. I thought you two went home an hour ago." They discussed Jackson's plans to come over the next Saturday to do some yard work. Then Carrie gave them the heads up about the girls' upcoming tee-ball games.

Sam sipped his glass of tea. "You know, I always thought it was odd that Toby didn't play baseball, as much as he loved other sports. I guess you knew he was a star running back for L.S.U. How about you, Jackson? You look athletic. You ever play baseball?"

Jackson shrugged. "I played some."

Bill chuckled. "Jackson pl—"

"So when does ball season start around here?" Jackson shot him his classic cease and desist look.

"It starts the end of March, about a month away. Opening day is a big deal here," Sam added.

Bill and Jackson made plans to attend before saying their goodbyes. Bill settled into Jackson's truck for the drive home and buckled his seatbelt before turning to his nephew. "I played some? What the hell was that all about?"

"It was high school and a little bit of college."

"A little bit of college?" Jackson's modesty still amazed him. "You had scouts for the major leagues watching you."

"Keep it to yourself, Uncle Bill. Nobody wants to hear about any of that, or why it didn't happen." He shifted in his seat under Bill's gaze.

"What could it hurt, Jackson? It's not like you've tooted your own damn horn about it all these years. And that bitch, Chloe, isn't around anymore to kick you down about throwing your shoulder out before you hit the big time."

Jackson's jaw clenched. "Don't say her name around me. That part of my life is over with, and so is baseball."

Bill lowered his sunglasses to look down his nose at his nephew. "You know, this system of yours—of not dealing with things—not wanting to talk about it to anyone. Well, hell, boy. That can't be healthy."

"Healthy or not, it's how I deal."

"I'm just saying, maybe it'd do you some good to vent a little about all the crap you've put up with over the years."

"Vent? It's not like you don't already know what a cold-hearted bitch she was."

"I don't know. Maybe you and Giselle could vent to each other. Kind of a mutual commiseration thing. A group therapy for just the two of you." He paused. "Maybe let her read that letter your lawyer brought over. You know, the one you won't show anybody? There's bound to be something eye-opening in that thing. Something that'll set you free from all that pent-up hatred."

Jackson braked at a four-way stop and looked both ways before shaking his head. “Trust me, Uncle Bill. That’s one thing that will *never* happen.”

Chapter Sixteen

New Beginnings

Bill followed Jackson into the Kenton ballpark at a quarter to eight the morning of opening day. He looked around the crowded park. "Damn! Kenton's serious about their baseball program. Look at this crowd."

"Sam said it thins out after the opening ceremony. Mac and Lex each have two games to play today, but I'm not sure about the times." Jackson stared at the groups of kids running around in uniforms. "I can't pick anyone out. They all look alike to me."

Bill laughed. "That's why I'm looking for Sam. That big guy will stand out in a crowd, no matter what he's wearing." He pointed. "There he is at the concession stand."

Sam looked up as Jackson called his name. "Hey, I'm glad you two could make it."

"Mac and Lex wouldn't have let us live it down if we hadn't. Did Giselle come?"

Sam shook his head. "No, she wasn't feeling up to it. Carrie said she'd be checking up on her all day in between catching up with some things that she had to do at the house. The girls are here already. They'll be excited to see you two."

They headed toward the stands and within seconds, Bill heard Jackson's name being called as Mackenzie, Lexie, and four other children ran up to them.

Lex threw her arms around Jackson's legs. "My Jackson's here! You came to watch us play?"

Jack hugged both girls then reached down to lift Lex in his arms. "I told you we would, didn't I?"

"Mama doesn't feel well, so I'm glad we have you."

"I'm glad too, sweetie."

Bill watched the exchange, his heart full. His nephew had spent a couple of Saturdays at Giselle's home doing yard work, had obviously bonded with the two little girls. Bill placed his hand gently on Mac's head and pulled her to him for a hug.

As soon as the opening ceremony finished, Lexie's team took to the field. Jackson and Bill spent the next three hours watching Giselle's girls and Carrie and Sam's grandchildren play ball—cheering when any one of them made a good play.

After the morning games, they headed as a group over to Sam and Carrie's for grilled hot dogs. Carrie greeted Bill and Jackson in the kitchen. "So, what'd you two think of opening day?"

Jackson grinned. "I can't wait for the second round to start. I'm having a blast."

Bill gave her a hug. "Me too."

"I'm glad you two are enjoying it. Grab a plate and serve yourselves, buffet style." She pointed to a cooler. "Canned drinks are in there."

After eating, the Broussard men brought Mac and Lexi to their house to see their mom and rest up for the next games.

Giselle looked up from where she sat with a cup of coffee. Pale faced, with dark circles under her eyes, her wraith-like appearance a complete shock to Bill. But the girls' reaction to her disturbed the hell out of him. They entered the room and shut down, all previous signs of animated joy gone, their light doused, subdued by their mother's sadness. Bill sat beside Giselle at the table and took her hand. "Hey hon, how are you feeling?"

"Hi Bill. I'm okay." She turned to her daughters. "How were the games?"

"They were good, we both won," Mac said, quietly.

"Yeah, we both won," Lexie repeated. She lifted her shoulders and let them drop, as she released a deep breath.

Giselle gave them a smile, one that fell far short of sincerity. If Bill had noticed, surely her daughters had also.

Jackson sat at the table across from her. "Maybe by next week you'll feel well enough to make one of their games."

"Maybe so."

"Mac hit two home runs, and I hit the ball off the tee twice, mama," Lexie told her.

"That's great, sweetie."

"Jackson said that daddy was watching, so we did it for him. Ouch!" Lexie turned, ready to fuss at her sister for jabbing her in the ribs. She stopped when Giselle suddenly left the table. Within seconds, she'd disappeared into the guest bedroom, closing the door behind her.

"I told you not to talk about daddy," Mac hissed at her sister. "It makes her cry."

Lexis's little face crumbled as she turned to Jackson for comfort. He picked her up and seated her on his long legs as she turned her face into his broad chest and sobbed. He held her close. "Don't cry Lex. Your mom's just hurting right now."

"I'm s-so-orry Jackson, I th-thought she'd b-be happy that daddy was w-wa-watching us-s," Lexie sobbed into his shirt. "I won't s-say d-daa-dd-dy a-g-gain."

"Maybe, just for now, Lex," Jackson told her.

What? Bill grunted and sent him a look, seething with disapproval.

"Uncle Bill—not now."

Bill sighed then turned to the older child. "Mac, do you think you'd like to rest?"

She nodded, walked to her bedroom, and closed the door.

"How about you, Lex?" Jackson whispered. "Think you could take a little nap for me?"

"I want to st-stay with y-you," she sniffed.

Bill felt helpless, clueless as how to handle this. Finally, Jackson got up with her and asked if she wanted to sit next to him on the sofa.

"C-Can I get M-Mac?" she sniffled.

He nodded and put her down so she could get her sister. When the two girls came back into the room, Lexie snuggled up next to Jackson, and Mac took the spot beside Bill. Within a few minutes, both girls had fallen asleep on the large, comfortable sofa. Jackson followed Bill out to the back patio so they could talk without disturbing them.

"They shouldn't be afraid to talk about their dad," Bill seethed. "They should be talking about him so they can remember him without mourning. Giselle has to face this."

"We can't do anything, Uncle Bill. They're her girls."

Bill sighed, agreeing to disagree on the matter for the moment. After their naps, he and Jackson brought the girls back to the park for round two. They left them at the end of the day, promising to make more ball games.

* * * * *

Bill couldn't make it to Mac or Lexie's games that week, due to an out of town business trip. As soon as he made it in the next Saturday afternoon he drove to Jackson's place and let himself in the house. He stared at the flat-screen on the wall playing a children's program. "Hey, son—I thought you'd outgrown cartoons by now," he called out to his nephew.

Two little heads popped up from the sofa. "Mac, it's Bill!" Lexie squealed as she jumped off the sofa.

Mackenzie made it to him first, throwing her arms around his legs. "I missed you."

Bill knelt down to give them hugs. "Hey, ladies! What are you two doing here?"

"Jackson's taking us to the *movie-ater* at the mall," Lexie said.

"Can you come with us?" Mac pleaded.

"I sure can. Where's Jackson?"

"He was all hot and sweaty from mowing our lawn, so he's taking a shower," Mac explained. She pulled him by the hand to the couch and made him sit between her and Lexie to watch cartoons with them.

Jackson entered a few minutes later.

"Bill is coming with us," Mac explained.

Jackson grinned. "I thought you were out of town, or I'd have called you to help me. I'm kind of new at this stuff."

"I got back and came straight here. Where are we going?" Bill asked.

"The two o'clock feature at the mall. Let's go."

* * * * *

Bill had experienced lots of firsts in his lifetime, but he'd never had as much fun as he did during the trip to the 'movie-ater' that afternoon with those two little girls. After the feature, they passed out within five minutes of driving back to Kenton.

"Are they out already?"

Bill turned in his seat to check on them. "Yep—like a couple of just fed kittens. All that laughing must have worn them out."

Jackson nodded. "That, along with a little emotional upheaval earlier today. Poor things must be exhausted."

"What happened?"

"Giselle happened. I never thought I'd get to the point where I'd actually lose patience with her. But her treatment of those girls this morning . . ." He stopped, shook his head. "Poor babies."

"You gonna tell me what the hell happened or leave me hanging?"

"After we finished the yard work, I thought we could get Giselle outside by setting up the patio table. I picked up a couple of pizzas and chicken nuggets. The girls set the table up so pretty with flowers and everything. But when Giselle saw it, she freaked. Turns out they used to do that as a family and it brought it all back to her."

"In a bad way?"

"The worst. She turned on us all, asked her daughters how they could do that to her." He wiped his face. "The girls were heartbroken. I'm talking total devastation."

"Shit."

"Yeah. Shit."

"What'd you do?"

"Whatever I could to smooth things over. Not with Giselle, of course. She crawled back into her hole, and cried. I hugged the girls until they quit crying. Carrie came over to take them to the movies. Next thing I knew, she'd roped me into taking them for her." He tapped his steering wheel with the heel of his hand. "I mean, I know Giselle's sad. She's lost a good man, the love of her life. But she's missed out on three months of her daughters' lives. They need her."

"It's past time she got some help," Bill growled. "Hell, I'm surprised she let you take the girls to the movies after that episode."

"Seriously, I doubt she cares one way or the other who takes them where right now. I expect after her little outburst, she cried herself to sleep, and woke up as completely despondent as she has been for the last three months."

Bill spent the rest of the trip to Kenton wondering what he could do to help.

As soon as the Avalanche pulled into Giselle's driveway, Bill stepped out. He opened Mac's door, unbuckled her seat belt, and roused her from her nap. He kissed her on the forehead and lowered her to the ground so she could walk sleepily to the kitchen door. She waited there, as though afraid to go in.

Jackson released Lexie's seatbelt before waking her. Still half asleep, she automatically reached for his neck, wanting him to carry her inside. He smiled and kissed her cheek as he carried her to the door where Mackenzie waited for him.

Bill climbed back into the front passenger seat and closed the door before turning up an old George Jones song on the radio station. He looked up, saw Giselle appear in the doorway and say something that had Mac moving closer to Jackson.

He watched the back and forth exchange between Jackson and Giselle, fighting the urge to lower his window and eavesdrop. When Jackson lowered Lexie to stand on her own, she moved behind him with Mac, as though using him for protection—from their mother? He opened the truck door to the sound of Giselle tearing into Jackson, her tone bitter and accusing.

"You can't be their father, Jackson, they already have a father!"

"I'm not try—"

"Yes, you are. And I don't give damn what Carrie asked you to do. I'm telling you *I* don't want you to see them anymore. No more movies. No more ball games." She reached out and jerked Mac and Lexie into the house by their hands.

"Mama, nooo!" Lexie wailed.

"We love Jackson and Bill. Please don't make them stop coming to see us. They're all we have!"

The tone of desperation in Mackenzie's pleading had Bill out of the truck in a second. He approached the conflict in time to see Giselle glare at Jackson while answering Mac with a viciousness he didn't think she'd possessed.

"You have me. Now say goodbye, girls. You won't be seeing him again."

Mackenzie pulled free from her mother's grip and cried out. "Noooo! I hate you!" Giselle turned on her then but Mac didn't back down. "You don't even love us anymore. You should be glad that Jackson and Bill want to watch us play ball and take us to movies. I bet daddy's glad! Daddy would have wanted us to be happy. Daddy wouldn't have minded if we said *your* name. I wish—I wish—"

Bill braced himself as Jackson spouted a warning. "Mac! Don't."

"I wish it had been *you* to die instead of daddy!" Mackenzie screamed.

Giselle grabbed her oldest daughter by the shoulders and leveled a glare at her. "Not half as much as I wish it."

Mackenzie twisted out of her mother's grip, and ran crying to her room, slamming the door behind her. Lexie stood there sobbing, and Jackson reached out for her, Giselle clasped her shoulder, pushing her back and away from him.

"Go to your room, Lex."

Lexie's frantic gaze jumped from Jackson to Giselle, then back to Jackson, her eyes wide, her lashes wet with tears, her plump cheeks covered with them. The child's struggle all too palpable—leave Jackson or stay and disobey her mom.

Jackson's fists clenched—no doubt to keep from reaching out to comfort the poor kid. "It's okay, Lex. I love you."

"J-J-ackson . . ."

Bill's chest constricted at Lexie's pitiful little voice, so full of sadness.

"Your room, Lex. Now." Giselle issued the command through clenched teeth.

Her little mouth quivering, and without another word or glance in her mother's direction, Lexie ran to her bedroom in tears. Sick to his stomach, Bill kept quiet. If he tried to mediate now, Giselle would accuse them of ganging up on her. Horrified, he watched the rest of the scene unfold.

"Please don't take this out on them," Jackson pleaded with her. "Can't you see they're hurting as much as you are?"

"I doubt that," she snarled. "Because of you they don't seem to even remember their father. You've made sure of that, haven't you?"

Jackson shot back, his tone hard and angry. "Oh, they remember him, Giselle. Didn't you hear Mac? They remember exactly what a wonderful father Toby was."

Giselle shook her head. "You're trying to replace him. They don't even talk about him anymore!"

Before Bill could warn him against it, Jackson stepped forward and grabbed her shoulders. "They *can't* talk about him here. Those girls are terrified to speak his name around you, because when they do you run to your room and hide."

"It's because of you!" She pulled out of his grip and pushed him back, trying to close the door in his face.

Jackson pushed back on the door and glared at her. "For God's sake, Giselle, are you so wrapped up in your own misery that you can't see their pain? Or is it the fact that they turned to *me* for comfort that upsets you so much?"

Bill winced. *Well shit, son—why don't you throw a little more gasoline on that fire?*

Giselle's glare turned icy. "Don't try to turn this around on me. This is your fault. Now, I mean it, Jackson. Don't you come around my girls again." She slammed the door. A second later he heard it lock.

Jackson stood there, his hands clenched, his entire body tensed, with his mouth open. He placed both palms flat on the door.

"Don't, son," Bill said. "You'll only make it worse. You can't reason with her now."

Jackson turned on him, his face tormented. "Did you hear what she said? What Mac said?"

Bill couldn't speak with the lump in his throat. He nodded.

"Lexie tried to come to me, but Giselle wouldn't let her. She was crying, they both were, and I couldn't do a damn thing about it. I feel so—so frustrated and—helpless."

Bill nodded again, swallowed the lump to speak. "I know you do, and so do I, but we can't fix this tonight. Let's go home and sleep on it. I'll drive."

Jackson nodded, climbed into the passenger seat of his own truck. His nephew stared blankly out the window as they drove in silence back to his place. Once there, Bill waited until Jackson entered his home before getting into his own truck.

Bill drove home, still sickened by the scene at Giselle's. He stormed into his house and threw his keys onto the counter. He hadn't expected that reaction from her—and Jackson—good God. His nephew, even living all those years with that lunatic wife of his, hadn't been the least bit prepared.

But then, Jack had never really loved Chloe. Hell, Bill had known that as far back as the wedding. No way had his nephew totally invested his heart into that woman. Oh, the potential had been there, at first. But Chloe had crushed that with a lie and her demand for him to make a choice. His nephew, ever the gentleman, ever gallant, had thrown his hat into Chloe's ring. Totally committed to his wife, he remained steadfast and loyal to the end.

But Mac and Lexie—those two little girls had crawled into both his and Jackson's hearts, found their spots and taken up permanent residency. Jackson had only been trying to help. Trying to fill a void. Not the void left by their father's death—but their mother's. Because sure as shit, taking a blow like that to your soul, losing someone *that* close to you, your other half—well, that pain felt like death. Worse than death, for a while.

His nephew didn't know that.

But Bill did.

He picked up his phone, punched in Carrie's number, and waited. He heard her voice on the other end of the line and took a deep breath.

"It's time."

* * * * *

They rang her bell the next morning. Giselle opened the door, and stared at him.

Bill stood tall, straight, hat in hand. "Hello Giselle."

She shot him a suspicious glare. "Bill."

He slapped his Stetson against his thigh, more than a little nervous at the task he'd taken on. "Honey, I've got something to tell you that may help you to gain a little perspective—"

She raised her hand. "Don't say you know how I feel, because you couldn't possibly."

Bill smiled. "You don't know how badly I wish that were true. What I'm about to tell you, I've not told to another living soul in close to four decades. How about you let Carrie take the girls to her house for a while?"

She squinted slightly, and her brow furrowed—revealing the war within her. A battle between her curious nature and her need to be left alone in her misery. She turned to her daughters, who stood waiting like two beautiful, somber, little porcelain dolls, and gave them a nod.

Mackenzie approached Bill for a hug, sent her mother a glare, a dare to stop her. Bill wanted to cheer for her little act of rebellion but kept quiet. It wouldn't do to give Giselle any more material for the wall she'd already constructed against common sense.

Lexie stopped in front of him, stole a glance at her mom. Bill leaned closer to hug her tightly.

"Tell Jackson I love him," Lexie whispered in his ear.

He smiled at her, brushed his hand over her plump, tear streaked cheek. "He already knows, but I'll tell him anyway."

Her lip trembled as she nodded, setting her golden curls into motion.

Carrie stepped forward to give Giselle a hug. "I don't know what he's got to say, but hear him out, honey. I know he's got your best interest at heart, or he wouldn't be here." She turned toward her truck, pausing long enough to squeeze Bill's arm and whisper a hasty "Good luck."

Alone in the kitchen with Giselle, he took the seat she offered him along with a mug of steaming coffee. She settled herself across from him at the kitchen table and waited.

Bill calmed his inner turmoil and began to speak, trying to keep his tone emotionless and steady. He told her about leaving home after graduation, travelling across the country and finally finding Lorraine. Talking about their first months together brought a smile to his face, one that turned to tears when he described the horrific pain of losing his wife and unborn child. Speaking the words brought it all back. He closed his eyes against the image of his wife in the casket, cradling their son.

Bill faced her then. "Both she and our baby died and I never got to say goodbye." He put his head down for a moment to wipe his eyes. "I lost them two days before Christmas."

Giselle choked on a sob, raised her hand to cover her mouth.

He continued in a monotone voice, lost in the past. "My father in law flew my brother, Jamison, to Washington state to pick me up and drive me home."

He described meeting Elise, his new sister-in-law, and how happy she and Jamison were with their newborn son. How she placed Jackson in his arms and how having to take care of that baby changed everything for him—put it all into perspective.

Bill stood up and walked to the window overlooking the back yard. "My nephew and I had a strong bond. Five years later, when Jamison and Elise died in a car accident, of course I chose to raise him." He exhaled and wiped his eyes with his handkerchief.

Giselle couldn't choke back her sobs. "I'm so sorry, Bill."

"My boy would be two months younger than Jackson. We were going to name him William Clayton Broussard, Jr., because Lorraine insisted that any boy with that name would be destined to grow up as fine as his daddy."

His voice broke slightly and he wiped his eyes again. "It's always a part of me, Giselle, but I had to move on. I had to leave it behind me so I could live the life I knew she wanted for me. I guess that's why I never bothered telling Jackson." He returned to his seat at the table.

She wiped her eyes and sniffed. "Jackson doesn't know?"

"As he got older, I didn't see the need. And after his folks died—well, it was him and me, and that's all that mattered. He was my boy after that. I've never let him forget either of his parents. They were wonderful people. Jackson doesn't remember much, but he remembers some." He placed a hand over his heart. "He knows enough to keep a part of them here, where they belong."

"Did he grieve for them?"

"Oh sure. We both did, but there's nothing as bad as a child losing his, or her, parent. You see, that's why Jackson relates to your girls so easily. He understands that they need to be able to talk about their dad, so that when they think of him, they can remember the joy he brought to their lives. I never met Toby, but from what Jackson says, he was a wonderful father and husband. You owe his daughters the chance to remember him with love.

So, you see, I *do* know your grief. I know you've lost the love of your life, but you're not done living. You'll find love again."

Giselle shook her head. "You didn't."

"I never found anyone willing to put up with me and Jackson in those early years, and he had to come first. Once I went in with a pal of mine and started a new oil company, I got too busy to settle down. That's not to say that I haven't had my share of female companionship, but nothing serious."

He flipped his hat to examine it. "I been thinkin' lately, maybe it's time I find someone. One of these days, you will too. Hopefully, it will happen sooner for you. Until then, you take care of those girls. In time you'll think about Toby and it'll hurt less. Eventually, you'll only remember the good times and none of the pain. In my opinion, the Lord does that so we don't die of sadness." He paused to sip his coffee.

Giselle reached out to touch his hand resting on the table. "I'm sorry, Bill."

"It's alright, hon. I just want you to understand that God puts people in our paths for a reason. I know the reason he put Jackson and me in yours was so we could help your girls through this. When they're with us, they talk about all the fun they had with their daddy. We allow them to remember him with love, with joy in their hearts. And isn't that what you want for them?"

She choked up at his words, able only to nod at him.

"Then, for God's sake, don't make them feel like they can't speak of him in their own home where you were all so happy. Put *their* grief before your own, and yours will disappear."

Giselle's head dropped forward on the table. Her tears, quiet at first, progressed into long, loud, body-wracking sobs. The kind that free the soul of suppressed sadness and excruciating pain.

Bill wrapped her in his strong, comforting arms, and held her while she cried.

Her sobs subsided eventually and she wiped her swollen eyes. "My babies," she groaned. "What have I done to my poor children?" She turned tear-filled eyes to Bill. "How can they ever forgive me?"

Bill handed her a box of tissues. "Hon, they'll be so glad to have their mama back, they'll forget everything else."

"Mac said she hated me. She was right, too, when she said Toby would have taken better care of them if I'd been the one to go. He never would have let this happen."

"What happened was meant to happen. It's all tiny threads woven into the fabric of your life. It's all part of God's plan and you have to trust he knows what's best for you. Mac didn't mean it any more than you did."

"I pray you're right, Bill." She groaned again. "I said such awful things to Jackson. How can I ever face him?"

"Don't worry about the rest of us. We all know what you were going through. He just wants to see you back to your old self so you can tend to your daughters. Those girls of yours sure have found a place in our hearts."

Giselle wiped her eyes. "I know you both mean a lot to them, and you two are welcome to be a part of their lives."

"Thank you for that." His voice deepened with emotion. "I know they don't have a grandpa of their own, but I'd be honored if you'd let me treat them as if they were my grandchildren."

She studied him. "Are you sure, Bill? What if Jackson meets someone and has children of his own? Wouldn't you want *them* to think of you as your grandfather?"

Bill stood, stretching his tall frame to his full height. "Of course, I would. People have more than one set of grandchildren all the time; by blood, by marriage, or by adoption. I have enough love to spare for as many grandchildren as I'm blessed with." He placed his hat back on his head. "And for God's sake, please give me a reason not to be so damn jealous of Sam Langley."

Giselle slapped her hand over her mouth to stop the laugh that popped out of her. She looked up at Bill, and let it burst forth. She finally stopped laughing, sat back in her chair and dabbed at her eyes with a tissue. "Oh, that felt good." She squeezed his hand. "I don't know how to thank you." She quieted then smiled. "How would you like it if my girls started calling you Grandpa Bill?"

Bill grinned. "Make it 'Paw Paw' and you've got yourself a deal."

She nodded. "Paw Paw, it is."

"Paw Paw Bill—I do like the sound of that. Thank you, hon, you've made me one happy old man today. Just wait until I tell Sam."

"You're not old, Bill. As a matter of fact, Carrie's said on countless occasions if Sam hadn't stolen her heart, she could really go for some Bill Broussard, but you didn't hear that from me."

Bill sucked in his breath and grimaced. "Playing second fiddle to Sam Langley isn't quite the ego boost I was looking for, but I guess it'll have to do." He sat back down in his chair and stretched one of his long legs out in front of him. "What's the story with those two? Why didn't they ever have any children together? They've been together long enough."

"By the time they met, their children were older and Carrie couldn't have kids anymore. Those two really do have their own love story, though. Maybe she'll tell you about it someday."

Bill gave her a nod. "I bet that's a story I'd find interesting. Should we call her back now?"

She nodded and made the call. Within five minutes, they heard the slam of car doors in the drive.

They stood and hugged. When he pulled away, Giselle placed her hand on his face. “Thank you, Bill.”

“You’re welcome, hon.” He turned to the door. “I’ll leave, so you and those girls can have some privacy.”

“Oh, but can you wait around for a few minutes? I want you and Carrie to be here after I straighten things out with Mac and Lex.”

He nodded. “I’ll send them in to you.”

Bill met the others out on the patio. Mac and Lex went to him, both casting cautious looks at the closed door. He embraced both girls, assuring them—encouraging them to go to her. Once they’d gone inside he turned to Carrie. “She’ll be fine now.”

Carrie reached out to cover his hands with her own. “I don’t know what you told her, but I know it had to be difficult for you, and I’m so thankful.”

He gave her a sly look. “Enough to leave Sam for me?”

She pushed his hands away and laughed. “Be serious, Bill.”

“It don’t cost a thing to ask, and all you can do is turn me down one more time.”

Carrie wiped tears of laughter from her eyes as she gazed up at him. “You and Jackson should put a patent on those sexy grins of yours, you know. They’re absolutely irresistible.”

He raised a brow as he pulled the patio chair out for her. “Have you reconsidered?”

“Nearly irresistible,” she corrected, as they sat at the patio table. “I’ve already found the love of my life, but that doesn’t mean we can’t find someone for you. You interested?”

He pulled his hat off and placed it on the glass topped table. “Maybe it’s time. Got anyone in mind?”

“I’d have to think on it.” She leaned her elbows on the table and tapped her tooth with a fingernail. “Hmm … what kind of woman would be right for you?”

“I could do with a young grandmotherly type, kind of like you.” He sent her a wink.

Carrie chuckled as she shook her head. “I appreciate the compliment, honey, but, you can do better. Have you thought about someone young enough to give you a child of your own?”

Bill's brow furrowed as he pondered the question. "I'd like that, but I really didn't think it was an option for me."

"Why not? You're healthy, aren't you?"

"My doc just told me I had the heart of a man twenty years younger. I don't smoke, I lift weights, and swim laps every day to keep in shape, I only drink occasionally, and I do all my own work around the ranch."

Carrie leaned back in her chair and crossed her arms loosely. "At the risk of inflating your ego, you and Jackson are two of the finest looking men I've ever known. When it comes to sex appeal, you easily hold your own against men half your age."

"You really think so?"

"Yep, and I think you should consider children," she said.

Bill sat back in his chair. He ran a hand through his hair and released his breath in a slow hiss. "All right then, let's do it. My life is in your hands. What do you need me to do?"

She smiled and gave his hand an affectionate pat. "Sit back and watch the gears turn, Bill. I'll take care of you."

The door flew open and Mac and Lexie burst through, giggling and grinning from ear to ear. The two little girls ran to Bill's outstretched arms, as combined squeals of "Paw Paw!" filled the air.

"Is it true? Are you our Paw Paw now?"

Bill beamed down at them. "I am if you want me to be."

"We've never had a Paw Paw before," Lexie said.

Mackenzie raised hopeful brown eyes to Bill. "Would that make Jackson our uncle, or our daddy—" She spread her hands, "Or what?"

"How about if you just call him Jackson, for now?" Giselle offered. "I'm sure he'd be fine with that."

"We have a Paw Paw Bill, *and* a Jackson!" Mackenzie squealed. "I can't wait to tell everyone that my birthday party is going to be at my Paw Paw Bill's house."

"Paw Paw Bill's *ranch*," he corrected her.

Mackenzie's eyes grew large with excitement. "Lex, our Paw Paw has a real ranch with cows and horses."

"And mini horses and piggy goats!" Lexie contributed.

"And a pond we can fish in," Mac finished.

"I also ordered paddle boats for your party," Bill added. "They'll be ours to keep so you can use them anytime."

Mackenzie threw herself at him again. "I can tell already, you're going to be the best Paw Paw in the world." She turned to her mother. "Can we call Jackson? I can't wait to tell him we're his family now."

Giselle sucked in her breath and made a face. "Um, not just yet. I think I need to speak to him first then I'll let you talk to him. You two go inside with Bill and Carrie, okay?"

Bill followed the girls into the kitchen, his shoulders sagging with relief. Carrie joined him seconds later, all tension erased from her face. "I think she'll be fine, now."

"I think you're right. Thanks again, Bill."

The kitchen filled with excited chatter until Giselle entered.

Lexie faced her mom. "Did you talk to Jackson, Mama?"

"No sweetie, he must still be sleeping. I'll call him later."

Lexie's face crumbled in disappointment. "I bet he's still *appressed* after yesterday. Can we go see him?"

Giselle brushed her daughter's bangs back from her pixie face. "I think I need to talk to him first before you see him again, Sweetie."

"Can you hurry, Mama? He looked so sad the last time I saw him."

"I'll keep trying, Lex, I promise." After Lexie ran off, Giselle turned to Bill. "I think I need to go over there. He sounded out of it, like hung-over or something."

Carrie threw Bill a cautious glance. "I don't know if that's such a good idea. The last time I talked to him, he said he was on his way to an all-nighter with a bottle of Crown. Sounds like he accomplished his goal."

Bill frowned. "Jackson hardly ever drinks. He had to be hurting to pull one that bad."

Giselle chewed on the corner of her thumbnail. "I can't stand this. I need to apologize to his face."

Carrie's gaze shifted from Giselle, to Bill, then back to Giselle. "I really wish you'd let him sleep it off."

Giselle paced the floor between them and her fridge. "I feel guilty, Carrie. Can you understand that?"

"You could follow me over there," Bill suggested. "That way I can be there to make sure he's okay. He was some kind of upset when we drove home yesterday."

Giselle grabbed Carrie's hands. "Could I bother you one more time to watch the girls for me? You can bring them to your place."

Carrie released a long sigh. "All right, but this goes against my better judgment."

Giselle clasped her hands together. "Thank you. Let me get my purse."

* * * *

Bill pulled into Jackson's drive thirty minutes later, followed closely by Giselle. He rang the doorbell several times without getting an answer. Using his key, he let himself and Giselle inside.

"Wow. I love what he did in here," Giselle whispered.

Bill collected the nearly empty bottle of aged ninety-proof whiskey he'd given Jackson last Christmas. "New furniture. Old whiskey. Said he was gonna save it for a special occasion." He turned to Giselle and grinned as he raised the bottle in the air. "Congratulations." She had the decency to look ashamed. He sniffed at the half empty glass on a sturdy end table and made a face. "Straight." *Oh. Shit.*

Bill turned to her, prepared for the worst. "Might be a good idea for you to wait outside. I need to see what kind of shape he's in."

She nodded and stepped outside.

Bill walked down the hallway, calling out to his nephew. He got to the bedroom, heard the shower cut off in the attached master bath. "I'm here, Jackson!" he called through the door. It opened seconds later and Jackson emerged, freshly shaved and showered, a towel wrapped around his hips.

Jackson brushed by without looking at him, using a hand towel to dry his dripping hair. "Excuse me. I'm thirsty as hell." He sounded like he'd gargled with a mouth full of gravel.

Bill chuckled under his breath. He'd awakened sounding like that more mornings than he cared to remember. He paid a quick visit to the restroom while he waited, surveying the condition of the bedroom on his way there. No signs of liquor and the bed still made. Jackson had probably passed out on that big leather couch of his. He'd just finished his business and zipped up when Jackson re-entered the bedroom, his face flushed.

"I don't know why the hell Giselle's here, but the neighbor's dog went after her," he growled.

"Shit!" Bill flew out of the room, as the bedroom door slammed behind him. He entered the living room, saw Giselle leaning against the front door, her face as flushed as Jackson's. That damn dog's incessant barking and snarling carrying through from the other side of the heavy slab of oak.

Her gaze locked on his as she pointed over her shoulder toward the door. "There's a dog. A big dog."

"Are you hurt? Did he bite you?" Bill walked toward her and the door.

"N-no-no," she stammered, still plastered against the door.

He gently moved her away from the door then jerked it open, lunging for the stupid dog. "Get out of here you son of a bitch!" It ran off, saving Bill the trouble of kicking its ass all the way to the curb. "Every stinking time I come over here, that dog's loose. I kicked it in the face once so he's got enough sense not to come after me."

He closed the door and faced her but Giselle didn't answer, her gaze had already locked on Jackson's as he re-entered the room, wearing jeans and a white T-shirt, feet bare, his hair uncombed. She jumped when he barked at his nephew. "That damned dog is a menace!"

Jackson ignored him, walked up to Giselle and stopped. "Are you okay?"

She nodded, looking away from him as a blush crept up her neck. Jackson's gaze stayed on Giselle's as Bill attacked the subject of the dog again.

"Who does that damn Doberman belong to, Jackson? That's the third time this month I've seen him out of his yard and off his leash, and I don't even live here."

Jackson finally tore his gaze from Giselle to look at him. "I've been meaning to talk to my neighbor about him."

"What if Mac and Lexie had been here?" Bill demanded.

Jackson's gaze travelled from Bill, to Giselle, then back to Bill. His tone hardened. "Why would the girls be here?" His gaze landed once more on Giselle. "Come to think of it, why are *you* here?"

Bill watched, fascinated at their silent perusals of each other. It came to him that Giselle had seen Jackson half-naked only moments before. Besides being blessed with good genes and an athletic frame, Bill had worked out with his nephew enough to know he was no slouch in that department. He wondered suddenly if the towel had come loose. *Nah—if it had Jackson wouldn't be standing here.*

Bill studied Giselle, recognizing the lustful gaze of a woman when he saw it. He wiped his face, trying to conceal the smile as the situation played out before him like a Saturday evening matinee. The vibes in this room—the pure animal attraction—thick enough to provide that Danielle Steel broad with enough fodder for an entire series of romance novels. And they sure as shit didn't need him in there as a third wheel.

He slipped out of the room, as quietly as he could, leaving the two of them to work things out amongst themselves. He waited until he got to his truck and started it before letting the low chuckle roll over him. By the time he backed out of the drive, it'd developed into a full-blown guffaw of laughter. He pictured the two of them alone in that room together—her, staring at Jackson, standing there in nothing but that towel. He almost called Carrie to let her know, but decided it was too damn juicy to do anything but keep it to himself.

Chapter Seventeen

Celebrations and Awakenings

Bill had just opened his door when the phone started ringing. He grinned, seeing Carrie's name flash across his caller ID. "Hello, hon."

"You really need to get a cell phone, Bill! I'm dying over here, wondering how it went with Giselle and Jackson. Was he all right? What happened when y'all got there? Did she talk to him?"

Bill tackled her questions in chronological order. "I don't *want* a damn cell phone. He was good and hung over. His neighbor's Doberman went after her but she's fine. And finally, they were talking when I left."

"You left them alone together?"

He chuckled. "Trust me, it was the right thing to do. Don't worry about either of them, Carrie. It'll be golden from here on out."

"You sure?"

"I've got a gut feeling," he said. "They'll be fine."

"Oh, okay then. I trust you. We'd put off our annual Mother's Day lunch until Giselle was out of her funk because they've spent it with us the last few years. We decided today was a good day to celebrate, so I'm calling to invite you and Jackson over for lunch. Sam and the boys are outside barbequing now. Come on over whenever you're ready. It's BYOB."

"Sounds good Carrie." He ended the call and pictured Jackson and Giselle as he'd left them less than fifteen minutes earlier. Hell yeah. He wouldn't miss their next meeting for the world.

* * * * *

Nearly two dozen people attended Sam and Carrie's backyard barbeque. Their house, deck and yard nearly burst at the seams with all five of their kids, including spouses, and every last grandchild.

Jackson checked his watched. "Where the hell is Giselle?" he asked for the dozenth time that day.

Bill studied his nephew, still grinning over what he'd witnessed earlier that morning. "Maybe you ought to go over to her house and pick her up." He wondered what the odds were of Giselle answering *her* door, fresh from a shower, and wrapped in a towel.

"That's actually a good idea." Carrie approached the two of them. "Why don't you go see if she's awake, Jackson?"

Bill sent Carrie a grin when his nephew jumped out of his chair to do her bidding.

Carrie's gaze narrowed on Bill. "What's up with that smug grin?"

"Not a thing." He watched Jackson disappear around the side of the house. Damn, but he'd have given anything to witness the towel scene earlier this morning.

She shook her head. "You're hiding something. And I bet it's juicy."

He'd contemplated telling her when Jackson appeared far sooner than he should have, holding Giselle's arm protectively as he escorted her to the back yard.

"Look who's here, everybody!" Jackson called out.

Lexie got to her first "Mama! Jackson and Paw Paw came."

Giselle stole a glance at Jackson before answering her daughter. "I see that, Lex. Have you eaten yet?"

Mac approached. "No, Sam just finished cooking the barbeque."

Bill and Carrie exchanged a glance as they observed the small group of four interacting.

Carrie spoke first, as though pulling the thought directly from his own mind. "That would be a good thing, wouldn't it?"

"Yeah. It would." He watched the younger women in the family as they swarmed around Giselle the second Jackson left her side.

* * * * *

The post-barbeque conversation gravitated to baseball, especially since seven of the eight children in attendance were playing in the recreational league.

Jackson took the empty lawn chair between Giselle and Bill. "Are you feeling up to making some of the girls' games yet?"

She nodded. "I'll make them from now on."

"And speaking of baseball," Carrie announced, "I heard this year's Summer Sizzler tournament has been scheduled for the second Saturday in August. Sam, they want you to call the games. You up to umpiring in hundred-degree heat again this year?"

"I guess I'll live for one day," Sam groaned.

Jackson leaned forward. "How are the teams formed?"

"Area contractors form teams by cities," Sam explained. "I've seen years when we have five or more teams, and I've seen some lean years when only two showed up. I know the Lake Coburn team could use some new blood."

Bill decided to shine a little light on his nephew. "You know Jackson played some college ball." He planted his gaze on him. "Are you going to play this year?"

"You played college ball? Where'd you play?" Amanda's husband, Joe, asked.

Jackson cleared his throat and mumbled an unclear reply.

"I'm sorry, I didn't understand you, Jackson. Who'd you play for?" Joe repeated.

"L.S.U." Bill answered for Jackson. "Louisiana State University."

"Really? What year was that?" Joe asked, as everyone leaned forward to listen.

"I only played one year, nearly twenty years ago."

Bill grinned. *Too humble, considering the kid's accomplishment.* "But it was a hell of a year," he added.

"What position?" Joe asked.

"I pitched, until my injury."

"Wait a minute—my step dad and I went to watch L.S.U. play around that time," Joe said. "They had a freshman pitcher who blew his shoulder out after pitching a no-hitter the last regular game of the season. A Broussard, and real tall. Was that you?"

"Afraid so," Jackson admitted.

"All this time you've worked with Carrie and Sam and we didn't know. Man, you were a hell of a player. That shoulder injury of yours was a tragedy."

Jackson shrugged. "Unfortunate—not tragic."

"So, that's it. You never played again?"

"Nope. That ended my short-lived career. After I had the surgery and completed physical therapy, they wanted me to play first base, but I only ever wanted to pitch. Besides, they already had the best first baseman." He shrugged. "That's when I changed my major to engineering. I hadn't really thought about what I'd do with my life until then."

"If you hadn't blown out your shoulder, we never would have met you," Carrie said. "So, are you thinking about playing?"

"I just might. Do they call practices? I'm kind of rusty," Jackson admitted.

"Practices!" Sam laughed. "No, they just show up and pray they don't hurt themselves. Relax, you're in good shape."

Amanda coughed. "Understatement." A ripple of laughter ran through the women.

Talk of baseball eventually turned into an impromptu backyard game of baseball using equipment Sam had accumulated in the past couple years he'd maintained the town's baseball park after retirement. Everyone joined in, except for Carrie, her youngest granddaughter, Ava, and Giselle, who acted as the cheering section. Jackson proved he hadn't lost any of his athletic abilities, hitting several over the fence, to his team's delight.

When it finally broke up, Jackson and Bill volunteered to drop off Giselle and her girls. Bill hugged them and promised to be at their next game, then returned to his seat to observe Jackson and Giselle at the door. They spoke, but her gaze darted all over the place—landing anywhere but on Jackson until she finally stepped inside, closing the door softly in his face.

Jackson stared at the door for a second, then turned and caught his gaze. He lifted both arms and dropped them before making his way back to the truck. He climbed in behind the wheel, threw the truck into reverse and backed out of the drive, his face tight with worry.

"What's wrong?" Bill asked him.

"I have no idea."

"What do you mean? Did she say we couldn't go to the game on Tuesday?"

Jackson backed out onto the street and put the truck into drive. "No, we're picking them up on our way in."

"What is it, then?"

"I don't know. She won't look me in the eye."

Bill could only imagine the thoughts running through Giselle's mind. "She keeps seeing you in that towel."

"I doubt that," Jackson mumbled.

Bill's chest rumbled with laughter. "I'm telling you, she keeps seeing you in all your glory. Didn't you see her ogling you? She couldn't force herself to turn away. The temperature in that room must've jumped twenty degrees. Got so hot I had to leave the premises."

Jackson turned on him. "Yeah, we noticed you'd left."

"Humph. I'm willing to bet it took a while. The two of you were so deep in it, I could have been doing one of Mac's cheers in a corner and you wouldn't have noticed."

Jackson shook his head. "It's got to be something else that's bothering her."

Bill dissolved into side-splitting laughter. "Whatever you say, Jackson."

* * * * *

Bill accompanied Jackson to Mac and Lexie's games the next couple of weeks. They always picked up Giselle and the girls on the way. Eventually, Giselle relaxed around Jackson and the two of them developed an easy banter. Bill had to miss a week's worth of the girls' ballgames, three games total, due to a business meeting. He returned, anxious to see them again, but found Jackson as frustrated over Giselle as ever.

"She barely speaks to me," Jackson explained. "She's afraid people will get the wrong idea if we're friends, like she's moved on from Toby's death after just five months."

Bill figured it had to be more than that, so he called Carrie to catch him up to speed on the situation.

"It was all innocent, really," Carrie explained to Bill. "Two adults, Giselle and Jackson, taking four hungry little girls to supper at a local restaurant after a ballgame. But Giselle overheard the town tramp making snide remarks—insinuating that she and Jackson were *seeing* each other with Toby barely cold in his grave."

"So, Giselle pulled away from Jackson," Bill finished, "to keep people from thinking she'd thrown the memory of her dead husband aside for someone new." He got it now… Giselle's refusal to share rides, to speak to Jackson, or sit near him in the bleachers. "Nothing we can do but wait it out."

Weeks of waiting turned into more than a month. Jackson, frustrated with Giselle's coldness, spent more time at the gym, his bulging muscles proof of diligent work-outs. Bill played the part of silent observer, his patience pushed to the limits. He planned Mac and Lexie's joint party, eagerly anticipating the event, and feeling in his gut that it would be pivotal in bringing everything to a head.

The Saturday before the party showed promise of a beautiful day for Mac's first tournament of the season. Jackson and Bill were halfway there when Jackson's phone rang. "It's Giselle." He put the phone on speaker.

"My car won't start! I tried to call Sam, but I can't get a hold of him, and everyone else is either on vacation or at the tournament already."

"Sam and Carrie are in Gardiner for the day, I know that for certain," Jackson told her. "It's probably just the battery. We're only a few minutes from you, so just hang tight."

Ten minutes later, Jackson lowered the hood of her SUV. He placed the dead battery in the bed of his truck. "If you ride with us to the tournament, we can pick up a new battery for you and install it when we get back later this afternoon." He used a wipe from a package in his truck to clean his hands. "You should be safe enough," he muttered, glaring at her. "Bill will be with us the entire time."

Stiff backed, Giselle thanked him and buckled Lexie into a booster seat in the back seat of Jackson's truck.

"I want Paw Paw Bill to ride in the back with me!" Lexie cried out.

Bill complied and sat back there, thrilled to watch the exchange as Giselle slid into the front seat next to Jackson. He grinned. *This should make for an interesting prequel to the birthday party.*

* * * * *

"Has Jackson been working out?" Gretchen asked.

Bill crossed his arms and grunted at Carrie's daughter once they reached the field where the girls would be playing. "It seems like every time I call him, he's at the gym."

Lauren joined them and dropped her folding chairs on the ground. She reached over to give Bill a hug. "I just saw Jackson on the way back to his truck. He's definitely been working out."

Bill chuckled. “He’s trying to stay busy—I guess it keeps him from thinking about things too much.”

“Here he comes.” Gretchen pointed, and they all turned to watch him. He walked up, loaded down with at least six strapped bags containing folding chairs, no sign of breathing hard or breaking a sweat.

“Who wants a chair? I brought everything I had.”

“I’ll take one.” Gretchen reached for one. “Let’s set them up under the tree for some shade.”

Jackson set the chairs in a line and sat down in one on the end. After everyone else had taken a seat, Giselle took the remaining one next to Jackson. He got up immediately to go to the concession stand. He came back with several bottles of water and passed them around, before asking Bill to switch chairs with him.

Giselle smiled at Bill when he sat beside her, but she couldn’t hide her hurt feelings. Within minutes, Lauren’s little girl, Ava Grace, made her way over to Jackson to flirt shamelessly with him. By the time the game began, the toddler wouldn’t sit with anyone but him.

When someone suggested Jackson needed to have kids of his own one day, Bill had to agree. He’d noticed Giselle watching the interaction between Jackson and the little girl—had even recorded some video and pictures on her digital camera. She finally weighed in.

“I told him we could find him a wife so he could have some of his own, but he insisted he could find his own woman.”

“That’s right, when I’m ready to move, I will. Don’t you worry about me.” He riveted his gaze on Giselle.

She adjusted her sunglasses and looked at Bill. “Speaking of which, ladies, we need to find someone for this fine-looking gentleman on my left.”

Lauren spoke up. “How about Ms. Clair Bertrand.”

Gretchen leaned over to look at her twin. “Ms. Clair from admitting? She’s too old for Bill. We need to find somebody younger, who can give him children. Right, Bill?”

He shrugged. “I’d like kids, but if it doesn’t happen I’ll be satisfied to have someone of my own. I’ve got Mac and Lexie, and I’m sure Jackson will furnish me with a great niece or nephew one day.”

"Hmph." Jackson mumbled something unintelligible under his breath.

"What was that, son?"

"I said I hope that happens real soon, Uncle Bill," Jackson piped up.

* * * * *

Later, on the way home from the tournament, Giselle sat in the back seat with Mac and Lexie. Jackson and Bill installed the new battery in her truck, and she thanked them both when it cranked up easily. She avoided any kind of contact with Jackson, but hugged Bill before she went inside her house, closing the door behind her.

"Well, that's interesting." Bill climbed into the truck and buckled his seatbelt.

"What's that?" his nephew asked.

"She can barely look you in the eye."

Jackson shifted to reverse and backed slowly out of her driveway. "Noticed that, did you? I have no idea what I did to piss her off this time."

"Giselle's not pissed. She's attracted to you."

Jackson hit the brakes at the intersection and faced him. "You are so off the mark on this one, Uncle Bill. That lady can't stand the sight of me."

Bill released a loud sigh and shook his head. "One of these days you're going to learn to listen to me. I'm telling you, she's attracted to you. And don't even try to deny you feel the same way."

Jackson's gaze turned hard. "She's the widow of a good friend. I only try to help her out when she lets me, and only because Toby would want me to."

Bill dragged the fingers of one hand roughly through his hair, frustrated as hell with all this denial. "Bullshit! You can lie to yourself if you want to, but you can't lie to me. I know what I see."

A car behind them blew the horn and Jackson turned toward the highway. "Fine, dammit. I'm attracted to her—a fat lot of good it does me. Are you happy now?"

Bill gave a loud guffaw of laughter. "I was right."

Jackson threw him a disgusted snort. “You always are, you old coot. And it’s damned disconcerting, if you want to know the truth.”

“Dis-con-what? Talk English. I’m just a simple man.”

“It’s ass-chapping, okay? It chaps my ass, the way you’re always right.”

“I’m just older and wiser in the ways of the world.”

“Yeah. What the hell ever.”

Bill put his head back and laughed. “It’s like Sam always says, Son. There’s *all* kinds of smart.”

“Maybe so, but I think you’re wrong about Giselle being attracted to me. If she is, she’s got a hell of a way of showing it. I’m about fed up with her damn attitude.”

“An intelligent man would try to see it through her eyes. Think about it, Jackson. Toby’s been dead for just over seven months and she feels guilty for being attracted to another man, not to mention terrified of what others will think. If you’d been sitting where I was, you’d have noticed she was a bundle of nerves by the end of the day.”

Bill shook his head, slightly annoyed at his nephew’s foot-dragging handling of the situation. “Your generation has mastered the art of wasting time. I’d have thought you and Giselle would see the senselessness of that after what you’d both gone through. By the way, you hurt her feelings when you switched chairs on her.”

“I didn’t do it to hurt her feelings. I just didn’t want to embarrass myself. There’s no way I could stare at those long, tanned legs of hers all day and not—you know.” He adjusted himself. Bill responded with a low chuckle that escalated into a knee slapping belly laugh. Jackson adjusted the adjustment, obviously annoyed at Bill’s reaction to his predicament.

Jackson gripped the steering wheel with both hands. “You don’t know, man. Every time I see her lately, it’s agony. You have no idea how much I dread tomorrow.” He shook his head slowly. “For me, the only thing worse than seeing Giselle—Is *not* seeing Giselle.”

Bill yawned, and leaned against the door. He lowered his hat over his eyes and crossed his arms to catch some shut-eye. The first step to fixing a problem? Admit you have one. He figured

Giselle and Jackson had both tackled that today. It would be interesting as hell to see how the rest of this story unfolded.

Chapter Eighteen

Someone for Bill

The first luminous rays of dawn broke on a cloudless sky, promising a glorious day for Mac and Lexie's party. Guests started arriving around eleven thirty to food tables, loaded down with barbeque and side dishes. Servers urged everyone to line up, buffet style.

"Paw Paw!" Mac and Lexie ran to Bill.

"There are my two birthday girls!"

"We wanted to come and thank you for doing all of this for us," Mac said. "I can't wait for the paddle boat rides."

"We'll start them right after lunch, so you'd better go eat." Bill smiled as he watched them run off.

Giselle approached and gave him an appreciative hug. "Bill, the girls are thrilled. I don't know what kind of day they would have had without this."

Bill knew she referred to her daughters' first birthdays without their dad. He placed his hands on her shoulders. "Jackson and I would do anything for you three. You know that, right?"

"I do, and I love you for that."

His smile widened. *But do you feel the same way about Jackson?*

Carrie joined them. "Come on, you two, let's get in line."

As they settled down at a table with their plates, Jackson approached with one of the most beautiful women Bill had ever laid eyes on. His nephew introduced her as Gwen—Bill didn't get the rest of her name because he was too focused on the fair complexioned, dark-haired, blue-eyed beauty. About 5'8" and curvy—the kind of curvy that a man could snuggle up to. He figured Jackson had brought her here for him.

Bill glanced over at Giselle, noticed the frown playing at the corners of her mouth, and decided she could use a healthy dose of jealousy. Gwen, who had a seven-year-old named Alyssa in Mac's grade, sat beside Giselle. She took the initiative and introduced herself to her. "Hi, you're Mac and Lexie's mom, right?"

Giselle nodded, her mouth a little tight. "Giselle Granger, nice to meet you, Gwen."

"Same here. Alyssa was thrilled with the invitation to the party. Thank you so much."

"Sure." Giselle's brow furrowed, as though she didn't quite remember inviting the woman.

Bill watched the scene with a vested interest. As the conversation between Jackson and Gwen deepened, so did Giselle's frown. *Nothing like a little competition to fuel the fires of interest.*

"So, Gwen," Giselle picked up a barbequed rib. "Where's Alyssa's father? Is he at home?" Conversation at the table came to a grinding halt, followed by an uncomfortable silence. All eyes turned toward Giselle.

Gwen cleared her throat before elaborating on that particular line of questioning. "I'm actually Alyssa's aunt, Giselle. Her father was my younger brother, David. He and his wife were killed in a boating accident six years ago and I've raised her since then. She calls me mom because she doesn't remember her parents."

Giselle blushed, clearly ashamed of herself. "I'm so sorry. I didn't know. Do you have family around to help?"

Gwen shrugged. "My father died when I was in grade school, and my mom passed away from cancer three years ago. I've never been married. I was engaged at the time of the accident, but my fiancé said he didn't want to raise another couple's child." She raised both her hands and let them fall. "That was that."

Gwen's story nearly flattened Bill in its familiarity.

Jackson gave a low grunt. "I bet it's been rough for you two."

"It's not always easy. I mean, I make do financially as a single parent. I work as an accountant at the Kenton Hospital. The pay isn't great, but at least I'm home at a decent hour for Alyssa." She turned to Giselle. "You know how it is. I wish I could be home more for her. Do better for her."

Jackson reached out to place a comforting hand over her wrist. "Maybe one day that'll happen for you."

Bill had to hide his grin when Giselle practically winced at the sight. He smothered his laughter when she pushed her plate of food away. The sight of the man she wanted fawning over another woman had sure as shit killed her appetite.

He tuned in on Gwen, thirty-nine and dreading her fortieth birthday just around the corner.

Carrie leaned forward. "Don't dread forty—forty was fabulous!"

"Not when you're husbandless, with no children of your own. I thought by forty I'd have all that tucked neatly under my belt. Don't get me wrong, I love Alyssa as if she's my own daughter, but I didn't get to experience childbirth. I feel like I'm running out of time."

"You're still young," Carrie insisted. "There are still good men out there who wouldn't mind starting a family."

"Not in my experience," Gwen confessed. "The few guys I've dated don't seem thrilled when they find out about Alyssa, and she has to come first right now."

Carrie faced Jackson. "You'd be surprised at the method God uses to bring two people together."

And *now* Bill knew who to thank for Gwen's appearance . . . and the reason behind it. He nearly crowed when Giselle's face turned pale. The poor woman looked like she needed a barf bucket. *Nice touch, Carrie.*

"This food is wonderful, isn't it?" Giselle said, a little too forcefully.

Sam turned to Bill. "It sure is. Who'd you hire to cater?"

Bill smothered his laughter at Giselle's obvious attempt to divert the conversation away from any suggestion of Jackson and Gwen as a couple. "A business that does all of our oil company's parties. They're used to serving large numbers of guests, so this was easy for them."

Jackson sneezed into his napkin, turned his head and sneezed again. "Excuse me, must be allergies."

"You're probably getting Ava's cold," Carrie snickered. "I heard how you let her kiss on you at the ballpark yesterday. That child is shamelessly rotten."

"I told Lauren to tell Bryan he's been replaced."

Carrie gave her head an emphatic shake. "You obviously haven't seen her with her daddy yet."

"I bet she has Bryan wrapped," Jackson said. "All those curls and her big brown eyes."

Gwen turned to Jackson, her gorgeous blue peepers sparkling with curiosity. “Are you talking about that adorable Shirley Temple look alike running around here?”

“That would be Ava Grace, our granddaughter,” Sam said. “She’s only one of seven grandchildren. And here are two more of them.”

Emmelia ran up with Allie and Lexie. “Can we go on the boats now? Is it time yet?”

“I want to see the little mini horses!” Allie said.

Lexie jumped up and down. “I want to see the piggy goats!”

Emmelia’s brow furrowed with lines of confusion. “What’s a piggy goat?”

Bill joined in on the laughter before explaining. “*Pygmy* goats are goats that stay small. I’ll tell you what, kids; give me five minutes to finish eating, and then we’ll start showing everybody the animals.”

“Okay,” Lexie said, before the three of them ran off.

Gwen looked around. “I didn’t know there were animals like that on this place. Who owns this ranch?”

Bill raised his hand, just about ready for to assume the leading man role. They obviously had lots in common. “That’d be me.”

“Cattle or horses?”

“A little of both,” he answered. “Do you ride?”

“Not in years, but I used to practically live on a horse.”

“I never would have thought that by looking at you,” Jackson said. “You don’t seem like that type of girl.”

“Afraid I am.” Gwen flashed his nephew a dimpled grin that had Bill sucking in his breath. Damn, he loved women with dimples. *One more thing to thank Carrie for when he got the chance.*

“It’s been awhile for me, too,” Jackson said, about riding.

Bill sat back in his chair. “Don’t let him fool you. He’s a natural horseman, and you don’t forget that.”

Jackson shook his head. “No, if you want to see a natural on a horse, it’s that man right there.” He pointed to Bill.

Gwen leveled her gaze on Bill. “Did you teach your son everything you knew about horses?”

"Jackson's my nephew, my brother's son. But yes, I tried to teach him everything I knew." He wiped his mouth on a napkin. "About riding, anyway."

Gwen's gaze flashed back and forth between uncle and nephew. "My goodness, you two look enough alike to be father and son, but I guess you've heard that before."

"My older brother, Jamison, and I looked a lot alike." Bill jerked his head toward Jackson. "Our story is similar to yours and Alyssa's. Jackson's parents were killed in a car accident a couple of months before his fifth birthday; I've thought of him as a son for thirty-three years."

"How old were you at the time?"

"I was twenty-four."

"But, that would make you fifty-seven years old." Gwen shook her head. "There's no way you could be that age—I thought you were in your mid-forties."

Bill had heard enough. The pretty lady had just handed him the ball and he planned to run with it. He beamed at her as he stood and made his way around to her side of the table. "Looks like we have a lot in common. How about we go find those girls, along with your Alyssa, and show them some animals?" He offered her his arm.

She took it and rose from her seat. "I'd love to."

The two of them were practically attached at the hip for the rest of the afternoon. She proved to be as knowledgeable and comfortable around the livestock as she'd claimed, turning into Bill's right hand when introducing the children to the animals. It didn't take long to realize he wanted to see a lot more of Gwendolyn Perry.

At day's end, Giselle approached Bill and hugged him. "I'm overwhelmed, Bill. You've made this day so special."

"Well, the three of you make me feel special every single time we see each other. It feels good to be able to return the favor." Mac and Lexie ran toward them and he leaned over to catch both girls, lifted them easily in his arms.

Mac laid her head on his shoulder. "Thank you for the best day ever."

"This was the best birthday party I've ever had, Paw Paw. I love you so much!" Lexie hugged his neck tightly.

"I love you too, my girls. The animals, the pond, and the boats are always here for you. You can come over anytime and bring your friends, too."

Mac's eyes sparkled with joy. "Even my new friend, Alyssa?"

"Sure, and tell her pretty mama to come along, too, while you're at it."

Mac's eyes widened with childish curiosity. "Do you like Miss Gwen, Paw Paw?"

Bill gave her a nod. "I sure do. Do you think I have a chance with her?"

Lexie nodded vigorously. "I heard her tell Carrie you were a fine looking hunkaman," she said in an exaggerated whisper. "I don't know what a hunkaman is, but I think it means she wants to be your girlfriend."

"Do you really think so?"

Lexie gave him a single, emphatic nod. "I think you need to marry her."

A deep chuckle rumbled through Bill's chest as he set both girls on the ground. He removed his straw Stetson, and passed a hand through his dark hair before leaning toward Lex. "How about if I ask her on a date first? You know, just to make sure we're compatible?"

"Okay, but you better hurry, Paw Paw," Lexie warned. "Some other guy might start to think she's patable too."

Bill tweaked her nose. "I wouldn't want that to happen. Thanks for looking out for me." He watched them run off before turning to Giselle. "They're something."

Giselle poked him in the chest. "Well, they happen to think you're something, Paw Paw Bill. And so do I, but—I have to wonder how Gwen's going to handle being called *Maw Maw*."

He sucked in his breath. "We'll cross that bridge when we get there—if—we even get there."

She put her fists on her hips and laughed. "I think I'll put my money on *when*, rather than if, Bill. Good luck, Mr. Broussard."

"Thank you, Giselle. But I don't believe in luck. I do, however, believe in skills."

At six o-clock, they met up with the remaining members of Sam and Carrie's family. The children were all exhausted from playing hard, pink from too much sun, and quickly running out of fuel.

"Bill, this was a blast," Carrie said. "I'd have never guessed this was the first little girl's birthday party you'd hosted."

He waved off the compliment. "All I do is write out the checks and delegate all the real work." He removed his hat and looked around. "Has anyone seen Gwen?"

"She was hanging around waiting to speak to you earlier, but you were busy." Carrie pointed to the parking area. "Look over there. She and Alyssa are nearly at her car, but I bet you can catch her if you hurry."

"Excuse me, but I've got some 'patability' issues to iron out." He winked at Giselle then headed toward the parking area. He spied Gwen buckling Alyssa into the back seat of her car, and called out as he jogged over to her. She faced him and smiled. He slapped his hat on his jeaned leg. "Now, I'd have been real hurt if you and Alyssa left here without saying goodbye."

"Hey, Bill. You seemed busy—I didn't want to interrupt."

"Never too busy for you. Did y'all have a good time?"

"We had a wonderful time, didn't we sweetie?" Alyssa managed to nod between two huge yawns. "Whoa, she'll be out before I reach the end of the drive way." Gwen looked up at Bill. "I had fun, too. It was nice meeting you." She smiled and held her hand out to him.

No time like the present to start planning a future. He put his hat back on his head, took her hand, but held it and stepped up closer. "Gwen, would it be a waste of time if I called you for a date?"

She shook her head from side to side.

"Does that mean 'No, I wouldn't be wasting my time' or 'No, I don't want to date an old man like you'?"

Gwen's eyes widened. She swallowed before answering. "You would *not* be wasting your time, and I can think of several ways to describe you, but 'old' isn't one of them."

He smiled and pulled out his wallet, then handed her two business cards. "There's my phone number if you ever need to get in touch with me. I'd appreciate it if you'd write your number on the back of one of those so I could call you."

She reached into her purse, pulled out a business card from the hospital, and handed it to him.

He read her name and number on the card and grinned. “Even better.”

She studied his card. “Don’t you have a mobile number—a cell phone?”

“I never needed one before, but—” he swept his hat from his head again and stepped closer, “—if you promise to call me, I’ll buy one tomorrow.”

She nodded. “I promise.”

A light snort and snore from the back seat had them both leaning over to peek at Alyssa, already fast asleep. Gwen’s soft laughter had Bill’s stomach doing somersaults.

“I need to get her home.”

Bill moved in closer and when she turned to face him he felt her soft gasp on his face. “Well . . . I’ll talk to you later.” He leaned over and kissed her on the cheek then pulled back a bit. He moved back in and kissed her lightly on the mouth. Bill hovered for a moment over her lips, waited for her to open her eyes again. He wanted her to see how much he wanted her. She did, then raised a hand to her cheek, flushed with a shade of pink that looked damned good on her beautiful face.

The strongest physical pull he’d ever encountered with a woman nearly knocked him to his knees. Aching with need, he gripped her car door with one hand and cleared his throat. “Gwen, I think I should tell you that I’ve waited a long time to look for a lady to share my life with. Once I think I’ve found her, I plan on moving ahead quickly. I’m not getting any younger, and time is too precious to waste. How do you feel about that?”

She gazed up at him. “I feel the same way, but . . .” She placed her hand against his chest when he attempted to move in for another kiss. “I don’t want to waste my time either, so—I do have a few questions.”

Please let me give her the answers she needs to hear. He raised his hand and rubbed his thumb softly along her bottom lip. “Fire.” *A double entendre if ever one existed—he practically burned with need for this woman.*

She swallowed. “Are you looking for a long relationship?”

Tell her the truth. “I’m looking for a rest of my life relationship.”

She closed her eyes, seemed to prepare herself for the next question. “Would you have a problem with Alyssa?”

"Absolutely not, she's a wonderful little girl."

Her eyes flew open at his answer. She swallowed again. "How would you feel about having more children?"

The truth worked before. Would it again? "All for it. As many as you want. As soon as you want."

"Oh, dear God." She released her breath in a sudden rush.

He leaned in and kissed her again, this time holding nothing back. When he finally pulled away, they were both drawing in ragged breaths and trembling. He rested his forehead against hers. "Just so you know, I'm okay in all departments."

Gwen's eyes widened. "I bet you are."

It took some effort to let her pull away from him. But she slid in behind her steering wheel, turned her key with shaky hands. She closed her door and lowered her window before looking up at him again, her blue eyes shining with an invitation he couldn't refuse. Bill leaned over, rested his arms on the opening of her window. "I'll give you a couple of hours to settle in before I call."

"That would be perfect."

He leaned into the window, gave her one last kiss—a little something to follow her home—let her know the seriousness of his intentions. He straightened, watched her place a trembling hand on her gearshift, and put her car into drive.

He stood there until the tail lights of her sedan disappeared in the dust, knowing that wasn't the last he'd see of Gwendolyn Perry. He wanted her in his life, wanted to make life easier for her and Alyssa. He turned away from the dust trail and started the walk back to the barn. He'd been out of the serious relationship status far too long. "Bill, ole boy—It's time to get your game on," he mumbled.

He met up with Sam and Carrie on his way back to the barn. He tipped his hat to them. "Carrie—Sam—I hope you had a good time."

"We had a great time, thank you," Sam replied.

"Did you enjoy yourself?" Carrie asked smugly.

He gave her a wide grin. "Best damned day I've had in a long time, hon." *No doubt thanks to you.*

She gave him a hug. "Good for you, Bill."

He whistled a snappy tune as he headed toward the barn, deciding to let her keep her little secret—for now. He approached Giselle, who stood staring out at the pond. When she mentioned she hadn't had a turn in a paddle boat, he told her to wait right there and he'd be back with her in a minute. Thinking the situation warranted a little intervention, he headed straight for his nephew, insisting he take Giselle and the girls out for a spin. Jackson grumbled but obeyed, heading reluctantly to where the three females stood waiting by the boats. Bill turned back toward the barn, whistling under his breath, and praying for another miracle.

* * * * *

Jackson rejoined him in the stable area later. "Well, you had yourself a good day, didn't you?"

Bill leaned on the pitchfork he'd been using. "Yep. A very productive day."

"Are you going to see Gwen again?"

Bill grinned. "As soon as I can. As often as she lets me."

"Do you really think you should be moving that quickly?"

"Son, it's like I told her, I'm too old to be playing games. That's just a waste of time and it's too precious to me now. Besides, as it happens, she feels the same way."

"Well, you're a big boy and a good judge of character, so I won't bother with the usual precautionary words." Jackson slapped his uncle on the back. "I hope everything works out for you."

"Me too, but I need to bother you for some advice, son."

"Like how to date in the new millennium?"

Bill chuckled. "What the hell would you know about it? You haven't been on a date since the nineties. Don't worry about me, I can still teach you some things about women."

"Then why haven't you dated recently?"

"Who says I haven't dated?"

"I haven't met any of them."

Bill turned toward his nephew. "Why should you meet them?"

"It seems like you'd want to introduce them to your family," Jackson mumbled.

Bill snorted. "They weren't exactly the type of women you bring home to meet your mama." He cocked an eyebrow. "And even if they were, you ain't my mama."

"Oh." Jackson looked slightly embarrassed. "What kind of advice do you need, then?"

"Who's the best carrier for a mobile phone?"

"I thought you didn't have any use for one," Jackson said.

"I didn't before. Now I do so Gwen can reach me."

"Welcome to the new century, Uncle Bill."

"I'm also buying a new truck tomorrow."

Jackson's eyes widened. "You're seriously getting rid of that old Ford?"

"No, I'm going to hang onto it for farm work. But the first time I go pick up Gwen for a date, I want it to be in my brand-new truck."

"Oh Lord, I can't believe it took a woman to get you to come into the new age. Good for you, old man."

Bill laughed and continued his previous chore of shoveling hay into horse stalls. "You know what they say, you're only as old as you feel—and today I don't feel a day over forty. So, how was your day?"

"Confusing as hell," Jackson growled, as he picked up a second pitchfork and tossed fresh hay into the nearest stall.

"That's because you won't listen to me."

"Your ass," Jackson snorted. "I let loose on Giselle in the boat when she made a comment I didn't care for."

"And that ended how, exactly?"

"She apologized. I told her I could find my own damn woman and I didn't need to be set up like, well, like you."

Bill stopped shoveling hay and looked at his nephew. "I figured as much when Alyssa and Mac met for the first time today." He wiped his brow and released a low chuckle. "I asked Carrie to find me someone. It's nice to know she's taking care of me."

They worked in companionable silence until Jackson spoke up. "You know, I know about the wife and baby you lost a long time ago."

Bill leaned on his pitchfork. "You do? It wasn't a big secret or anything, I just didn't see any reason to bring it up. How'd you find out?"

"I overheard you and mom talking about it the same day she and dad died. She was telling you it was time to find another girl."

Bill smiled at the memory. "Elise loved trying to set me up with some friend of hers." He faced the west, toward the setting sun. "New Year's Eve—Jamison made plans to take Elise dancing." He passed a hand over his face. "That was a bad time for both of us."

Jackson nodded, and leaned against the wall. "I told Giselle I'm tired of waiting for a family. I must have used up my reserve of patience on Chloe."

Bill picked up a length of rope and slowly wound it into a coil. He walked over and hung the rope on a hook near Jackson's head. "Maybe you're just tired of denying your feelings for Giselle."

Jackson met his uncle's gaze. "I've already admitted that I'm attracted to her."

Bill shook his head, "I'm not talking about physical attraction. I'm talking about the fact that you're in love with her. Are you ready to admit that?"

Jackson pushed away from the wall. "Don't start. Her husband was one of my best friends. I would nev—"

"You would never have acted on it as long as Toby was alive. Believe me, son. I, better than anyone, know that."

Jackson let his head drop. "I've loved her for so damned long. I *wanted* what she and Toby had. But I wanted it with *her*. I've loved her for three and a half years of my life now, Uncle Bill." He lifted his arms, let them fall heavily to his sides. "I don't know how to go on if I never get the chance—*Dammit!*" He kicked an empty bucket and sent it flying noisily across the wooden floor of the tack room.

Bill walked over to where the bucket landed, and picked it up. "What is it you're so upset about?"

"Now that you know and I've accepted it—well, shit!" he snapped. "What if?"

"What if, what?"

"What if she never returns the feelings? What do I do then?"

"Then, you do what we've been telling her to do for months. You move on, look for someone else to fill the void."

Jackson groaned and exited the stables. He paced slowly, both hands clasped at the back of his head.

Bill followed him out. "Don't worry, I doubt if anyone else besides me and Carrie know about this."

Jackson stopped and faced his uncle. "Carrie knows too?"

Bill shrugged. "We haven't discussed it, but I'd bet my last dollar on it. She's worked with the two of you forever." He placed a hand to Jackson's shoulder. "You don't die from disappointment, son, or a broken heart over unrequited love. Believe me, I know."

Jackson stared at his boots. "The last few years every time I looked at Chloe, I wished for Giselle. I knew it wasn't right. I couldn't help myself. Despite everything, I kept hoping that if Chloe had a child, things would get better."

Bill winced. "I know I probably shouldn't say this, but the thought of Chloe alone with an innocent baby always scared the living hell out of me."

Jackson faced his uncle again. "I know, but I'd have protected it, would have raised our child alone if push came to shove. My feelings for Giselle kept me going. Pitiful, ain't it? Carrying around a torch for a woman with two kids and already in a wonderful marriage. I didn't see the harm in holding out for a miracle." He rested one hip against the opening of the barn door. "The day I met Toby it threw me for a freaking loop, I tell you. To make matters worse, he turned into one my two best friends for the entire last year. Hell, I was happy he and Giselle were so good together. But even then, I wanted to be the one she loved." He crossed his arms against his chest and stared at Bill. "You have no idea what that's like."

Bill took his hat off and slapped it against his thigh, sending particles of hay and dust flying. "Oh, I think I can empathize with you some. You see, a year or so after my wife died is when your mom proceeded with her quest to get me married off again. The night you overheard us, I'd have said anything to get her off my back. I knew I couldn't have feelings for anyone else. Because just like you with Giselle, I'd fallen in love with your mother."

Jackson's gaze clashed with his.

"And just like you," Bill continued, "I never acted on it. I would never have dreamed of telling her or your dad. I was every bit as happy for your parents as you were for Giselle and Toby." He looked at Jackson. "I'm only telling you this so you'll know—I understand exactly what you went through then—what you're going through, now." He paused before speaking again. "I hope you don't think less of me."

Jackson snapped out of his dazed expression. "Of course not. But I'm just realizing now that you've lost the most in all this. You've lost two women you loved, as well as a child, and a brother. No wonder it took you so long to move on. Jesus Christ, Uncle Bill. How the hell did you manage?"

"I had you, son. You put everything into perspective for me. You always have."

Jackson gave Bill a brief nod before pulling out his wallet to hand him a business card. "Here's the wireless carrier I use, and I can't wait to see the truck you buy to impress Gwen. I sure hope you find happiness with her, because I can't think of another person who deserves it more than you do."

Bill glanced at the card, slipped it into his shirt pocket. "Oh, I don't know. I can think of one other man who's sure as hell due for some."

Chapter Nineteen

Creating the New Bill

Jackson released a long whistle as he walked up to Bill's new truck, a beautiful Super Duty Ford F-350, ready for towing, bronze in color and trimmed up in chrome. The King Ranch accessory package dressed up the eye-pleasing, luxurious interior. The seats were tan saddle leather, heated for wintertime comfort, with front and back climate control. The truck boasted a built-in GPS and a premium sound system. "Gwen will be impressed. I promise you. Hell, I'm even impressed. You're making me regret my Avalanche."

Bill took off his hat and passed his fingers through his dark hair. "I just want her to be comfortable."

"She will be. I nearly forgot. My new bike is coming in tomorrow, so I'm taking the day off," Jackson explained. "They're delivering it to my place tomorrow morning."

"What'd you get?"

"An Indian Chief Road Master. It's the motorcycle version of that truck." He cocked his head toward Bill's new wheels. "I'm hoping it'll be the perfect distraction to keep my mind off Giselle." He spotted Carrie approaching. "Look who's coming. This is going to blow her mind."

Carrie beamed at Bill as she approached. "If you're trying to impress a certain Ms. Perry, this should do it. It's not necessary, but a good-looking man like you belongs in a truck like this." She glanced inside the open driver's door and gasped. "This is *so* Bill Broussard."

Bill leaned over to hug her. "I haven't had a chance to thank you properly, for Gwen, I mean."

"You're welcome, honey. I heard her story and knew God put her in my path for a reason, and it had to be you. I only want credit if it works out, though."

"How about if I buy you lunch?"

She shook her head. "Not today, I've got errands to run. She called me this morning, you know. I hear you two had an interesting talk last night. A two-hour phone call?"

"Sure did," Bill admitted. "That much less to say next time I see her."

"A little less talk and a lot more action?" she teased, as Bill gave her an enthusiastic nod.

Jackson scratched his head. "Two hours? Hell, I can't get you to talk for five minutes on the phone."

Bill winked at him. "You don't look like Gwen."

Carrie grinned and turned to him. "Jack, are you going to lunch with Bill?"

"Yeah, we're going to choose a wireless phone and a plan for him before lunch."

Carrie's mouth dropped in obvious shock. "Next thing you know, you'll be setting up your own web page and surfing the net from your smart phone."

"I don't know about all that. I just want Gwen to be able to get a hold of me when she feels like talking. It'll be rough not being around her twenty-four, seven, now that I've found her. I've waited a long time for this."

"Oh yeah." Carrie sent him a knowing smile. "I remember those days. Not wanting to be separated from Sam for one single night. Good times ahead for both you and Gwen. I'm happy for you." She headed for the office, giving them a wave. "You two boys have a good lunch."

* * * * *

Bill slid his finger across the screen of his new phone and pulled up his contact list. Gwen sat right on top of his favorites list. He tapped her name and smiled.

"Hello?"

"Hey Gwen. Save this number. It's my new cell."

"Ah—good. I'll do that as soon as the call ends. How was your day, Bill?"

"Great. We still on for tonight?"

"Unless you've thought better of tying yourself down to a frumpy nearly forty-year-old with a little girl."

"Nothin' frumpy about you, lady—and I'm looking forward to seeing more of both you and Alyssa."

He made good on that, spent most of the next week in her company, either them at his ranch or him at their place. He always left them before nine p.m.—call him old school but they damned sure wouldn't sleep together with Alyssa under the same roof. Each evening, they tore themselves away from each other and went to their own corners. Once she'd put Alyssa to bed they'd talk on the phone for hours.

He learned everything he could about them in the next couple of weeks. Gwen lived on a tight budget, but sacrificed daily for Alyssa's sake. Bill couldn't wait for the day when he could do more for them. When Gwen mentioned she had vacation time coming to her, he decided to indulge them both with a trip. After asking their opinions, he made plans to bring them to San Antonio for a week of summer vacation fun.

They attended a ball game in Kenton one day after Giselle and her girls returned from a brief get-a-way to a nearby water park. When Giselle mentioned being leery of travelling alone with her girls, Bill and Gwen invited her to go along with them to San Antonio. Giselle wasn't crazy about driving in high volume city traffic and took Jackson up on his offer to go along and do the driving for her—with the understanding he'd get his own room, of course.

Bill watched the two of them carefully, recognizing all the signs of a mutual growing attraction. Now that he had Gwen, he wanted Jackson happy, as well. He figured this trip would benefit all four of them.

The day before their scheduled departure, Bill received a frantic phone call from his nephew.

"We have a problem, Uncle Bill."

"What's up?"

"Giselle has developed a bad case of food poisoning—no way she'll make the trip and I'm not leaving her like this."

Bill's mind worked, wondering how to salvage the situation. "We can take both girls along with us." *Jackson alone in a house with Giselle? Even with food poisoning, that could work.* "I don't want Mac and Lexie to miss out on this. They've been looking forward to it."

"I know they have, but I also know you and Gwen deserve some time alone, too. I've asked Gretchen and Caleb to go in our places and take Gretchen's two girls since they're all friends."

Bill didn't have a problem with that and neither did Gwen. San Antonio proved to be a wonderful experience for couples at night. After two days spent as a group, Gretchen and Caleb offered to take Mac, Lexie, and Alyssa for an entire twenty-four hours to give Bill and Gwen some 'couple' time to themselves. Bill waited until that evening to take his lady for an arm-in-arm stroll on the Riverwalk. He'd chosen a particular spot earlier, waited until they reached it before facing Gwen.

"Hon, what do you really think of us—" He paused to wave his finger between the two of them, "—together?"

She stepped closer, stood on her tip toes to give him a kiss. "Surely you can tell, Bill. I adore us as a couple."

"Perfect answer." Bill grinned and pulled a small embossed leather covered box from his pocket before lowering himself to one knee in front of her. "Would you make me the happiest man in the world by becoming my wife?"

Her eyes wide, she covered her opened mouth with one hand as he took out the solitaire diamond engagement ring. "Oh, my God. Yes! Yes, I'll marry you!"

He stood and slipped the ring on her finger, pulled her close for a kiss and hugged her tightly afterward to scattered applause from approving onlookers. She pulled away and covered her face, a hint of embarrassment from the attention they'd received.

"Is that you, Cowboy?"

Bill turned at the sound of the voice he'd only heard over the phone in the last twenty-eight years, the last time nearly six years earlier when she'd called with news of her own engagement. He studied the face of the woman before him, her hair cut in a short, sassy style, with a few more lines around her sparkling eyes and smiling mouth. Slightly heavier than when he'd first met her, Maggie Hannigan. Still stunningly beautiful and voluptuously curved woman. More importantly, she looked healthy and happy. "Maggie? I'll be damned."

She released the hand she clutched and gave him a hug. "It's so great to see you again!"

"You also, Mags." He hugged her back before turning his attention promptly back to Gwen. "I want to introduce you to my new fiancée, Gwendolyn Perry—she just said yes."

Maggie laughed, her eyes sparkling with obvious delight at the news. "I just saw that, but I have to admit, I didn't know it was you until afterwards." She faced Gwen. "I'm Maggie Hannigan-Bowers, Gwendolyn. Congratulations, and it's wonderful to meet the woman who's going to finally domesticate Cowboy, here. I'm thrilled for both of you."

Gwen smiled at Maggie. "Thank you, Maggie. I don't think I've heard him mention you before, so I'm not quite sure how you two know each other…"

Maggie smiled at Gwen. "Bill Broussard is the best friend I've ever had—there for me when I had no one else. You're getting a wonderful man."

Gwen beamed at Bill. "I know. I'm a lucky woman."

Bill pulled her close again. "I think we're both lucky." He cleared his throat and faced the man standing beside Maggie, extended his hand. "Bill Broussard."

The man reached out and gave Bill's hand a vigorous shake. "I'm Maggie's husband, Matthew Bowers, and if you're the same Bill Broussard I've heard about, thank you. I'm grateful."

Bill smiled at the man and gave Maggie a wink. "Friends take care of each other. Just make sure she's happy and that's thanks enough."

"Will do, man. Will do."

The four parted ways, and Bill and Gwen headed in the opposite direction.

Gwen looped her hand through his arm again. "What was that her husband said about being grateful?" She teared up when he filled her in about Maggie's affair and subsequent suicide attempt. "I'm glad you were able to help her out. She looks happy now."

"Seems so," he agreed.

"Cowboy, huh?" Gwen sent him a sidelong look.

Bill laughed nervously. "From the first day we met she called me that." He faced her, wanting to make sure she understood the situation. "There was never anything more between us other than sex. And even that transformed into nothing other than a good friendship."

She studied him, finally nodding. "I believe you." She turned and started walking again. "Only…"

"What is it?" he said, not quite convinced.

"Oh, that nickname—*Cowboy*. I guess I'm just wondering how much *riding* you've gotten in over the years."

Bill stopped her then, bent her over his arm to kiss her. He finally let her up, breathless—and, from the look in her eyes—wanting him. "The only thing you need to worry about is that this stallion is off the stud list, for good."

She nodded, swallowed, before answering with a weak, "Okay…"

They ended up back at the hotel, celebrating their engagement with champagne and strawberries ordered from room service. Later that evening, exhausted and sated, they collapsed into Bill's single king-size bed.

"Oh, my goodness!" She gasped against the pillow. "Nothing wrong with that, Cowboy…"

"Nothing at all," he panted. He waited for his heart to stop pounding in his chest. "And I think you just broke this stallion."

Her eyes grew serious. "Enough to keep you from sniffing out fillies from other stables?"

"Baby." He pulled her to him, and planted his hand firmly on her backside. "Marry me and I promise you I'll never set foot out of our own paddock—or out of our own stable."

She kissed him gently, her eyes welling with tears. "That's what I wanted to hear, Cowboy."

* * * * *

Bill had just walked back into his house and thrown his dirty laundry into the washing machine when his landline rang. He picked it up and drawled an exhausted but happy 'hello' into the phone.

"Hey, Uncle Bill, how was the trip?"

"Outstanding. It was nice to be able to do something like that for those two. Gwen's had to work hard to raise Alyssa. Things you and I take for granted are luxuries to them."

"I imagine they've had a rough time of it."

"Yep, but we did some—talking—when Gretchen and Caleb took all the kids for one night. Gwen and I have discovered we're *compatible*—In several different ways," he murmured.

"You don't say," Jackson replied, his voice containing more than a hint of laughter. "So, when's the wedding?"

Bill couldn't wait to blow his nephew's mind. "I was about to call you to talk about that. I've asked her, and she's said yes. Think you could be my best man?"

"Sure, I will. I'm happy for you, for Gwen, and for Alyssa. They can't ask for better."

Bill stared at the phone in his hand. He'd expected some kind of resistance from Jackson. He grinned, thinking Giselle's bout of food poisoning may have been beneficial to his nephew as well. "Thanks, son. We've chosen August 31st, the Friday night of Labor Day weekend. That way we can have a quick honeymoon. She's planning to ask Giselle to watch Alyssa for the weekend. You know," he took a short pause. "We've discussed trying for children right away." Bill's voice filled with emotion when he spoke. "Alyssa gave us her blessing and asked if she could call me daddy. You can't imagine how much that means to me."

"Oh, I think I can. You don't have to tell me how those little girls can tug on your heart strings."

Bill chuckled at his nephew's comment. "No, I guess I don't. How was your weekend? What did you two do once Giselle got over the food poisoning?"

"Oh man, it was great. We rode the Indian a couple of days, went to Red's club on Friday and spent Saturday with him. I brought her swimming at your place this afternoon. By the way, Red's a little disillusioned that his bachelor mentor has gone over the deep end over a woman."

Bill laughed at that. "Yeah? Well you can tell old Red he doesn't know what the hell he's missing."

* * * * *

Mid-August

If he'd stopped to think about it, Bill would have realized things were moving along too damn smoothly. He was happy with Gwen and Alyssa, soon to be his wife and adopted daughter. Giselle had finally faced her feelings for Jackson, and the two of them were a couple, every bit as happy. Their pasts should have told them not to get too comfortable—prepared them for some form of disaster in the making.

The first hint of it came in the form of a phone call from a frantic Giselle one morning after her girls had returned to school.

"Bill, this is Giselle. Is Jackson with you?"

"No, he isn't. Is something wrong?"

"Yes. No. I don't know for sure. Maybe it's nothing. I'm here at his house; his bike is missing and his house was unlocked, the garage door left opened, his truck and house keys left on the cabinet. All the things he'd never do."

"I don't think it's reason to worry." He waited through her pause, his chest tightening with concern.

"I left here about two hours ago. It's a long story, but I told him I couldn't see him anymore, Bill. I've realized how foolish that was, and I came back to tell him. He's not answering his phone. I don't know, but I've got a bad feeling. I think he needs help. Can you help me find him?"

Well hell. "Sure honey. I bet he's just riding somewhere around here to clear his head. Why don't you come meet me?"

"I will, but start looking right away. I'll check some roads we've ridden on going toward your place."

Bill left immediately, searching for signs of Jackson's bike in his area. Finding nothing, he headed back to his ranch. As soon as he pulled to a stop next to Giselle's SUV, she got out and jumped inside with him.

"Anything?" she said.

"Not a thing. He doesn't answer for me, either." He headed back down the drive. "You know, he may be just riding and can't hear his phone."

She twisted nervously at her fingers. "He needs help, Bill. I know it. I can *feel* it. What's worse is that he doesn't know yet." She wiped an escaped tear from her face.

"Doesn't know what, hon?"

"That I love him. I love him so much, and I want to marry him. I want to have his babies, and I want us to be a family. One big, happy family." She shook her head anxiously. "Wherever he is, he's thinking there's no hope for us." She covered her eyes and released a tortured groan. "When I left him, he was devastated, Bill. He begged me not to walk away from him, and I did. I hurt him so badly. I'm such a fool."

Bill laid a hand on her arm, hoping to comfort her. "Things will work out, you'll see." *Please God, let it work out.*

"Where could he be?" she sobbed. Giselle dug in her purse for a tissue, picked up a photo of something and clutched it close. "He and I went riding the other day and there was this pond. There were cattle and a few head of horses grazing in a pasture, and ducks and geese that stay there year-round." She pivoted to stare at him. "Do you know where that is? Have you checked there yet?"

Bill knew the place. "I know what you're talking about and I haven't checked there, but it's only about five miles from here. Do you have reason to believe he's there?"

"No, it's just a feeling." She put her head down. "Oh God, keep him safe," she whispered, clutching the photo tighter.

Bill pointed to the photo. "What is that you have there?"

"I cleaned out Toby's office this morning and found this in an envelope." She handed him a snapshot of Toby and Jackson together. "I'll never forgive myself if . . ." Her voice trailed off, leaving the dreaded thought unspoken.

Bill reached over and put a hand on her shoulder. "He'll be all right, Giselle. He's strong."

She lowered her head and hot tears fell from her eyes. "But he's so alone. And he thinks he'll stay that way."

Bill studied the snapshot with one hand. "The time and date stamp says this was taken on February 28th. That's Jackson's birthday."

"That's right, it is."

"We'll find him, don't worry. Okay, this is the road."

"I remember it! How far is it to the end?"

"About six miles, but the pond is a couple of miles up."

She pointed at something on his dash. "Is this a GPS?"

Bill nodded. "If he needs help, they'll find us."

They stopped talking so they could keep watch for any sign of Jackson's bike. They'd both been scanning either side of the roadside ditches when Giselle called out to him. "Look out!"

He had to slam on his brakes and skidded off toward one of the ditches to avoid hitting a dead cow in the road. The truck came to a jerking halt. "Are you okay?"

Giselle didn't answer, just pointed at the ditch and jumped out of the truck. She ran to the twisted heap of metal that had been Jackson's motorcycle. "He's here somewhere, Bill!" She called his name every few seconds as they began to search through the pasture's waist high grass. It took another minute or so before he heard the two sentences that sent both relief and a feeling of dread running through him.

"He's here! Get Air Med out here—Hurry!"

Sensing her urgency, Bill ran to his truck and sent the call through, along with the coordinates. He ended the call and ran back to where Giselle kneeled in the grass. He approached the bent and broken body of his nephew and had to stop the automatic need to cuss up a storm at the sight of him. The compound fracture…bad enough with the jagged bone protruding through the skin of his left shin. But his head, good God—his head injury looked extremely bad. No telling what kind of internal injuries or bleeding going on inside him.

Bill kneeled next to his nephew. "I called in the GPS location. They'll bring them right to us."

"How long, Bill?" She clutched Jackson's hand.

He shook his head. "She said it'd be within six minutes. Jackson's strong, hon. If anybody can survive this, it's him."

They talked to him, assured him—for five more agonizing minutes before they heard the Air Med helicopter's approach. Bill stood and waved his arms.

Giselle had to let go of Jackson's hand and move aside to let the medics do their work. It took another couple of minutes to stabilize and load him into the chopper.

As they readied to leave, she leaned over him. "Jackson, you have to be strong now. Don't you give up. I love you! Fight for us. Do you hear me? Fight for us!" She turned to the nearest medic. "Where are you taking him?"

"The trauma center at St. Luke's is the best around. They're already waiting for him."

She and Bill ran back to the truck. She made phone calls while Bill broke every speeding law on the way to the hospital. She called Carrie and Gwen, then Gretchen, Lauren, and Amanda. She thanked Amanda for offering to collect Mac and Lexie from the bus and take them to her place. After ending that call she turned to Bill. "Do you have Red's number?"

"I think Jackson programmed it into my phone for me."

She pulled up his contact list, found his name, and hit call.

"Red . . ." That's all she could manage before she broke down and handed the phone to Bill.

"Red, it's Bill Broussard. Jackson wrecked his bike. It's serious; he's got a bad head injury, a compound leg break, and surely some internal injuries."

"What the hell happened?"

"As far as we can tell, he hit a cow on one of these back roads around my place. The cow's dead, the bike's totaled, and it looks like Jackson flew about thirty feet into a pasture. I don't think he hit the pavement, and the pasture was pretty thick with tall grass. Maybe that softened the impact some. I didn't see a helmet, did you, Giselle?"

"Yes, it was that half-helmet that he likes to wear. It must have flown off," she said, between sobs.

"Listen, I'll leave here in about five minutes. What hospital?"

"St. Luke's on South Ryan."

"I'll see you there. Put Giselle back on the phone."

Bill handed her the phone. "He wants to talk to you."

She hit the speaker button. "Red?" she sobbed.

"You listen to me, hon. He's strong and he loves you. He'll be fine. I know he will."

"He has to be. I can't—I can't lose him, Red."

"You won't. I'll see you in an hour or so."

Before Bill's truck rolled to a stop, Giselle had jumped out and sprinted to the door of the hospital. Bill threw it in park and chased after her. They'd just been given the information when Carrie rushed through the doors.

Giselle hugged her. "Sixth floor, Carrie. He's going into surgery soon."

Carrie took Bill's arm while they waited for the elevator. "How bad, Bill?"

"It's serious." He described the injuries. "The medics suspected brain swelling from the head injury."

She seemed to take it in stride, nodded and turned to Giselle. "He's a strong man. He'll be fine, you'll see."

They took the elevator to the waiting room and began the long, agonizing wait for information on the man they all loved in different ways.

Giselle opened her purse. She rummaged around, growing more and more frantic. "Where is it?"

Bill pulled something out of his shirt pocket and held it out to her. "Maybe you're looking for this."

"Oh, thank you!" She hugged the snapshot to her. "I was afraid I'd lost it."

Carrie leaned forward. "What do you have there?" She inhaled sharply at the picture Giselle held up. "I took that—right before I told them they were stinking up my house. I'd forgotten I'd given one to Toby. It wouldn't have helped to give one to Jackson. He'd have had to hide the damn thing." She covered her mouth and suppressed a sob. "What happened, Giselle?"

"It's my fault, Carrie. If I hadn't put off cleaning out Toby's office for so long, none of this would have happened. I wouldn't have overheard the conversation I heard this morning."

"What conversation?"

"One of the women claimed that Toby and Chloe were having an affair."

"That's ridiculous," Carrie said. "Toby would never have done that."

"I know that now, but I guess I went a little crazy," Giselle admitted. "Besides, Jackson let me read the letter Chloe left him and it proved he didn't sleep with her."

Carrie faced them, wide-eyed with curiosity. "You read the letter?"

Giselle nodded. "It explained a lot of things. Like why Chloe was after Toby in the first place."

Carrie paused a moment before asking. "She knew Jackson was in love with you, didn't she? Of course, she did. She was a mean little bitch, but she wasn't stupid." She glanced over at Bill. "If the two of us could tell, she had to have known."

Bill nodded as he took the photo from Carrie and studied it again, flipping it over to read the back.

Me and Jackson, after whipping his ass in hoops again, thanks to my lucky cap. They don't make men any better than Jack—I'd trust him with my life.

"I'm sorry I never met him, he sounds like a wonderful man," Bill said.

Giselle turned tear-filled eyes on him. "Every bit as wonderful as Jackson is."

"This is a sign, you know, a sign that Jackson's going to pull through." He smiled down at her. "Jackson loves you and those girls more than anything. He'll fight like hell to live."

"He has to, Bill." Giselle allowed herself a final sniff, then wiped her eyes free of tears. She lifted her chin. "I will *not* lose Jackson."

He smiled and pulled her to him for a hug. "There's the spunky girl that Jackson fell in love with."

"How did you both know?" Her gaze bounced from Bill to Carrie. "He said the two of you have known for years."

Bill couldn't keep the grin from his face. "His eyes lit up every time he talked about something you did to put him in his place at the office. One day I asked him why he didn't apologize for humiliating you during some meeting and be done with the whole business. He insisted it was worth keeping you pissed off at him just to see your beautiful green eyes flash with anger. That's when I knew he was in love with you."

Giselle turned expectantly to Carrie. "And you?"

Carrie sniffed then sighed loudly. "One day at the office you were telling Joan, Barbara, Tina, and Catherine a story about your girls. I think it was when Mac tied Lex up to your four-poster bed in a sheet and told you to bring her back to wherever you got her."

"I remember. We were standing around Joan's desk. After I finished the story, I saw him leaning in the doorway of his office drinking a cup of coffee. I expected him to fuss at me for keeping everyone from their work."

Carrie shook her head sadly. "He was listening. I caught him watching you before you noticed him. The look on his face was so intense. I could almost hear him thinking how badly he wanted that, and suddenly I knew he wanted it with you. I started to pay closer attention after that, and all the signs were there. He was in love with you. Poor guy—trapped in that mess with Chloe, and knowing how happy you and Toby were. Then Toby and Jackson became such good friends. He probably figured he could keep his feelings hidden as long as you weren't speaking to him." She released a long sigh. "Looking back on it, I wonder how he managed to put one foot in front of the other some days."

"When you've never had it, you don't miss it," Bill said. "Jackson and Chloe had a half-ass decent year of courtship together, but it blew up a couple of nights before the wedding. He had to choose her over his best friend. It didn't take him long to realize he chose wrong. Chloe knew it too, and never let him forget it. That was one sadistic little tramp."

Carrie shook her head. "He never lost Red as a friend, Bill. They got together every chance they could the last several years. Red always understood."

"It ate at Jackson. I don't know how he put up with her," Bill growled.

They turned, as a tall, blonde man in green scrubs walked into the waiting room through the surgery doors. “Excuse me. Is someone here for Jackson Broussard?”

Giselle jumped up to meet him. “We are.”

Bill stuck his hand out. “I’m his Uncle, Bill Broussard.”

“Of course, you look just like him,” the doctor said. “Mr. Broussard, I’m Dr. Collins.”

Bill stared at the man, struggling to remember where he’d seen him before.

“I used to play ball with Jackson at LSU,” Dr. Collins said. “An old teammate of ours called to ask if I could get some info to you. Scott McAllister?”

Bill pushed aside any misgivings. If Red had called him, surely the guy checked out.

“Oh, Red—God bless him!” Carrie said. “What can you tell us? Are you his surgeon?”

“No, but I’ll be watching to see what’s going on and I’ll come in here periodically to keep all of you informed.”

Giselle stepped forward. “What can you tell us now?”

“He’s got a compound fracture of the right tibia—that’s the shin bone, a fracture of his left arm, and they’re seeing some internal bleeding that needs to be taken care of. The most serious injury is his head. There’s swelling in the temporal lobe of his brain. We don’t know what’s causing it yet, but they’re going to remove a piece of the skull to relieve the pressure. Once they open him up, they’ll be able to trace the bleeder and take care of it. After that’s under control, they’ll tend to the other injuries. This should take several hours, so don’t get discouraged if the surgery goes on longer than expected. The good news is Jackson’s in excellent shape and his heart is strong.”

Giselle nodded. “Thank you so much.”

Dr. Collins nodded and left the room.

Carrie touched her shoulder. “You see? It’s because of you that he’s in such good shape. If you hadn’t made him so crazy, he wouldn’t have gone to that gym every day. It was fate.”

Giselle gave her a tight smile. “Maybe so, but it’s also because of me that he’s in here today.”

Sam entered the room to support Carrie. Then Gwen arrived, settled into Bill’s open arms and made everything more bearable for him. After another thirty minutes, Giselle went to find the chapel. When Collins entered the surgical waiting area, Carrie called Giselle's phone to let her know. She burst through the doors two minutes later, accompanied by Red, her eyes noticeably redder and more swollen.

Giselle approached the doctor. "What's going on, Dr. Collins?"

"They've removed part of the skull and found a subdural hematoma inside the temporal lobe." He explained the procedure for correcting the situation to the group. "It'll take a few days to know whether or not there's been enough significant damage to cause loss of function."

Giselle spoke, her voice strong and determined. "There won't be."

The doctor looked at Red and extended his hand. "Scott."

Red stared stonily at the man for a few moments before taking it. "Tanner."

Red's reaction to the man gave Bill total recall. Jackson's wedding, the best man substitution, and remembering what that bystander had said about seeing Chloe and Tanner together during the reception. He pictured Red tampering with the future doctor's license plate out in the parking lot. The asshole had left the scene, oblivious to the fact his personalized plate read *Dick-MD.*

Dr. Collins assured them he'd speak to them again as soon as he knew more, and exited the room.

Red turned to Carrie and hugged her. "Hello, sweetheart."

She hugged him back tightly. "I'm glad you could make it here to suffer along with the rest of us."

"He's like a brother, I had to come."

Carrie stepped up. "What's the deal with you and Dr. Collins?"

"Wait a second," Giselle said. "Did you call him Tanner? Is that *the* Tanner Collins?"

Bill grunted. "I thought he looked familiar. He stepped in as best man when Chloe claimed you tried something with her."

Red shivered, clearly revolted by the thought. "I didn't, you know."

"Of course I knew, and so did Jackson. But why the hell would you call *him*?"

Red scowled. “I knew he worked here. I told him if he didn’t do this I’d give him the ass whipping he deserved fifteen years ago.”

Bill’s grip tightened on Gwen’s hand. He loosened it and clenched his jaw instead, thinking he’d like to get a piece of that action himself.

* * * * *

Jackson came out of the surgery fine and asked for Giselle. Dr. LeBlanc took her to see him in recovery, and she returned a few short minutes later, smiling—thrilled that Jackson had been conscious enough to propose to her.

She looked around, her tears a mixture of relief and joy. “I said yes, of course.”

Bill stayed long enough to speak to Jack once in his own room in the hospital’s critical care unit. Once he knew for sure his nephew would be fine in the care of his new fiancée, he’d asked Gwen to follow him back to his place.

As soon as she’d entered his home he’d pulled her to him, needing the closeness. They’d gone to his bedroom for a session of love-making that left them both weak with satisfaction and relieved they hadn’t lost another loved one that day. The entire experience had given Bill a new appreciation for life.

He lay there, his and Gwen’s legs still entangled, and wrapped in sheets. “Marry me, Gwennie.”

She turned her head, smiled lazily at him. “Haven’t we already had this conversation? I said yes, remember?”

He rolled over on his side, rested his head on his elbow. “I know, but I don’t want to waste another two weeks waiting for you to become my wife. I don’t want to spend another night without you in my bed. I want you and Alyssa here with me. Let’s find a JP and do it now—tomorrow at the latest. Then I’ll start the adoption proceedings immediately. What do you say, babe?”

“That sounds pretty good to me. Maybe I can get a half-day or even a day off of my job to get it done.”

He took a deep breath and prayed for the best. “I don’t want to offend you, honey, and you keep on working if that’s what you want to do. This is only an offer. If you’d prefer to quit your job, it’s okay with me. I’ll take good care of you and Alyssa.”

“You mean it Bill? I’ve always imagined how nice it would be as a stay-at-home mom.”

He kissed her, leaving her breathless again. "Of course, I mean it. I'd love nothing better than to keep you barefoot and pregnant—only because I know that's what you really want."

"Well, hey there, Cowboy—" She maneuvered her body until she sat astride him. "You sure know how to make a girl's evening."

She took her own turn in the saddle that night, and he sure as hell didn't complain. Any kind of second chance at happiness was a rare occurrence in life—and he'd be a damned fool not to make the most of it with a woman as wonderful as Gwen.

Chapter Twenty

Bells Will Be Ringing

Gwen & Bill

December, 2014

Gwendolyn Broussard leaned in close to put the finishing touches to mascara framing her blue eyes. She caught her husband's handsome reflection as he approached from behind. Tall, tan, and built to perfection thanks to a combination of good genes, a daily swim regimen, and hard work, Bill Broussard looked far closer to her forty-one than his own age of fifty-nine years.

"Hey, handsome." She smiled as he nuzzled her neck.

"Good morning, babe. Did you sleep okay?"

"Uh huh." She capped her 'ultra' lash lengthener and dropping it into the drawer. She pulled her thick dark hair back away from her face and bound it with a clip. Spinning around, she buried her face in his broad, rock-solid chest. "Mm, you smell delicious."

Laughter rumbled throughout his upper torso. "Thank our daughter for that. It was my birthday gift."

"Alyssa insisted on picking it out herself, too. I had no idea she'd zero in on the most expensive cologne in the mall." Gwen lifted her face for a kiss, dragging her fingers through his abundant locks of russet hair, peppered with just enough silver to achieve the distinguished gentleman look he wore so well. She pulled back, staring into striking blue eyes, nearly as luminescent as the digital numbers glowing from the small clock she kept on the bathroom counter.

"I hope you made the coffee extra strong this morning. Somebody kept me up way past my normal bedtime last night," she said, thinking of the hours of pleasure he'd treated her to the night before. *It's all about you tonight,* he'd insisted, refusing to take any pleasure for himself, but instead, giving her plenty.

Bill gave her the devilishly handsome grin she'd fallen for two and a half years earlier. "I didn't hear any complaints at the time."

"You bet your ass you didn't." She looped her arm through his as they headed for the kitchen. She indulged her senses with one last sniff of him before stepping away to pour two cups of fresh coffee.

He gave her a playful tap on her rump. "Speaking of gifts, that Christmas tree looks entirely too bare without any gifts underneath. And you know the only thing I like seeing *nek-ked* around here is you."

She handed him his mug and leaned against the kitchen cabinet. "I don't think you like seeing me naked nearly as much as you like saying the word that way."

"Hmph! If you bet on that, you'll lose your retirement."

"I don't have any retirement."

"You don't need it. You have me."

"I do, don't I? And even if you didn't have money to burn, I'd still be crazy about you. I hope you know that."

"And here I thought I was nothing but your sugar daddy." He winked at her. "I may not have money to burn, but I think I have enough to indulge you every now and then."

"You've indulged me every day since I met you, just by your love and generosity, and I adore you for that." Steam rose from her cup, temporarily clouding her view of the Christmas tree the three of them had decorated the night before. "And you're right about the shopping. I guess I've put it off long enough," she groaned.

"I've never known a woman who hates to shop the way you do." He brushed the back of his hand softly along her face.

"I'm one of the very few," she admitted. "How does tomorrow evening sound? I have to drop Alyssa off at Giselle and Jackson's place to spend the night with Mackenzie and Lexie. Giselle said they'd bring her home Saturday evening."

"You mean you're subjecting her to an entire night and day over there? How'll she survive?"

"I know, right? Getting to play with her best friends and their adorable twin baby brothers? Giselle loves it when she goes, says she doesn't have to lift a finger to tend to the boys the entire time she's there."

Bill swallowed some coffee and grunted. "I don't know how she does it, Gwennie. I stopped by their place yesterday to drop a tree off and went inside to help Jackson set it up. By the time we'd finished, Jamison and Justin had both climbed halfway up the built-in entertainment center at least a half dozen times. Jack plucked 'em both off and set 'em on the floor like he did it all the time."

"He probably does. Giselle says they have definite futures in rock or mountain climbing."

"They come by it honestly." Bill shook his head and chuckled. "Their daddy used to do the same damn thing, and Lord those boys are the spitting image of him at that age."

"They are some handsome little men, aren't they?" Gwen gushed. "Their hair is turning darker every day and their eyes are already so blue. They'll be breaking hearts all over the place."

"Oh, I imagine their parents will teach 'em all about treating women with the utmost respect. I tried my best to do the same with Jackson after Jamison and Elise passed on." He became glassy-eyed, as though trapped in memories from the past. "It was a real pleasure raising that boy, but it breaks my heart that the twins will never know how wonderful their grandparents were."

Gwen placed a hand on Bill's shoulder. His eyes glistened with unshed tears, and a tender ache squeezed her heart. Bill Broussard didn't cry, even when discussing his late brother and sister-in-law. *Something's off here.* "Are you okay?"

He wiped at his eyes and turned to look out the window. "Feeling a little guilty I have it so good. You know, most times I don't feel the loss of my older brother so much, but days like these . . ." He drifted off and shook his head.

Once again, a cold fog of apprehension clouded her Christmas spirit. She stared at his stiff back, seconds away from asking exactly what he kept from her. Before she could organize her perceptiveness into a question, his phone rang.

He drawled into the phone, sounding more like himself. "Bill Broussard here. What can I do for you?"

Gwen listened to the one-sided conversation, anticipated some problem with the truckload of hay he'd ordered for the cattle. By the time he'd finished she'd brushed aside her paranoia.

He gulped the last of his coffee. "I've got to go, Gwennie. It looks like the hay's coming a day early. I need to make sure the loft is cleaned out and ready for it. Let's go ahead and plan for that shopping trip tomorrow evening."

"Roger that." She saluted him, making him laugh. Before he turned away, she grabbed his belt loop and gently jerked him around. "Are you feeling okay, Bill?"

He gave her another of those sexy grins that turned her stomach to a fluster of anticipation.

"You worry too much." He reached for her. He kissed her then—an indulgent, satisfying, tongue-delving kiss from a man sure of himself—the type of kiss that always left her breathless, wet, and weak-kneed with wanting him.

By the time she fully regained her wits, he'd already left the house. When she realized he hadn't answered her question, he'd already pulled his truck out of the drive.

* * * * *

Bill revved the engine on his Ford truck and pulled out, feeling guilty for the second time that morning. Once he'd driven around to the back of the barn, he parked under the loft opening. If the descent from his truck caused him to wince at the now familiar hitch in his lower region, the trek up the stairs to the loft was downright torture. He gazed out the loft opening toward the house, breathing a shallow sigh of relief at the realization that Gwen wouldn't follow him to the barn.

He settled into the work, taking a full hour to clean out the loft; sweeping and pitching out the old hay into the bed of his truck. By the time he'd finished, Gwen had left the ranch to take Alyssa to school. He took a few minutes to sit and rest before flipping open his cell phone, praying he hadn't put this off too long, already. A quick scan of his phone list got him Red and Tiffany McAllister's home number. Within seconds of punching the call button, he had the lady of the house on the line.

"Tiffany, you're just the gal I need to talk to. I need the name of a specialist. It seems I've got a problem that needs tending to…"

* * * * *

The next afternoon, Bill sat in his truck, still somewhat in shock over the prognosis. Dr. Moss's words came back to him like a phone call with a sketchy signal on a backwoods road.

Ultrasound verified it's a tumor...within the left testicle...definite removal...biopsy... possibility of testicular cancer.

He wiped his face and let his head fall back on the leather headrest. "Hell's bells..." he mumbled, trying to imagine a right time to tell Gwen. Since their marriage, they'd both longed for at least one child of their own. The doctor had also informed him during the visit that this could cut her chances of conceiving by half, if not more.

He slapped the leather-wrapped steering wheel with the palms of both hands then gripped it hard, wishing he'd told his wife of his symptoms earlier. He hadn't expected this. A hernia maybe, bad enough for a man like him. Four little words—*possibility of testicular cancer*—had as much destructive power as a nuclear warhead.

Already planning, he used the slow drive back to their ranch to form a mental list. Thoughts on how best to take care of his wife and adopted daughter filled his mind; ways to make sure neither of them wanted for anything, in case—well, just in case. He'd made a will, of course, but had neglected to set up a trust fund for Alyssa's education.

"Tomorrow—I'll do that *tomorrow,"* he whispered, wondering, for the first time in his life, how many tomorrows he had left.

* * * * *

A shiver travelled up Gwen's spine as she watched her husband step out of his truck. He faltered ever so slightly as one boot touched the ground. He recovered quickly, as though trying to hide how badly he hurt. She swallowed the lump in her throat, pushed back the feeling of apprehension she hadn't been able to shake since the doctor's office had called yesterday to confirm the appointment. She'd asked them to call his cell to verify instead, and somehow stopped herself from questioning Bill. He'd tell her if it was important.

Stepping back from the window, she crossed her arms tightly and waited for him to come to her. Her senses operated on full throttle—the lit bayberry scented candles suddenly overpowering, the ticking of the antique grandfather clock may as well have been gun shots, the artificially heated air stifling and stuffy. The seconds it took him to breach the entrance felt like an eternity.

When he finally entered, closing the door softly behind him, his gaze found hers immediately. He stood silently, as though trying to search for the right words.

She clenched inwardly preparing herself for something—just what she couldn't tell. She hadn't seen him this affected since they'd made the trip to Washington state a few months ago to visit the grave of his first wife and infant son—his first since the day he'd buried them. Terrified at the sobering reaction from her man's man of a husband, she swallowed the scream building from deep in her diaphragm.

He cleared his throat with a deep rumble.

"Tell me," she said, truly astonished the words had come out in anything but hysterical screaming. He didn't answer, so she continued, if for no other reason than to keep from exploding. "The doctor's office called yesterday to confirm your appointment. I Googled him and I know he specializes in male specific cancers." She took a deep breath. "Please don't tell me you have prostate cancer."

"No, I have a tumor in one of my—you know—tea bags." He lowered his hand to draw attention to his nether region. "It'll have to be removed and biopsied before they know if it's cancer."

Gwen drew in a deep breath and released it slowly. "Jeeze, I never thought I'd be so relieved to hear those words coming out of your mouth."

"You're relieved they have to cut off my left nut?" he asked.

"I'm relieved it's not prostate or pancreatic cancer. Testicular cancer has a much higher recovery rate. Didn't your doctor tell you that?" She hurried over to wrap her arms around his waist. He buried his face in her hair and held her tight.

"He may or may not have, but in his defense, I kind of quit listening once I heard I'd be one nut shy of a pair. That's not the kind of thing that sits well with a guy."

"I guess not. Did he say when?"

"I'm scheduled for Tuesday morning and he suggested I make a deposit in the bank—in case it affects the old swimmers," he stammered, shifting uneasily.

"Swimmers?"

"Sperm bank."

"Oh, in case the count lowers, you mean." She struggled to keep her breathing even. *Still no hysterical screams—amazing.*

"Also, in case the treatment renders me sterile."

"You won't have any treatments. You *don't* have cancer." She pulled away from him and placed her water glass and coffee cup in the dishwasher and slammed the door shut harder than she meant to.

"Babe…"

"You don't have cancer. It's a benign tumor." She wiped down the spotless granite countertop with a damp dishcloth, willing him to be cancer free and healthy—forever.

He reached out for her. "Babe…"

She let him pull her into his arms. "What?"

"We have to discuss some things in case the results come back—"

She arched one brow, a silent dare to continue in the same dangerous direction.

"—not quite in my favor," he finished.

She pulled away and turned her back to him. "I refuse to have this conversation with you, William."

"Gwennie, come on."

She turned on him then. "No, dammit! I will not—cannot—fathom a life without you. It can't happen! I can't survive something like that." She clasped one hand over her escaping sobs.

* * * * *

Bill stood silently, watched his wife, usually a model of tranquility and strength, fall apart before his eyes. He moved in to hold her, knowing she'd need a moment to get it out of her system. After a minute, she sniffed loudly and wiped her eyes.

"Okay now?"

She nodded.

"You're probably right, you know, but even if you aren't, it'd take something a hell of a lot bigger and more bad ass than a little old tumor to tear me away from this place. I haven't had near my fill of you."

She nodded tearfully and hid her face in his chest. "I know," she said, her voice muffled from the fabric of his flannel shirt.

He held her close, rocking her gently from side to side as her frantic panting leveled off. When she calmed, he planted a kiss on top of her head. "I love you more 'en anything, Gwen, and you're probably right about it being a benign tumor."

"I am right, you'll see. Are you hungry? I baked lasagna for lunch."

He played along with her abrupt change of subject. "Great, I'll need sustenance for the Christmas shopping."

"We're not going." She caught his gaze. "Don't even try to tell me you aren't hurting, either. You've been soft-stepping around here for nearly a week, you stubborn, *stubborn* man."

"I have, but I'm fine on level ground. Long as I don't have to climb stairs, I'll be fine. Besides, once I have that surgery, I doubt I'll be doing much moving around for a week or so. A tree with no gifts under it for that long would be a damned sorry sight."

* * * * *

Later that afternoon, Bill claimed the one free table at the mall's packed food court. He set two glasses of sweet tea onto the glass topped table and lowered himself gingerly onto a wrought iron chair decorated with a scrollwork fleur de lis pattern. He sipped on one tea, savoring the blend of sweet, lemony goodness, letting it temporarily satisfy his growling stomach.

He waited for Gwen to join him, thought about his idea for her Christmas gift. After today's reaction to his news, every item of jewelry in the mall had paled in comparison to the love he felt for that woman. The notion had come to him as he'd passed up a group of women, a future bride and her maids, he assumed, gushing about wedding and honeymoon plans. Within moments, he'd formed a plan and called Giselle to enlist her assistance. His niece-in-law's whoop of excitement had verified the enormity of his decision.

Now if he could just get past this tumor business. He had things to do.

"Hey handsome, are you looking for me?" Gwen approached him from behind and leaned over to give him a peck on the mouth. She sat beside him, her eyes widening with delight as she accepted the glass of tea. She pulled from the straw, rolling her eyes in pleasure. "Raspberry infused, sweetened with honey. Mm—my man knows what I like."

"I believe I do. Where are all your bags?"

"They're in the truck already. I didn't want to haul them all over the mall. Are you as hungry as I am?"

“Starved.” He took her hand. “Hope we can find a decent place to eat without an hour long wait.” He stared down his nose at her. “So, what’d you get me for Christmas?” Her velvety laughter cut through the noise of the crowd to wash over him like warm water.

“I would never presume to buy your Christmas gift with you anywhere near the vicinity.”

Bill didn’t miss her furtive glance around his chair at the floor. “You lost something, Gwen?” He gave her an innocent smile.

She cleared her throat, shaking off his comment. “I only wondered if you’d hit some of those great sales I did after we went our own way earlier. I found some bargains at Dillard’s on fragrances for Giselle and Carrie’s girls.”

“Fragrances? Is that all you found?”

“I found some other items as well. I obviously did better than you. You want me to suggest a few things?”

Bill shook his head. “Nah, I’ve got a handle on it. I believe I’ll surprise you this year.” If there was one thing he knew about his wife, it was that she couldn’t stand the waiting. The worst part of Christmas for her was him keeping a secret from her, especially about gifts. He’d learned their first Christmas together not to put her gifts under the tree until Christmas Eve at the earliest.

She pulled her chair closer to him. “Any chance I can change your mind later on tonight?”

“Under normal circumstances, I’d say you’re welcome to try, but I don’t think I could handle it tonight.” He shifted uncomfortably in his chair. “And you *know* how I hate to turn you down.”

She paled suddenly. “Oh, Bill! I’m so sorry. For a moment I completely forgot.”

He pulled her closer for a quick kiss. “Then this little shopping excursion was a success.”

* * * * *

Gwen snuggled nearer to Bill, smiling as he pulled her closer, even in his sleep. She lay still, listening to the sound of his heartbeat, steady and strong. For a moment, she let herself wonder what she would do if the news from the biopsy wasn’t good. Within seconds, terror suffocated her. She tensed, clamping down on her jaw to keep from dissolving into tears, choosing instead, to repeat the three-lined prayer that had been a part of her subconscious for nearly a week.

Dear Lord, please don't let it be cancer. Please don't take him from me when it took me all these years to find him. Please Lord, give us all strength.

Bill's procedure had been textbook perfect, according to the doctor, and he hadn't had much discomfort after the first day or two. But the waiting had been hell. Tomorrow was the day—biopsy results by tomorrow. If it was cancer, he'd need another surgery to determine whether lymph nodes in his abdomen had been affected. That would lead to more waiting for results, then determining what course of action to take.

Although the office wasn't open on Saturdays, the doctor had pulled strings so they wouldn't have to wait until Monday to hear, one way or the other.

She flexed her jaw, forced herself to relax—to breathe deeply. She'd normally rolled onto her back by now, her optimal sleep position, but she couldn't bear to end the physical contact with him.

After what felt like an eternity, her eyes drifted closed of their own accord and she fell asleep, still clinging to her husband.

* * * * *

Gwen pulled on leather gloves and grabbed the grooming mitt and body brush from the kit in the tack room. The soft nicker of several horses, her personal favorite's most recognizable, carried over the wind howling outside. She smiled, made her way over to the stall where she knew he'd be waiting for a brushing and his treat.

His gray nose appeared first, followed by the great white head of the stallion, Bill's wedding gift to her, two years ago.

"Hey good looking." She reached for his velvety muzzle. "How's my boy today?" His relaxed head posture and gentle nickering let her know he'd looked forward to her visit. Every other horse in the remaining stalls seemed to look on with envy, as though they sensed the closeness between Knight and his mistress.

Gwen slipped inside the stall and approached him, wrapping her arms around his neck for a hug. His great neck lowered and twisted slightly to the position that always made Bill shake his head in awe, swearing the horse was hugging her back. Determined to get her back into riding, Bill had asked a local horse trainer to find the perfect ride for his new wife. Knight was only one by-product of her husband's generosity.

White Knight had been four years old when Gwen first set eyes on him—one of three possibilities. Their instantaneous and mutual connection had shocked everyone. Leah LeBlanc, the trainer who had found him for her, said she'd never before witnessed such an obvious link between a horse and human. Especially since the horse's previous owners had considered him a 'problem child'. They insisted he was fond of nipping anyone on the butt who got too close to him. Neither she, nor Bill, had seen any such behavior since acquiring the animal.

Leah insisted that he'd been waiting to have Gwen as his mistress since the day of his birth.

Gwen slipped the grooming mitt over her leather gloves and smiled at the thought as she brushed down her horse. Each swipe of her arm relaxed her, dissipating any and all negative energy along with the dust and particles of hay from his shaggy winter coat. This was her therapy. *This* is what enabled her to face Bill and not break down at the thought of hearing bad news from the doctor.

She finished his grooming then pulled out the plastic bag of sliced apples, the thing that made her a favorite with all the animals in the stables. She gave Knight several slices then made the rounds of the other animals, checking to make sure the stable hand had properly mucked out the stalls this morning. Gwen left the stable, securing the door behind her and feeling better for her brief period of hands-on therapy.

She entered the house through the mud room, stripping off her heavy coat, gloves, and the hat she'd worn to repel the frigid temps. South Louisiana, usually known for mild winters, was in the second week of temps dipping below freezing. Rare occasions such as these made her wonder how people put up with harsh winters in northern parts of the country and elsewhere in the world. Despite several layers of warmth, the high humidity levels had icy coldness slicing right through to her. Shaking off a chill, she walked into the kitchen and paused as all things good bombarded her senses. Cozy warmth, the delectable aroma of a steaming mug of hot cocoa brimming with miniature marshmallows, and the sight of her handsome man smiling as he held it out for her.

She grinned up at him, reaching for the mug. "A prime example of why I love you so much…mind reading! Will you ever stop spoiling me?"

"Not likely." Bill pulled her close for a one-armed hug while balancing the cocoa in the other, keeping it just out of reach. "I wanted you to remember this moment as something pleasant and not break down into tears, even though they'd likely be happy tears."

Gwen's breath caught in her throat. In true Bill style, he didn't make her suffer.

"The doc called while you were out. Good news, babe. Excellent news. No cancer."

She wrapped both arms around his lean waist, absorbing his warmth, enveloped by his goodness and love for her, and allowed herself to fully relax in the knowledge that her husband was healthy. "Thank you! Thank you, sweet Jesus."

* * * * *

As expected, Bill's plan to wait until after Gwen's daily ritual therapy session had worked. No tears at all, just as he'd hoped. He pulled her to their favorite spot in front of the fireplace, what he liked to call 'the *big-ass* chair' built for two. He waited until she'd finished her hot cocoa and lay snuggled beside him with her head resting on his chest.

"You good now?" he asked, hard-pressed to contain his excitement.

"Oh, yeah. I'm so good."

"I'm glad." He checked his watch. "Because I've got to get you somewhere in the next thirty minutes." He gave her bottom an affectionate pat as he urged her to stand. His wife gazed up at him, her face a study of complete unawareness—again, just as he'd planned.

"Where? What are you talking about?"

"You'll see when we get there. Now come on, Love, get your coat and purse. We're on a tight schedule here."

She grabbed her purse then held up one forefinger. "You'll have to give me a few minutes." She ran towards the master bathroom. By the time she came out her cheeks were flushed a bright pink with excitement. He helped her put her coat on, threw his over his shoulder, and reached for a bag he'd hidden behind the sofa.

She stared down at the piece of luggage. “What the heck is that?”

He shifted the bag he’d taken the time to pack, as per Giselle’s instructions, during Gwen’s time in the stable. “Never you mind, honey. Grab your purse and let’s go.”

* * * * *

Bill pulled Gwen’s Explorer up in front of Red McAllister’s club and parked. He grabbed the single piece of luggage and eased his way out of the truck to meet his wife on the passenger side.

“I wish you’d tell me what the hell’s going on,” she hissed at him. “You know I hate surprises.”

He took her hand and leaned in for a quick kiss. “Nope, you love surprises. It’s the waiting you find intolerable. Admit it, Gwen. You have no patience when it comes to waiting for anything—like birthday gifts, anniversary gifts, and especially Christmas gifts. I discovered that our first Christmas when you hounded me about that unlabeled gift under the tree until I about lost my mind.”

She grinned sheepishly. “I can’t help it if I have a curious nature. I get that from my mom.”

“Well, this time I took the waiting out of the surprise.” He walked her to the front entrance of Red’s club and made her stand off to the side while he peeked inside. He popped back out, unable to hide a grin. “Everything’s right on schedule. I knew Red could get the job done according to plan.” He held one door open for her and bowed at the waist. “After you, Madame Broussard.”

* * * * *

Gwen held her breath as she walked into the darkened club. The thud of the door closing was followed by several clicks, and suddenly the room was awash with light—thousands of tiny crystal clear, white, and red lights. Every square foot of the ceiling sparkled with lights, either alone or wrapped in tulle. Every corner of the room had been graced with gorgeous red and white poinsettias. A huge flocked Christmas tree took center stage at one end of the room, wrapped in lights and overloaded with red and gold ornaments.

“This place is gorgeous,” she whispered. “But what’s it for, Bill?”

“It’s for you, Gwen. It’s all for you. When we went shopping the other night, I saw a group of women, all giddy with excitement. It wasn't hard to figure out it was a bride and her bridesmaids. I started thinking that you'd waited so long to get married, but you never got a real wedding. So, I planned one for you. I hope you don't mind."

"All this is for a wedding?" she asked, certain her eyes were about to pop out of her head.

He nodded, his eyes sparkling with laughter, and accompanied by an ear-to-ear grin. "Yep, for *our* wedding. That is, if you'll have me again. And not by a Justice of the Peace this time, but officiated by two men of God—Father Carlos from our Catholic church here in Lake Coburn, as well as Pastor Jack from the Baptist church in Kenton. So, what do you say, beautiful? Will you marry me again?"

Through tear-filled eyes, she gazed up at the man who'd stolen her heart at a children's birthday party. Each day brought a new reason to love her gentleman *Cowboy*, as well as to be thankful to God for bringing them together.

"Of course, I'll marry you again." She locked her hands at the back of his neck, welcomed the feel of his arms encompassing her, surrounding her with delectable warmth. He pulled back just far enough to seek out her mouth, giving her a mind-blowing kiss. She pulled away at a sudden thought. "What time is this wedding?"

"In two hours," he said.

"I don't have a dress fit for a ceremony like this, Bill. I don't have anything I need to get ready for this."

"Sure, you do." He brought two fingers to his mouth and released a loud, shrill whistle. Within moments, several women poured out of the hallway to greet her.

"Oh, my gosh!" She squealed at the approach of several of her dearest friends in the world. Carrie Langley, who had decided a couple of years back that Gwen and Bill would be perfect together, approached her, followed by Leah LeBlanc. Giselle and Carrie's girls followed, with Tiffany McAllister and her sister-in-law, Annie, bringing up the rear. Alyssa came running up to her from another doorway. "Oh sweetie, you were in on this too?" Gwen wiped away emotional tears.

"Yes ma'am," Alyssa beamed. "I have a pretty dress, too, but it's not *nearly* as pretty as yours is, Mama."

"I have a pretty dress?" Gwen raised her hands to her face.

Giselle took one arm and turned Gwen toward the hallway. "Just wait until you see it, Gwen. Your husband has excellent taste. It'll look fabulous on you."

Gwen let the cluster of women herd her toward the area they'd exited from a minute earlier. She stopped at the end of the hallway and turned, searching the expanse of room to find her husband where she'd left him—his gaze still locked on her, and still grinning. "Don't go anywhere."

Bill saluted and gave her a wave. "Don't you worry, babe. I'll be here."

She raised her hand in return. "Love you, Cowboy."

His grin broke into a beaming smile. "Love you too, Gwen."

* * * * *

Gwen stood in front of the full-length mirror in the powder room. She slid her hands down both sides, smoothing the off-white satin gown that glittered with delicate crystals and beadwork. She met Giselle's gaze in the mirror and smiled at her friend.

"Gorgeous," Giselle said, in a near reverent whisper. "Uncle Bill will be absolutely blown away."

Gwen raised her hands to her cheeks. "I still can't believe he pulled this off without me knowing a thing. God, I love that man."

Giselle smiled. "I know you do. He's a good man, and he loves you so much."

Wiping a tear from her eye, she nodded. "I've felt it every day of my life since we've been together."

Carrie approached quietly, as though afraid to ruin the moment, and placed a hand on her shoulder. "It's time sweetie. Can I go cue the DJ now?"

"We have a DJ?"

Carrie raised a brow. "Of course. Your man left no stone unturned. He even picked out the music we're walking out to."

Gwen opened her mouth to say something then clamped it shut.

"What? Don't you trust his taste in music?" Giselle smothered a laugh.

"Well, it's just that I know his favorite song is *Dinosaur* by Hank Williams, Jr. You think it's too late to make a request?"

Carrie shook her head slowly. "Sorry, but he said it's non-negotiable."

"Do you know what he chose?"

"Not a clue, but I have it on good authority that you'll love it. Now come on everybody, let's line up. It's time to start the party." Carrie stepped outside.

Gwen lined up behind the other women, preceded by Alyssa in her beautiful flower girl dress. Bill had spared no expense on this shin-dig—he'd done it all for her, and she intended to have a wonderful time. She caught Carrie's curious look as soon as the soft piano chords began, followed by Adele singing *"To Make You Feel My Love"*. Gwen gasped, fighting hard not to dissolve into tears, even as she saw Carrie nod in satisfaction.

"What's wrong, Mama? Don't you like the song?" Alyssa asked, concern plastered all over her face.

"I love this song, sweetie." Gwen wiped another tear from the corner of her eye. "I just can't believe he remembered—"

* * * * *

Bill adjusted his tie for the umpteenth time, checked his boots for scuffs…again…and looked toward the hallway…again…with the same results as the previous fifty glances. Gwen had never been one to leave him waiting, until today.

"What the hell's taking her so long?" He flashed a look in the direction of both men of the cloth. "Sorry."

"Das okay," Father Carlos said, in his thick Columbian accent.

"Totally understandable," Pastor Jack commented, smothering a laugh.

"I don't understand what could possibly be taking so long. You don't think she's getting cold feet, do you?" A firm hand landed on his shoulder, and he turned to see Jackson grinning at him.

"Relax, Uncle Bill. She married you once. Why wouldn't she marry you again?"

"Bill, quit mining for trouble," Daniel LeBlanc scolded. "Have you stopped to consider that she's waiting for two o'clock? You know, the time we told everyone it would start?"

Bill checked his watch. "I've got two minutes till; how about you?"

"For the tenth time, our watches show the same as yours." Jackson slapped his uncle on the back. "Calm down, it's almost time."

Carrie chose that moment to appear just long enough to motion to the house DJ. Within seconds, the song Bill had chosen especially for his wife filtered through the space from several speakers. Suddenly, he wondered if he'd made a mistake. Maybe she would have preferred to pick something out for herself, like her own dress, or the very least, her wedding music.

He watched nervously as one by one the women exited the hallway, making their way slowly to where Bill stood waiting with the two church officials.

Bill beamed with pride when Alyssa began her journey, dropping red rose petals delicately along her path. He looked up expectantly toward the hallway as his bride made her first appearance. A collective gasp—well-warranted—resounded from the wedding guests and well-wishers. His wife was a vision…more so because of the look of unadulterated joy on her face. She glowed with happiness—an obvious match for his own feelings, because if he was any happier, he'd have to explode to make room for it.

By the time she reached him, the song was rolling to its heart-achingly touching conclusion. He couldn't have planned it better if he'd had a musical technician on his payroll.

She stopped directly in front of him, and his breath caught as he tried to speak. "My God," he whispered, awestruck at her beauty. Giselle had helped him, suggesting styles she knew Gwen would prefer. Ultimately, the choice had been his. He didn't know a sweetheart from a modified Queen Ann neckline, but he damn well knew what he wanted to see her wearing. There wasn't a doubt in his mind he'd chosen correctly. He knew by her genuine smile, the ease in her facial expression, the regality with which she carried herself that she approved of his choice one hundred percent. Damn if he hadn't found the perfect dress for his bride.

She took a step closer, holding the bouquet of blood red roses he'd chosen for her, beaming up at him. He took her arm and looped it through his own before resting his hand over hers.

"You ready to do this?" she said.

"Honey, I been chomping at my bit for more than an hour waiting for you to walk out of there. And if you don't believe me, ask any one of these guys." The men around him all chuckled in agreement.

Together, they turned to face Father Carlos and Pastor Jack, who took turns reading the scripture. Between the two of them, they were very thorough in making sure that Gwen and Bill were joined in the holiest of matrimonies.

Finally, Father Carlos raised his hands, saying the words Bill had been looking forward to hearing. "*We* now pronounce you man and wife…" while Pastor Jack finished it off for him. "And *you*, my friend, may now kiss your bride."

The two of them came together, obviously neither ashamed of showing their affection in a roomful of people. She looped her arms around his neck, while he pulled her close, molding her body to his. Bill, figuring they'd waited long enough for this moment, did a thorough job of kissing his bride. He slacked off only upon hearing Alyssa's delighted giggles, finishing up with a hug then another short kiss to seal the deal.

Gwen's eyes sparkled with excitement. "Bill, can I show you something?"

"Here? In front of Father Carlos and Pastor Jack?" The wedding party snickered in amusement.

She smiled up at him. "Oh, absolutely." Gwen reached for her bouquet that Giselle had held during the ring exchange. "I have my own little wedding surprise for you. It was going to be your Christmas gift, but considering all this…" She waved at their room full of guests." She placed the bouquet between them and gently parted the filler flowers with one hand. "There, do you see it?"

Bill strained his eyes, trying to figure out what was hidden among the petals. "What is that?"

"I don't know. You tell me, Bill. What is that?"

Puffed up with curiosity and determination, he dug for the elusive flash of white—the man-made item that didn't belong in the natural beauty of her bouquet. Finally, he parted two roses and found what he was looking for, some type of plastic strip placed strategically amongst the flowers. He lifted it halfway out then froze, staring hard at it. "Does this mean what I think it does?" he asked, his heart thumping wildly and filled with hope.

"It depends." She turned the item so he could see the highly visible plus sign. "If you think it's the positive end of a battery, you'd be wrong. *But* if you think it's a pregnancy test strip, and it means we're adding to our family, then you would be completely correct in your assumption."

"Oh God," he murmured, brushing her mouth with a tender kiss before touching his forehead to hers.

"Now keep in mind this isn't exactly official yet. It could be a false positive…I mean it's just a home pregnancy test, but, Merry Christmas, anyway, Bill," she whispered.

"Merry Christmas, Gwennie."

The masculine clearing of distinctly different throats had the both of them looking up at the two men waiting for them to finish their private talk.

"*Escuse* us," Father Carlos said, with a wide grin.

"Ahem…would it be possible to make an announcement?" Pastor Jack added. "Ladies and gentlemen…Mr. and Mrs. William Broussard." The room erupted in applause.

Bill smiled at their guests before turning his gaze back toward his beautiful wife. "Babe, it doesn't get any better than this."

She cocked her head to the side. "I disagree. Something tells me it's going to get a lot better than this."

* * * * *

Two days later, Bill barely let his truck roll to a stop before jumping out to meet his wife and daughter. He'd been in Houston on business when she'd called him, telling him the test had obviously been a false positive. She'd taken two more this morning and both had produced big, fat negatives. He hurried inside, knowing he'd find her trying to put on a brave face. Sure enough, she was baking Christmas cookies with Alyssa, trying to stay busy.

"Daddy's home!" Alyssa screeched, running up to throw her arms around him.

He hugged her back and let her show him the large cowboy cookie she'd made for him, complete with hat and boots. "Heck, if that tastes half as good as it looks, I know it'll be delicious. Thanks, baby girl, it means a lot to me." He waited for her to go back to decorating the other cookies before pulling his wife gently by the hand to their bedroom for some privacy.

"I'm so sorry, Bill." She hung her head. "I should have waited until I knew for sure. All I did was jinx it for us."

He folded her into his arms, giving her a big bear hug. "No such thing as a jinx, honey. And never apologize for being an optimist. We both knew at the time it was just a home test."

"I know, but you did so much for me that day, and I was happy I could give you something back," she sobbed.

"Don't cry, Gwennie. Just because it hasn't happened yet, doesn't mean it won't. Now look, we have a wonderful honeymoon creeping up on us during the Christmas Holidays. Watch if it doesn't happen then."

"We've been trying almost two years, Bill," she sniffed, clearly heartbroken over this latest in a string of monthly disappointments.

"Hell, babe, all *that* means is we get to keep on trying." He nuzzled her neck. "Don't forget about that good size deposit of swimmers I put in the bank. If that's what it takes, that's what we'll do. I ain't stopping until one of us is pregnant."

* * * * *

They took Alyssa out of school two days early for the Christmas holidays so she could spend the first part of their honeymoon with them. They spent three fun filled days in north Texas at an enclosed, temperature-controlled waterpark. Afterward, they dropped Alyssa off with Jackson's family in Galveston, who'd planned their own holiday vacation to coincide with Gwen and Bill's.

As soon as they were on their own, they hopped on a ship for a seven-day cruise through the Gulf, the Western Caribbean, and all its lovely ports of call.

Tanned, toned, and totally relaxed, they made it back to the bayou state just in time for Christmas at Jackson and Giselle's place. After an afternoon of good food, good company, and tearing open gifts in a crowd that size, they couldn't wait to get to their own home.

Within minutes of having taken her bath, Alyssa was sound asleep in her bed. Seated before the roaring fireplace, the mellow sound of Charles Brown singing "Please Come Home for Christmas" poured softly from the speakers, Bill motioned for Gwen to meet him on the double recliner.

"Mmm…I don't know which version I like of this song the best—Mr. Brown's or The Eagles'." She pulled an envelope from her purse then snuggled up next to her husband under the downy soft throw.

"One version's just as good as the other. It's my favorite non-religious Christmas song."

"Mine too," she admitted. They sat quietly, listening to the music as the fire snapped and popped, casting shadowy reflections on the wall. She curled her arms around his waist, groaning in satisfaction. "Can I thank you again for the best time I've ever had in my life?"

"It was my pleasure."

She ran her hands over his chest, remembering numerous instances of languid pleasure, and released a low groan. "It wasn't all your pleasure, I can assure you." His deep rumble of laughter stirred something inside her, making her want to recreate one of those nights, in particular. She smiled as she pulled the envelope out from under the throw. "I picked this up for you on the boat, babe. I hope you like it."

He pulled a card from the envelope, laughed at the cartoonish image of a cowboy and cowgirl couple smooching in front of a Christmas tree decorated with stars and horseshoes, the words Merry Christmas spelled out in colorful lights. He opened the card, catching the slip of paper that fell out of it before it hit the floor. He read the card from cover to cover and smiled, thanking her with a kiss. "What's this?" he asked, flipping on the lamp so he could read the slip of paper.

Gwen studied his face as he read, wondering if he was catching it all. "What do you think?" she asked, when she couldn't stand it anymore.

"I'm not sure I can read this handwriting. Who's Dr. Wells?"

"He was the doctor I went to on the ship to get something for sea sickness."

"Yeah…so?"

"He told me he couldn't give me anything for sea sickness if I was pregnant. I told him we'd been trying but no luck yet. When I explained about the false positive he insisted I take another one, just to be sure, before prescribing something for the nausea."

Bill squinted, as though struggling to read the doctor's squiggled notes.

She reached over to point something out. "You see under the word diagnosis—"

"It says six times…no…six weeks…I can't make out the next word." He stopped suddenly, and gazed at her. "Pregnant? Six weeks pregnant?"

She nodded.

"But is he sure?"

"When the test came out positive, he did a pelvic exam to be sure."

"And?"

"There is absolutely no doubt about it, Bill. We're having a baby—somewhere around July 22nd."

A beaming smile transformed his face from shock to absolute joy. "And you've known about this…how long, now?"

"Since the second day on the boat." She beamed with satisfaction. "And you said I couldn't keep a secret—"

Chapter Twenty-one

Christmas Blessings

Christmas Eve, 2015

Bill heard the ruckus outside and shifted his infant son to his left arm. He pulled open the door before his nephew could get to it.

Jackson stood there, balancing an armload of packages. Before he could speak, he whipped his head around. "Jamison! Justin! Don't run through that puddle. Get in here—get in here before you get your shoes—stop! Don't! Aaahhh . . . damn . . ." he finished. His head fell forward in defeat as he turned and headed for the huge Christmas tree in one corner of the room.

One dark-haired boy ran in, a flash of red and black plaid flannel, his brown western boots sopping wet and leaving a trail of muddy water. Bill reached down to scoop him up in his free arm. "Gotcha, little man!"

The child gave him a toothy grin, his blue eyes sparkling with good-natured mischief. "Hey, Paw Paw!"

"Hey yourself, twin—and Merry Christmas."

"I'm not Twin, I'm Jamison!"

"I'll have to take your word for it." Bill chuckled. "I still can't tell you little stinkers apart."

"I'm cuter than Justin," the blue-eyed imp insisted.

"Says who? You look exactly the same. Now sit your butt down right there and take your boots off before I hang you upside down for messin' up my floors."

"But my feet will be cold if I can't wear my cowboy boots!" Jamison wailed.

"Then you should have listened to your dad and not run through the puddle."

Giselle finally made it inside, twin two's wrist gripped tightly in one hand. "I've got extra socks and shoes for them." She gave a slightly hysterical laugh. "I pretty much travel with their entire wardrobe these days. Sheesh!"

Bill grinned at her flushed face. "Never doubted it for a second, hon. Nice of you to join us."

"At least I managed to get to this one before he ran through that same puddle," she huffed, slightly out of breath. "Now stay in the house, Justin. It's too wet and cold to play outside today."

Bill leaned over to speak to the child dressed identically to his brother but for the green and black plaid flannel shirt. "Merry Christmas, Justin."

"Merry Christmas, Paw Paw!" He tore off in the direction of the tree the second his mom released him.

Bill hugged Giselle tightly in his free arm, mindful of her baby bump. "How you feeling?"

"I *feel* pregnant for my fifth child. But the morning sickness has ended already so that's good."

Bill winked at her. "Are we sure it's not another set of twins?"

Giselle exhaled and cupped her hands around her belly. "Yep. This little girl is all by herself." She smiled suddenly and reached for the baby in his arm. "Give!" She cuddled the chubby infant to her. "Hey baby boy. You are growing so fast and looking more like your handsome daddy every day."

Bill's chest puffed out with pride at the sight and sound of his five and a half-month-old son cooing and drooling in Giselle's arms. "David's growing like a dandelion in a pile of cow manure." He stepped toward the door in search of Mac and Lexie. "Where are you hiding my granddaughters?"

"They attended the same post hayride sleepover at Gretchen's last night as Alyssa did, remember? They'll drop all three of them off on their way out of town in a few minutes. Carrie's entire family is spending the morning at her mom's place in Gardiner."

Bill nodded. "That's good. Carrie said she didn't know how many more Christmas's they'll have with Ms. Elaine." He turned as his beautiful wife entered the room, looking radiant and sexy as hell in black jeans and a red form-fitting sweater. "Hey gorgeous, we have guests."

Gwen stopped to grace him with a kiss before giving both Giselle and Jackson a welcoming hug. "I love this," she gushed.

"All of us spending Christmas Eve here and waking up together as one big family. This should be fun!"

Bill watched the two women as they turned and entered the kitchen together, as close as sisters, despite their actual step-aunt/step-niece relationship.

He helped Jackson unload their vehicle, a full-sized family SUV with three rows of seats. It took two more trips to bring in all the gifts and food items.

"I think you forgot the kitchen sink." Bill closed the rear door after grabbing the final casserole dish. He peeked under the lid and smiled. "Please tell me this is Tiffany McAllister's recipe for banana pudding."

Jackson approached, grinning from ear to ear. "You know it is. My wife will not be denied when it comes to pregnancy cravings. I predict she'll make no less than six more of those before our daughter is born."

Bill heard Giselle screech and tell one of the twins to *"Get off of that, boys. It's not a jungle gym!"* He laughed through Jackson's groan. "And she deserves every bite of it."

Jackson shook his head as they entered the house, his gaze automatically seeking out the two active little boys. "Honestly, Uncle Bill—I don't know how the hell she does it. Those two never stop."

"They're exactly like you were at that age—except there are *two* of the little climbing, speed demons." Bill closed the door against the damp December rain. "Anyway, it's our jobs to make sure our wives don't feel overwhelmed. And your wife is happy—anyone can see that."

"Mac and Lexie are huge helps, too." Jackson placed the casserole dish on the kitchen's granite counter top.

"They are the best big sisters and mama's little helpers ever," Giselle piped up.

"Is that the pudding?" Gwen asked, her eyes glazing over. "Are you gonna make us wait for it?"

"Nah," Giselle said. "Go ahead and help yourselves."

Bill grinned at his wife. "Oh, I don't think she was talking about me when she said 'us'. Should we tell them now, babe?"

Gwen's face transformed with her radiant smile. "We're pregnant again!"

Giselle's mouth dropped open. "Are you sure?"

Gwen nodded. "I've already been to my OB—another July baby. I hope this one waits until the due date of the twentieth and doesn't declare its independence on July 4th!" She took a deep breath and released it in a rush. "I never imagined when I met Bill that I'd have *two* babies a year apart from each other." She brushed a happy tear from the corner of one eye. "I'm so blessed."

Bill curled one arm around his wife's shoulder and pulled her close. "*We're* blessed."

The sound of car doors slamming had them all facing the front door as three young girls burst through the opening.

Mac reached Bill first, throwing her arms around his waist. "Merry Christmas, Paw Paw!"

Bill leaned over to hug the ten-year-old girl, whose promise of heartbreaking beauty increased daily. "Hello, beautiful girl and merry Christmas to you, too." He released her so she could hug her "Emgee", the nickname they'd come up with for Gwen. His wife had suggested Maw Gwen, but Mac had declared her too young for that tag and had shortened it to M.G., which, ran together, became a single word, *Emgee*—and it stuck.

"Hey Paw Paw!"

Bill reached down to lift eight-year-old Lexie into his arms for a hug. "Hey sweet girl. Did you have a good time at Ms. Gretchen's?"

She gave him her signature pixie grin. "I sure did. Her baby, Lilly, is still sweet. She's not old enough to be bad like our brothers yet. But Ms. Gretchen says she has definite *potential*, whatever *that* means."

Bill laughed at his granddaughter's continued flair for dramatic Lexi-isms that never failed to amuse. "Well, she would know, wouldn't she?" Setting her down, he squatted beside Alyssa, wrapping her in a big hug. "Good morning, beautiful. Did you also have a good time playing with baby Lilly?"

She nodded and hugged him back tightly. "And I kept our secret, too," she whispered in his ear. "Even from Mac and Lexie. And you *know* how hard that was for me, daddy."

"I'm proud of you for that. But you know what, sweetheart? I think you can go ahead and tell them now." He straightened and searched out his wife's gaze.

Alyssa clapped her hands together and looked from Bill to Gwen. "I can?"

Gwen nodded her consent, her eyes glittering with happy tears that matched the smile on her face.

"Mac! Lexie! Guess what?" Alyssa grabbed each girl by a hand. "We're having another baby in July."

Mac squealed with delighted laughter while Lexie looked from Bill to Gwen and back to Bill. All the adults in the room held their collective breaths, anticipating some quip to erupt from her at any second—something that would make them remember this moment forever.

"Well . . ." She put her hands on her hips. "When you two learn how to do somethin', you sure learn it good!"

Bill's chest rumbled with laughter as he pulled his wife in front of him. He wrapped his arms around the woman he adored, and breathed in the sights and sounds around him. "That's right, baby girl. We surely do."

Chapter Twenty-two

A Legacy of Love

Christmas Eve 2018

Bill sat in his corner of the big, overstuffed couch, his feet propped up on a large ottoman, surrounded by the serene ambiance of Christmas. Serene only because David and Yvette, three and two respectively, were sound asleep in their beds. Alyssa, now thirteen, had just helped them haul all the gifts under the tree—enough to let the little ones think that Santa had passed. Their oldest daughter had since gone to bed, leaving her parents alone, the only two awake in the house.

Thoughts of his three children had him wondering how much of their lifespans he'd live to witness. He wasn't a fool. At sixty-two, even with his exercise regimen and healthy eating habits, his chances of out-living anyone in his immediate family were slim at best. He hoped he didn't, anyway. He'd lost enough people in his lifetime and didn't want to be around to lose anyone else.

He'd taken precautions to provide for his family. Neither he nor Gwen lived large, both preferring the simple pleasures of life. He supposed that came from them having to wait so long to get what they truly wanted out of life—that being family. Family mattered to them—material possessions didn't. As a result, he'd amassed life insurance policies, college funds, and lucrative investments. When his time came to leave this earth, his family would be well cared for, financially speaking.

He heard his wife puttering around in the kitchen, making them hot cocoa. Hopefully, they could relax and rest enough to fuel them for tomorrow. They had a long day of celebrating with Jackson's family, now seven members strong with the last addition of little Elise, four months older than their youngest, Yvette. She entered the room and placed two mugs on the end table.

"Thanks babe." He grabbed the remote for the sound system and hit play, starting the little self-indulgent Christmas playlist tradition they'd started a few years earlier. It had all begun with two versions of their favorite Christmas song, "Please be Home for Christmas". The playlist had grown from versions by Charles Brown and The Eagles to include others by Sheryl Crow, Jon Bon Jovi, Martina McBride, Aaron Neville, and Kelly Clarkson. He cocked his head. "You want to dance?"

Gwen smiled and dropped beside him on the couch. "Maybe in a bit. I think I'd like to snuggle first if it's okay with you." She practically purred with satisfaction when he tucked the cashmere throw over the two of them.

They sat there, staring into the fireplace as the flames crackled, casting cozy combinations of glowing light and shadows in the otherwise darkened room. They sat, not speaking through two complete versions of the song, letting the honeyed melodies and cherished lyrics wash over them.

She finally spoke up, pulling him from his memories of the past. "A penny for your thoughts, Cowboy."

He smiled, tucking her close to his side. "I'm just sitting here thinking about Jamison and me as kids, before our mom died. Life has sure thrown some surprises my way—both bad and good. The good started outweighing the bad the moment you entered my life." The Eagles' version of the song started up—he stood slowly and reached for his wife.

Gwen smiled and took his hand, let him pull her up against him. She wrapped one arm around his waist and lay her head on his shoulder, rested her open hand on his chest. They swayed slowly from side to side. She waited through a few more lyrics before speaking again. "You have been such a blessing to me."

"You, as well, hon. It blows my mind to think how different my life is now from that very first Christmas without my mom."

Her soft laughter filled the space between them. "I know what you mean. I'd begun to lose all hope of having babies of my own." She sighed in total contentment. "But, here I am—the forty-four-year-old mother of two toddlers and a teen-age girl."

Don Henley crooned softly in the background about no more sorrow … no grief or pain … and being happy once again.

He pulled her closer, smiling at the lyrics. "And I'm the sixty-two-year-old father of those same three wonderful kids—and I am happy." He stopped dancing and stared into her blue eyes. "I know I've got you to thank for it."

ABOUT THE AUTHOR

Award winning author, Lori Leger, adores writing stories set in southwest Louisiana, where good Cajun cooking, helping your neighbors, and saying 'y'all' is as normal as hurricanes, heat, and humidity. She has twelve full-length novels, two novellas, and five short stories published in four series: La Fleur de Love, its spin-off, Halos & Horns, one stand-alone Christmas suspense published with The Wild Rose Press.

She's contributed to the Sweet & Savory Cookbook of Amazon Authors, published by Top Ten Press. Lori also has an article published in the non-fiction book Writing After Retirement: Tips From Retired Writers, published by Rowman and Littlefield Publishers, and edited and compiled by Carol Smallwood and Christine Redman-Waldeyer.

Her fourth novel in the Halos & Horns series, "One Year to Forever" won 2015 Romance Novel of Excellence award from InD'tale Review magazine.

BOOK LIST

LA FLEUR DE LOVE SERIES
Some Day Somebody (Book 1)
Last First Kiss (Book 2)
Hart's Desire (Book 2.5 – A Novella)
Brown Eyed Girl (Book 3)
Heaven in Your Eyes (Book 4)

HALOS & HORNS SERIES
Green Eyed Temptation (Book 1)
Sarah Smile (Book 2)
Meagan's Marine (Book 3)
One Year to Forever (Book 4)
Tinseled Up in Texas (Book 5)

PRIME OF LOVE SERIES
Running Out Of Rain (Book 1)
Hanging On To Hope (Book 2)
Settling For More (Book 3)
Bells are Still Ringing (Book 4)

Full Circle Love
(Four short stories about one couple, Cat and Zach, taken from the Seasons of Love Anthology series)

Christmas 911 – Stand-alone Christmas suspense with **The Wild Rose Press**

Lauren Gayle became a **USA Today bestselling author** in October of 2019 with her first novella, *A Southern Lights Christmas*, Book 1 of the SOUTHERN LIGHTS SERIES, available only until January 2019 as part of the **Christmas at Mistletoe Lodge** boxset.

Look for Lauren's Inspirational SOUTHERN LIGHTS SERIES in both digital and paperback format by the end of summer 2020.

A Southern Lights Christmas – Southern Lights (Book 1)
Southern Landing – Southern Lights (Book 2)
Southern Retreat – Southern Lights (Book 3)
Southern Redemption – Southern Lights (Book 4)